Exiles in Time

Books in the *After Cilmeri* Series:
Daughter of Time (prequel)
Footsteps in Time (Book One)
Winds of Time
Prince of Time (Book Two)
Crossroads in Time (Book Three)
Children of Time (Book Four)
Exiles in Time
Castaways in Time
Ashes of Time
Warden of Time
Guardians of Time
Masters of Time

The Gareth and Gwen Medieval Mysteries:
The Bard's Daughter
The Good Knight
The Uninvited Guest
The Fourth Horseman
The Fallen Princess
The Unlikely Spy
The Lost Brother
The Renegade Merchant
The Unexpected Ally

The Lion of Wales Series:
Cold My Heart
The Oaken Door
Of Men and Dragons
A Long Cloud
Frost Against the Hilt

The Last Pendragon Saga:
The Last Pendragon
The Pendragon's Blade
Song of the Pendragon
The Pendragon's Quest
The Pendragon's Champions
Rise of the Pendragon

A Novel from the *After Cilmeri* Series

EXILES IN TIME

by

SARAH WOODBURY

Exiles in Time
Copyright © 2013 by Sarah Woodbury

This is a work of fiction.

All rights reserved. No part of this publication may be reproduced, stored in a retrieval system, or transmitted in any form or by any means without the prior written permission of the author, nor be otherwise circulated in any form of binding or cover other than that in which it is published.

Cover image by Christine DeMaio-Rice at Flip City Books

To Dad
I think you would have
liked this one

A Brief Guide to Welsh Pronunciation

c a hard 'c' sound (Cadfael)

ch a non-English sound as in Scottish 'ch' in 'loch' (Fychan)

dd a buzzy 'th' sound, as in 'there' (Ddu; Gwynedd)

f as in 'of' (Cadfael)

ff as in 'off' (Gruffydd)

g a hard 'g' sound, as in 'gas' (Goronwy)

l as in 'lamp' (Llywelyn)

ll a breathy /sh/ sound that does not occur in English (Llywelyn)

rh a breathy mix between 'r' and 'rh' that does not occur in English (Rhys)

th a softer sound than for 'dd,' as in 'thick' (Arthur)

u a short 'ih' sound (Gruffydd), or a long 'ee' sound (Cymru—pronounced 'kumree')

w as a consonant, it's an English 'w' (Llywelyn); as a vowel, an 'oo' sound (Bwlch)

y the only letter in which Welsh is not phonetic. It can be an 'ih' sound, as in 'Gwyn,' is often an 'uh' sound (Cymru), and at the end of the word is an 'ee' sound (thus, both Cymru—the modern word for Wales—and Cymry—the word for Wales in the Dark Ages—are pronounced 'kumree')

Prologue
November 2016
Cardiff, Wales

Callum

"We found them." It was Agent Jones, the new man, who so far had done a better job of keeping his composure in the current crisis than most of his superiors.

"Where?" Callum said, holding his dripping hands above the sink. Callum's employer, the British internal security service known as MI-5, no longer stocked paper towels. Callum needed to run the drying machine, but the conversation with Jones came first.

"Fueling up at a petrol station south of Builth Wells," said Jones.

"So we have them," Callum said, not as a question.

Jones paused before speaking. Callum sensed him arranging and rearranging his sentences in his head to find a way to tell the truth in the most efficient and least painful manner. "We didn't catch the image in real time, sir. It's from an hour ago."

Callum slammed his fist onto the counter. "What road were they on?"

"The A470, sir."

"I want to see the images. Set it up. I'll be there in a minute."

"Yes, sir."

Callum dried his hands and was back in the conference room within the allotted time.

Agent Jones stood at attention to the right of the screen that filled one wall. The images of their fugitives took up half the space: Meg Lloyd; her husband, Llywelyn Gruffydd (who claimed to be the last Prince of Wales); and Goronwy, whose surname they hadn't yet determined.

"So they're headed back to Chepstow." Callum nodded to Jones, who tapped a square in one corner of the screen showing a map of Wales. He highlighted the southeastern portion of the country and enlarged it to fill the screen.

"They must have taken that trackway from Devil's Bridge," said Agent Natasha Clark, pointing to the unnamed road that ran through the Elan Valley. "No cameras, which is why it took so long to find them."

"Not much of anything out there but sheep," said Jones, "though at least the road is paved."

"It couldn't have been fun in the dark," Natasha said. "They must have felt desperate to take that road."

"We made them desperate," Callum said.

The initial pickup had been handled badly, not by Callum, but by Thomas Smythe, a fellow security service agent. Although the file on Meg was Callum's, and had been for six months, his boss had bypassed him for the lead on the case because Smythe spoke Welsh. Smythe didn't know anything about people, however, and had misjudged his quarry badly, going in heavy when he should have gone in light.

"They could be heading anywhere, not necessarily Chepstow," Callum said.

"If they didn't go north, Chepstow Castle is the most logical choice," said Jones. "They're trying to reverse what they did to come here."

According to Meg's brother-in-law, Ted, Meg had spent the last few years living in medieval Wales. She and her companions had started out earlier in the week in the Middle Ages, jumped from Chepstow's balcony that overlooked the Wye River, and gone from 1288 Chepstow to 2016 Aberystwyth in the blink of an eye.

"Does that sound as crazy to you as it does to me?" The last member of the team, John Driscoll, kicked back in his chair.

"From their point of view, it makes a certain kind of sense," said Jones.

Snorting his disgust, Driscoll tossed the papers he'd been holding onto the conference table. "A pregnant woman and two old men, one of whom has a heart condition, are running circles around us. How in the hell have they eluded us?"

"While Meg might be from this world originally," Natasha said, "Llywelyn and Goronwy are not. That reaches to the heart of our problem: they don't think like we do."

"I wouldn't have taken you for a true believer, Natasha," Driscoll said.

Natasha gave her fellow agent a sour look. "I'm not. Just keeping my options open."

"I can't believe we're even having this discussion. As if that's not crazy right there." Driscoll mumbled the words under his breath as he typed into his laptop.

"If we could focus on the mission ..." Callum said.

"Of course, sir," Natasha said. "All I'm saying is that if Meg is telling the truth—"

"Would you rather I put you on to infiltrating those Welsh nationalists in St. David's?" Callum said. "You could reveal everything you know about the return of the last Prince of Wales and they'd welcome you to their meetings with open arms."

That made Natasha laugh. "No, no. I'll take this case any day over that."

Callum checked his watch and then pointed to Jones. "Keep watching the cameras. If they're in Chepstow, or getting close, we need to know." He looked at the rest of his team. "I think we all should be involved in this."

Driscoll closed the lid of his computer and got to his feet. "I'll get Ted ready." He left the room.

Callum turned to Natasha and Jones. "I don't want to hear talk about anything but the task before us. We have a job to do, and we're going to do it."

"Yes, sir," Jones and Natasha said together.

The SUV pulled into the parking lot of Chepstow Castle a few minutes before seven in the morning.

Natasha rubbed her hands together. "It looks cold."

"It's November in Wales. What did you expect?" Callum unlatched the door and discovered that the driver had parked directly over a puddle. Having just responded curtly to Natasha, Callum refrained from chewing out the driver. They were all going to get a lot wetter than this before the day was over. Callum was still dressed in his regular work clothes: business suit, trench coat, and respectable shoes. Half an hour ago when they'd left Cardiff, he hadn't felt he could stop by his flat to collect his rain boots and hat.

The men who made up Callum's security team wore Kevlar under black trench coats. While it was standard policy to wear armor during operations like this, Callum hadn't seen the point for himself. As far as Callum was concerned, nobody was shooting anyone today, and certainly not pregnant women or men who thought they were nobles from medieval Wales. They weren't a threat to anyone but themselves, and even that was debatable.

In fact, this was a crap assignment, and Callum would be the first to admit it. MI-5 usually dealt with threats to national security such as the detection and apprehension of terrorists.

These people needed a psychiatrist. They certainly didn't need to be chased by a dozen agents from MI-5.

For this mission, Callum had brought two SUVs and a larger van, which he directed to park in the castle's rear car park. He then dispersed his ten men around the perimeter of Chepstow Castle. They could patrol the exterior until Callum got word that Cardiff had rousted the government official who managed the castle, and he had arrived to unlock the main door. Callum left Ted inside the second SUV with two agents to watch over him. There wasn't any point in getting him wet until the castle opened for business. Callum got back into his SUV himself just as his phone rang.

It was Jones. Callum put him on speaker and popped up the tablet that connected the SUV to the computer in the conference room back in Cardiff. His eyes went instinctively to a corner of the screen where Jones had pasted the picture of one of the girls who'd somehow gotten caught up in all this: Bronwen Llywelyn. She'd been an archaeology graduate student in Pennsylvania before she'd disappeared three years ago. Ted had met her and claimed that she'd gone back to the Middle Ages with Meg's son, David.

"What can you tell me?" Callum said. "Are we in the right place?"

"A camera caught their car coming into Chepstow earlier this morning," said Jones.

"When this is over, heads will roll," Natasha said. "You can be sure that Smythe's will be first, even if he is the current pet of Thames House."

Callum glanced at Natasha in the rear view mirror, surprised at the venom in her voice. He was touched if it was on his behalf but sensed there was more to it. Ever since he'd come back from Afghanistan, there were moments when Callum didn't trust his instincts, particularly with women. He wanted to ask Natasha what Smythe had done to her, but now wasn't the time.

"Just so long as the head that rolls isn't mine." Callum couldn't allow this mission to get out of control, not with junior MI-5 agents lurking in the wings, waiting for him to slip up. He walked a thin line as it was, having come back from Afghanistan with enough Post-traumatic Stress Disorder (known as PTSD) to feel like he had to hide it. The fact that everyone came back from Afghanistan with issues of one form or another meant that his obsessions were so minor they didn't prevent him from working. But he didn't care to advertise them either. As his American father had said, "Son, the war screwed you up, but not so much they feel they should mention it."

It might be, for example, that the goons deep in the belly of Thames House knew all about Callum's secret compulsion to wash his hands a little too often, even if the IT department swore they hadn't put cameras in the loo. Callum didn't trust them to tell the truth. Admittedly, that was an occupational hazard.

"The other news could be better," said Jones. "Chepstow is having a fair today—hundreds of people are expected."

"Bloody hell. We need to shut it down," Callum said.

But even as Callum spoke, Natasha was shaking her head from the back seat.

"Hold on, Jones." Callum turned to look at her. "What?"

"If nobody is here, if all Meg sees when she arrives is our men, she's smart enough not to approach. A crowd might be better," Natasha said.

Callum directed his voice towards the speaker again. "I take that back. We'll stick to the current plan."

"A crowd will give them cover," said Jones.

"But it will also make them think they're safe," Callum said. "We can't let them get away again."

"The men are good," said Jones. "They'll see to it."

"You've got the camera feeds?"

"Eight of them," said Jones. "The only difficult spot is the rear of the castle. The cameras in the car park are working, but the two that cover the west side are out. You'll have to mind that back gate in particular. That's where we're completely blind."

"The gate was locked when I visited Chepstow a few months ago," Natasha said. "I know because I wanted to use it but the custodian told me I couldn't."

"I doubt that something like that would have changed," Callum said, "but we shouldn't presume."

"Right," said Jones. "According to the plans I have here, the original entrance was destroyed and that gate is used only for maintenance."

"I'm orienting the men now," Natasha said, one hand to her ear piece. "They'll patrol there specifically."

Jones disconnected and Callum scrubbed at his hair with one hand, feeling every one of his thirty-four years. Natasha had deep circles under her eyes too, not surprising since neither of them had slept in twenty-four hours. If they stayed at this much longer, their boss would replace Callum's team with a different unit. Tired men made mistakes.

"Worst case, the river patrol has to scoop our fugitives out of the Wye," Natasha said.

"I'd prefer it didn't come to that," Callum said. "I can see the headline now: *Pregnant Woman Evades Security Service, Jumps into Wye River!*"

"Have you ever been inside the castle?" Natasha said.

"I dated a girl who brought me here soon after I arrived at Cardiff. It was summer, so warmer then." Callum checked the sky as he slipped his gloves back on. "Though admittedly, not by much."

Natasha nodded her head towards the entrance to the castle. Only three people had passed across their line of sight since they'd arrived. "Where should I set up the command post?"

"You'll be my point person here and coordinate with the team," Callum said. "I'll take the balcony when it comes to it."

"They'll never reach it," Natasha said. "We could use you elsewhere. Maybe on the battlement." She gazed up at the crenellations on the closest tower. The rain had turned the normally yellowish stone a dark grey.

"We've underestimated them from the beginning," Callum said. "I'd like to start thinking two steps ahead." The driver had left the engine running and the heat bathed Callum's face. Callum relaxed against the headrest. "We need to move to a less noticeable location. We don't want to scare them off before we've started."

It took until eight o'clock to contact the custodian of the castle. By then, the man was already on his way in. To top the morning off right, the rain started to fall again, though the crowd that had gathered to await the opening of the castle seemed unperturbed by it.

Natasha, talking through her headset, had been patiently directing the men. As the time neared eight-thirty, she tapped Callum's shoulder. "Have you noticed what everyone is wearing?"

Too late, Callum realized that the crowds not only would hide Meg, Llywelyn, and Goronwy, but would provide them an easier cover than he had expected: everyone in the crowd that was forming outside the castle gate wore medieval garb.

Callum grabbed the binoculars and put them to his eyes, focusing on one individual at a time as he worked his way through the crowd. It was one thing to find the three fugitives in broad daylight, but with the rain, hoods were up and cloaks were tucked tight under chins. Callum's men were going to have a hard time spotting them, even with cameras watching keenly.

Callum turned up his earpiece. "Driscoll, get Ted to the front gate. We need someone closer who can recognize them on sight."

"Yes, sir," Driscoll said. "But we risk Meg spotting him."

"Better that than to lose her entirely," Callum said.

"We can watch the crowd for anyone who balks as he approaches the entrance," Natasha said.

"I don't like this." Callum turned to Natasha. "I need a better picture of what's happening. I'm too far away."

Natasha put one hand to her ear, listening, and held up her other hand to Callum. Then she said, "The custodian has arrived and is waiting for you at the castle entrance."

"Excellent." Callum got out of the car, checked that his earpiece was working properly, and headed towards the castle gate. His trench coat with the collar up didn't fit in with the re-enactors, but at least he wasn't in black like his men. Their coats hid their firearms from the crowd, but they still looked like cockroaches on a bed sheet. At this point, however, it was too late to find them medieval clothing. It wasn't as if Callum could buy that kind of attire at Marks and Spencer.

Welsh gun laws were more than strict. People weren't used to seeing weaponry outside of their televisions. Callum didn't wear his gun openly either. He didn't want to intimidate the innocent onlookers more than he had to. Callum wanted this to be easy. It *should* have been easy from the start.

Callum eased through the crowd, smiling and nodding, trying to blend in and pretend he enjoyed medieval pageantry. All the while, he cursed the rain, the bad luck that had brought Meg to Chepstow on this day, the errant custodian who had only just arrived, and Smythe for his initial heavy-handed approach to their fugitives. Remarkably, Smythe had never learned that much more could be accomplished with honey than with vinegar.

As promised, the custodian was waiting for Callum at the castle entrance and unlocked the door as he approached. The custodian didn't immediately push the door open, however; he just stood there, gabbing at Callum. "I don't understand what this is all about."

"You don't need to," Callum said.

"If something untoward is going on, I need to know about it," the man said. His expression told Callum what he thought of this insult to his authority.

"No, you don't." Callum put his hand on the door and shoved it inward with enough force to knock the door handle from the custodian's hand. The custodian sputtered his disapproval, but Callum pushed past him and entered Chepstow's lower bailey.

He was alone for only a minute before a host of organizers and re-enactors followed. With them came Callum's men who would watch for Meg from inside the castle. Before they set about their task, Callum took them aside. "I want you on the walls and in the doorways between the baileys. We stay in constant communication."

"Yes, sir," the men said in unison.

Callum then did a complete survey of the interior of the castle, all the way up to the rear door. It was locked. He returned to the lower bailey and entered the gift shop, looking for the custodian. The man wasn't happy to see Callum, but he delegated the ticket taking to someone else and gave Callum his full attention. "Tell me about the back gate," Callum said.

"It's always locked," the man said. "Only the groundskeeper and I have keys."

"Is the groundskeeper here today?"

"He'll be along in a minute," the custodian said.

"Send him to me when he comes in," Callum said. "I'll be on the balcony off the wine cellar."

"Yes, sir."

Having little faith that the custodian would do as he requested, Callum asked Natasha to let him know when the maintenance worker arrived. He was sorry he'd rubbed the custodian the wrong way, but Callum had a job to do. It was ridiculous for the man to question how he did it.

Callum made his way through the kitchen, already busy with preparations for a medieval meal, down the stairs, and into the wine cellar. Chepstow Castle was in better repair than many ancient fortresses since it had never been taken by an enemy force in battle. Still, it wasn't what one might call habitable, having lost its wooden infrastructure—specifically the roofs to all its buildings and halls—centuries ago.

The room in which Callum found himself now, however, was built in stone. Contemplating the rain, he stood in the doorway to the balcony that overlooked the Wye River. He couldn't help but think about the men who'd lived here centuries ago when the cellar was full and the purpose of the castle was to stand as a last bastion of English strength against the miles of Wales to the west.

Seven hundred years ago, Llywelyn ap Gruffydd, the man Meg claimed was her husband, had died and Wales had fallen to England. Callum hadn't lived in Wales very long, but only an imbecile could have failed to notice how many Welsh people wished that had never happened. Callum stared at the puddles forming on the uneven stones at his feet. He wished he could speak to his father, who'd have had a thing or two to say about the day Callum was having.

From the back of the wine cellar, perched on a building stone that could have fallen off the balcony wall four hundred years ago, Callum called in to Natasha. "What do you see?"

"I —*crackle, crackle*—someth—*crackle, crackle*—"

"You're breaking up."

"I —*crackle, crackle*—"

"Forget it. It's my fault. I'm coming up."

Natasha was right that waiting for Meg in the wine cellar was a waste of his time, especially since the stones blocked the reception for his earpiece. Callum had allowed the knowledge that Meg had eluded them so far to cloud his thinking. He was ascribing superpowers to a pregnant former history professor burdened by two older men, one of whom was fresh out of hospital. If Callum hadn't felt that his job was somehow on the line, he would have laughed out loud at the absurdity of his situation.

Callum came out of the former great hall of Chepstow Castle into a dramatically changed scene. When he'd entered earlier, the castle had been just starting to fill. Now, an expansive pavilion had been set up in the center of the lower bailey. Tourists streamed through the gift shop, heading towards either the pavilion or the middle bailey, where Callum could hear a speaker welcoming everyone to Chepstow Castle. Three of Callum's men observed the movements of the crowd from the battlement, and two more stood in the doorway between the middle and lower bailey, checking the face of every person who went through it.

Callum tried Natasha again. "Where are we?"

"I've moved Ted and Agent Driscoll inside the gift shop," Natasha said. "Ted was getting restless and cold."

"How well can he see from there?"

"He can see better," she said. "We're having people remove their hats and hoods once they're inside—for security purposes."

"Excellent," Callum said. "No sign of them, I assume?"

"No, sir."

That wasn't excellent. While Callum had been speaking to Natasha, the speaker in the middle bailey had released the crowd, which surged into the lower bailey. A girl brushed past Callum lugging an iron pot. It was so heavy, she needed both hands on the handle to carry it. Steam rose from the liquid inside, wafting the scent of beef and barley stew in his direction.

Uncertain about his next move and sure that he was missing something important, Callum moved closer to the castle entrance. He spent a few minutes scanning the face of every tourist who entered the castle. With each person who passed by, Callum's irritation and suspicion rose, until he remembered that he hadn't yet spoken to the groundskeeper.

"Who's watching the back gate?" Callum said, cutting through the chatter amongst his men that came constantly through his earpiece. He hadn't cut them off earlier in large part because men standing around talking looked more natural than men glaring at the crowd.

"Agents Jeffries and Leon, sir," Natasha said.

"Excuse me, sir," Agent Leon said, "but Chapman and Stevens were assigned to the rear of the castle. Jeffries and I have been up on the wall in the middle bailey for the last thirty minutes."

"That's not right, sir. Chapman and I were tasked with watching the car park," Stevens said.

Bollocks. "Stevens, check the back gate. Jeffries, find the groundskeeper."

"They haven't slipped past us from the front," Natasha said. "I'm sure of it."

"I'm going to have a look at the cellar again as a precaution," Callum said.

Of all the times to screw up the assignments. That had been Natasha's job, but it was ultimately Callum's responsibility. If he couldn't stop Meg from jumping off the balcony, the head that would roll would be his. Callum trotted back into the passageway that led to the wine cellar.

Tourists' wet boots had made the stones slippery, and Callum was glad for the good tread on his rubber soled work shoes. No electric light or torch guided his feet as he descended into the darkness of the wine cellar, but as he neared the bottom of the stairs, dim light came from the doorway to the balcony. Callum reached it a second later and pulled up, stunned by what he saw.

"Stop!"

At Callum's shout, the woman—Meg—pushed back the hood of her cloak and glanced over her shoulder, letting the rain sweep into her face. Goronwy, the shorter, squatter, and greyer of the two men, already stood on the wall that overlooked the Wye River. He glared at Callum, who couldn't blame him, given that for the last twelve hours MI-5 had chased him across the length and breadth of Wales. All three fugitives looked as tired as Callum felt.

Goronwy's hand strayed to the hilt of his sword, but he didn't draw his weapon. Llywelyn didn't even glance at Callum. Instead, he hoisted himself up onto the stones to stand on the wall beside Goronwy. It wasn't a wide wall, either, maybe a foot deep. Both men balanced there securely, even Llywelyn with his gimpy heart.

"Please. Let us go." Meg clutched her skirt in one hand and gripped Goronwy's hand tightly with the other.

"Don't make another move except to step down slowly. I need you to come with me." Callum put a hand to his ear, noticing the absence of conversation, and realized that his earpiece had gone on the fritz again, blocked by the stones above his head.

Meg dropped her skirt and reached for Llywelyn's hand. "We can't. We have to go home."

While Callum watched, helpless to stop them, the two men lifted her onto the wall. Callum took a step forward, one hand out, fumbling with his other hand in the pocket of his trench coat for his phone. What he didn't do was pull his gun from its holster under his suit jacket. Callum needed to end this before it went further, but not with a bullet wound.

He pressed 'talk' and put the phone to his ear. As the phone rang, Meg, Llywelyn, and Goronwy sidled closer together. Goronwy and Llywelyn clutched Meg around the waist while she slipped her arms under their cloaks and held on.

Even as Natasha picked up with a distant *Hello?* Callum lowered the phone.

"Don't do it!" he said.

"*Sir?*" Natasha's voice came from Callum's phone.

Callum wanted to answer but the situation was too delicate. A wrong move by him might encourage them to jump. If Callum couldn't come up with the right thing to say, that headline on the front page of the national rag was going to be written after all.

Then feet pounded in the corridor above him, the metal fittings of boots rapping loudly on the stones. Callum didn't know if Meg heard the noise or if it was an instinctive twitch from him that gave the game away. As Meg bent her knees, Callum dropped his phone, took a step, and threw himself forward in a flying tackle. He managed to wrap his arms around Llywelyn's shins, but he was too late. Their feet had left the balustrade. Their combined weight and Callum's momentum carried him over the wall.

The water rushed four stories below him. As he fell, seconds passed as if they were days. He forgot to breathe. And then a great chasm of blackness opened beneath him and swallowed him whole.

Callum hit the river and went under.

Six Months Later ...

1

May 1289

Kings Langley Palace, Hertfordshire, England

Callum

Callum brought his sword down on David's shield and then sidestepped a countering move by mere inches. The king had gotten the jump on Callum early in the fight and had kept him on the defensive ever since. The two men drove back and forth—thrust, parry, block—until Callum's arm was shaking with the effort. For the mock fight, they were using blunted swords that were a half pound heavier than Callum's personal blade. The added weight made the fourteen years Callum had on David and the years of swordplay David had on Callum more evident with each minute that passed.

David's shield splintered. He dropped it, leaping to the attack with two hands on the hilt of his sword. Callum countered yet again, using his greater weight to push back until the two men grappled together, their faces a foot apart. They'd been going at it for half an hour now. David had cleared the small courtyard of watchers, but Callum could feel the eyes of the garrison on them, watching surreptitiously from the battlement and the top of the keep.

"Enough!" David shoved Callum away from him.

Callum dropped his sword and shield to the ground and bent forward with his hands on his knees, breathing hard. "Give up, do you?"

"I wouldn't want an old man to get hurt."

"You're only twenty," Callum said. "I wouldn't call that old."

David laughed and gazed at Callum with that particular expression he often wore—of amusement and intelligence and *am I really the King of England?* He didn't often turn it on Callum, and it made Callum straighten and forget the fight, instantly wary of what might be coming.

"You'll have muddy roads all the way north, unless this good weather lasts," David said.

Callum swallowed down laughter and incredulity. "So that's what this was all about? A test? You wanted to see if I was ready to go off on my own?"

"You've been cooling your heels as a glorified bodyguard since you came here," David said. "Today has been a long time coming."

"You're saying I'm to go to Scotland for you?" Callum clenched his suddenly shaking fists and took a step towards David.

"You speak Gaelic. How could I not send you?" David said. "I once stood in your shoes, you know."

Callum took in a deep breath and let it out, acknowledging that few men could understand Callum better than David. He had arrived in medieval Wales at the age of fourteen and grown to be the King of England. "That isn't something I could ever forget, even if others might."

"You could have told me how you felt," David said.

"You've had enough on your plate without worrying about me. I didn't want to make your life harder. But you're right. If I have to spend one more day with nothing of value to do, I might lose my mind."

"Then this is the right time for you to leave," David said.

In the early days of his sojourn in the medieval world, Callum had hoped that the near constant activity involved in learning this new way of life would be enough to sustain him until he could return to the modern world. But as the weeks and months had dragged on, it became increasingly clear that the opportunity for return was not going to be forthcoming—not from Meg, not from her daughter, Anna, and particularly not from her son, David, who had a kingdom to run.

Callum had come to accept that he was stranded in the Middle Ages for the time being. He hadn't asked Meg to take him back to the modern world, and after living for six months among these people, it seemed less likely with each passing day that he could. He understood that he would be able to leave only if an opportunity dropped into his lap. He couldn't plan on it. It would be a matter of being in the right place at the right time for once, as he'd been in the wrong place at the wrong time on the balcony at Chepstow.

By treating his life here as just another mission, and by living the life of a soldier again, Callum had also hoped to have banished the PTSD for good. But the enforced inactivity of late winter had unveiled new symptoms, worse ones. Callum dreamed every night of his old life in MI-5, or on bad nights, of the flash of exploding IEDs and death. He would wake with grit in his teeth, more tired than when he went to sleep. He'd taken to pushing himself physically so he could go to bed exhausted. If that didn't work, or Callum awoke in the night and couldn't go back to sleep, he would return to the hall and consume more beer than was good for him. A drinking companion was never hard to find in medieval England.

David hadn't said anything to Callum about his behavior. The king might be all of twenty years old, but he was still effectively Callum's boss. As odd as that was, David never took advantage of it, never threw his weight around, and never implied that he knew more than Callum about what was best for him. Even if he did.

Callum had spent much of the spring—when he wasn't learning impossible languages or practicing sword-fighting as he'd done today—riding with the garrison on patrol as if he belonged with the other men. Everyone knew Callum didn't. The men humored him, even accepted his company as his horsemanship improved, but he could never be one of them. Callum had finally concluded that he needed something real to do.

And it seemed that David, despite his total silence on the subject, had understood that too.

David tossed his weapon into a pile with Callum's sword and shield. Then he pulled off his gloves and sweat-soaked shirt, effectively giving Callum permission to do the same. The day had grown warm. David sat on a bench in the shade of a north-facing wall and leaned back, stretching his long legs in front of him. "From that first day at St. Paul's, I had every intention of using you. It was a matter of finding where your interests and mine aligned."

Until now, David hadn't asked anything of Callum, just provided: food and shelter, tutors, weapons training—anything that Callum thought he needed, and some things that he hadn't known he needed in order to take his place as a knight in medieval England. David hadn't said one word about Callum serving him.

But now ... now Callum had a task he could sink his teeth into.

Since Christmas, Callum had been catching up on all the British history that had bored him stiff in school. A matter of kings and crowns and untimely deaths, only some of which had turned out to be the same here as back in the old world.

David's current headache had to do with who would sit on Scotland's throne, empty since the death of the last king, Alexander III, in 1286. Scotland had been ruled during the three years since by a council of Guardians: two Scottish bishops, two Scottish lords, and two English noblemen. Callum's headache was keeping them all straight, but it helped that one of the English lords happened to be Gilbert de Clare, a strong ally of David. The other English lord had died and hadn't been replaced.

These Guardians had held the throne in trust on behalf of Alexander's last legitimate heir: his six-year-old granddaughter, Margaret. Fearful to wait until she grew up, her father, Erik of Norway, had sent the girl to Scotland to stand before her people as their queen. Margaret had died during the journey from Norway, however, before she could be crowned.

The girl's death had happened in the old world too, and King Edward had stepped in to mediate the succession. As the new King of England, it was David's task now, and all of Britain was counting on him to stop Scotland from going off the rails.

David tapped a finger to his lips. "I promised the Scots I would ride north to meet Margaret and speak before their Parliament, but I was hoping to put it off until the summer. Now that she's dead, I'm stuck with that promise and have a pressing need for a delegation. The Scots are still expecting me to come, but I can't go. You'll have to convey my regrets to them."

Callum went up on the balls of his feet and came down. "It's important to be here for the birth of your first child."

David scoffed. "You and I are the only men who think so. You should have heard the uproar among my advisors when I told them I wasn't going."

"The Scots might appreciate your lack of interference," Callum said.

"That's exactly what I explained to my council." David laughed. "The good news is that I have managed to turn my selfish desire into kingly magnanimity. By not journeying to Scotland now, I show the Scots that I mean what I say: I do not want their throne." He eyed Callum, still smirking. "You will have to do."

"What about Gilbert de Clare?" Callum said. "He could speak for you instead of me."

"He is overseeing his estates in Ireland," David said. "I sent him a message that he's needed, but communication being what it is, he may not have received it yet. I can't predict when he will arrive in Scotland."

"I will do my best for you, my lord." Callum bowed. He didn't bow before David very often, but this moment seemed to call for some formality.

"I trust you more than any of the other men I'm sending in the delegation," David said. "I'm counting on you to be my eyes and ears in Scotland. Bishop Kirby thinks he's the primary ambassador and will take all the responsibility for the mediation if he can—as well as all the credit for its success—but I don't trust him."

Callum met that statement with the silence it deserved, taking a moment to pour David a cup of water from a pitcher and hand it to him. Callum poured a cup for himself too, and they both drank. David had told Callum about the behind-the-scenes machinations that had taken place leading up to David's crowning as King of England. Kirby had forged documents attesting that Meg was the daughter of King Henry and Caitir, an illegitimate daughter of King Alexander II of Scotland.

Although David had declared time and again that the documents were fake, nobody seemed to believe him, especially since the Church had gone ahead and crowned him King of England anyway. Other claimants to the throne of Scotland now feared that those same documents gave David a right to the Scottish throne too, and that David would back up his supposed claim with military might.

"I have ordered Kirby to leave my rights out of this, no matter how acrimonious the negotiations become among the Scots." David poured the last of the water in his cup over his head and then brushed the wet hair back from his face with both hands. "Kirby has assented. I'm not getting involved in a war in Scotland. As you and I know, it would be a quagmire. Do try to head one off if you can."

"You're sure about asking Kirby to lead your delegation?" Callum said.

"The task should have gone to Archbishop Peckham, but he has been ill since the winter and is still recovering. Kirby begged for the job, and while his desire for it concerns me since it appears to me to be a thankless task, I don't want you to get sucked into the dispute. You are to stay free of bias towards any faction. Your job is to be a calming influence among the Scottish nobility, to ferret out what's happening behind closed doors and in the underbelly of the royal court, *and*—I want to know who killed Princess Margaret."

"She died of what sounds like the flu or pneumonia," Callum said.

David shrugged. "So they say. I'm reluctant to believe in so coincidental a death, even if it would take an awfully cold heart to murder a small child."

"It has happened before," Callum said. "Maybe recently."

"That's exactly my concern," David said. "It's bad enough that I never discovered if my predecessor, little Prince Edward, died of smallpox or was murdered. I don't want to place the crown of Scotland on the head of the man who ordered Margaret's death."

"I can't promise—"

"I'm asking too much, I know. Do what you can."

"Yes, my lord."

David smirked. "My title never sounds right coming from you, though it's not as bad as when my sister says it."

Callum smiled. "Yes, my lord."

Then David held up a hand, having one more thing to say. "To give you the stature you require in order to move freely throughout the north, I am awarding you the earldom of Shrewsbury."

All the air left Callum's chest. It was an outrageous gift and one he didn't deserve. David's advisors must have nearly had apoplexy when he suggested it. "My lord—you can't!"

"The Earldom of Shrewsbury was allowed to expire almost two hundred years ago," David said. "I can bestow it upon whomever I wish."

"I know for a fact that Humphrey de Bohun covets it for his son, William," Callum said.

"I've given Worcester to William. He didn't complain so I don't see why you should. It's a done deal. I signed the document this morning."

Callum was still staring at David, his mouth agape.

Then Lili appeared through the archway that led from the courtyard to the kitchen garden. She glanced at Callum and grinned. "I gather you told him?"

David stood, clapped a hand on Callum's shoulder, and strode past him towards his wife. As an excuse for David not to ride to Scotland, she was a good one. Less than a month remained in her pregnancy, and he was determined to be with her for the birth.

David had moved the court from Westminster Palace to Kings Langley so she could have sunshine and quiet as she waited. He had little of either himself no matter where he resided, although this was better than the stink and press of London. Even through Callum's very modern eyes, the London of the Middle Ages was crowded and polluted. Kings Langley couldn't compare to the mountains of Wales, but it was more like them than the city.

David took Lili's hand. "Are you well? Is there something you wanted?"

"I'm fine. I'm fine." Lili laughed at David's attentiveness. "I won't break, you know. I just came to tell you that the men on the wall can see Ieuan's banner in the distance."

"Finally!" David gestured that Callum should come with him.

Exiles in Time

Callum had met the rest of David's family at Christmas, after David's tour of England as the country's new king, but he hadn't seen any of them since then. In the Middle Ages, travel was dangerous and difficult. While David's rule had brought peace to England and its roads were for the most part safe, to travel a hundred miles still took three days on horseback. It was too much of a challenge for a woman with a new baby, of which David's family suddenly had quite a few.

A few weeks ago, David's sister, Anna, and her husband, Math, had welcomed a second son. They'd named him Bran after the original ruler of Dinas Bran, Math's seat in northeast Wales. Before that, in March, Meg had given birth to her twins, Elisa and Padrig. Neither woman felt comfortable leaving her children to travel to England.

Thus, the only family members who could make the journey from Wales for the birth of Lili's baby were Bronwen, a fellow time traveler; her husband, Ieuan (who was also Lili's brother); and their six-month-old daughter, Catrin.

Callum knew that childbirth was one of the events that seemed to precipitate time travel. He'd spent approximately one minute scheming as to how he might attend the births, on the off chance that one of the women *did* time travel home, but then discarded the idea just as quickly. What could he have done? Hovered over Anna or Meg as they labored, waiting for that moment when they might take him back to the modern world? It would have been an obscene request and he'd stayed in England rather than be tempted.

Callum accepted the clean shirt Lili had brought for him, slipping it on and buckling his real sword around his waist, before following David towards the gatehouse of the castle. They reached it just as the visitors came to a halt in the outer bailey.

Bronwen shot Callum a grin from the saddle as she handed Catrin down to Ieuan, who had dismounted first. "You're here!"

Callum moved to help her to the ground. "Why does that surprise you?"

"I don't know," Bronwen said. "You had the look a few months ago of someone whose feet were itching to hit the road."

"And so they are," Callum said.

Aaron, the physician for the Welsh royal court, held his hand to his lower back. "The journey from Caerphilly to London was quite enough for me."

"You are a steadfast companion, nonetheless, Aaron," Bronwen said, and then looked past him to smile at his son, "as is Samuel."

If Callum had thought the day couldn't be improved upon, he was wrong. Thanks to a long-term (clandestine) relationship with a Scottish woman who now lived in Carlisle, Samuel spoke Gaelic. Because Callum did too, Samuel had been one of the few people with whom Callum could communicate in the first months he'd lived in Wales. Like English and French, Gaelic had changed between the thirteenth century and the twenty-first, but Callum had more easily navigated those changes, and Samuel had been willing to help.

Although Samuel was of Jewish descent, at six feet tall, with light brown hair and the body of a soldier, he could be mistaken for a run-of-the-mill Englishman. Very often, he meant to be. Until the death of Edmund of Lancaster, King Edward's brother in whose company Samuel served before 1285, Samuel had denied his Jewish heritage and passed for an Englishman. In the new world David had created, such deception was no longer required. Not surprisingly, Samuel now served David instead of any English baron.

Samuel had lived his life on the outside looking in, pretending to fit in with Gentiles—and doing it so well that he'd never been found out. Despite the vast difference of time and culture between Callum and Samuel, Callum had found that he could relate to Samuel more than to any other medieval man and counted him as one of his few friends.

Callum strode over to Samuel and the two men clasped forearms. "Sir." Samuel bowed his head slightly.

"Welcome," Callum said.

"Thank you for coming, all of you," David said.

"Thank you for inviting us, sire," Samuel said, "but to what do I owe the honor of your invitation?"

"Earl Callum has agreed to join my delegation to Scotland." David shot Callum a grin. "He is to be my eyes and ears. I want you to be his."

Callum looked at David. "You've been planning this for a while, haven't you? Why didn't you tell me—?" He snapped his mouth shut as David tilted his head and gave him a questioning look. "Right." Callum turned back to Samuel.

"It would be my pleasure to serve you, my lord," Samuel said, and then paused, his eyes glancing towards David. "Did you say, *Earl*?"

David grinned. "Callum is the newly installed Earl of Shrewsbury."

"A wise choice, my lord." Samuel bowed, a smile twitching at the corner of his lips. "May I ask why you chose me for this journey?"

David narrowed his eyes. "Do you object to the post? You speak Gaelic and English, you're loyal to me, and you're good with a sword. Why not you?"

"You have other talents as well that make you particularly suited to the job," Callum said.

"Such as what?" Samuel said, but then nodded as he caught on. "Oh yes. That would be lying."

"It's a useful skill, whether or not the leaders of our respective religions would agree," Callum said.

David clapped a hand on each of their shoulders and shook once. "I, on the other hand, am very bad at it. Lili despairs of me because I turn red, stammer, and look down at my feet."

"I'm not sure that's such a bad thing," Callum said.

"When would you have us leave, my lord?" Samuel said.

"Tomorrow," David said. "Can you two work together?"

"Yes, my lord," Samuel and Callum said in unison.

"Good." David nodded at Samuel, indicating he was dismissed. With a final bow in the king's direction, Samuel and his father went into the hall. Then David turned to Callum, switching to American English. "He's a common soldier and can ask questions where you cannot. Between the two of you, I have a chance of getting at the truth."

Callum sensed that David had mentally checked Scotland off of his list of things to do. Callum had seen him create the lists, scribbling on scraps of paper he carried around with him at all times. Without warning, he would pull one from an inner pocket to tick items off or add new ones. Callum didn't know how David managed to keep so many balls in the air at once, even with two very efficient secretaries.

Meanwhile, Ieuan had fallen into a conversation in rapid Welsh with Lili. It would have proved too much for Callum, even if they had wanted to include him. Lili squeezed David's hand and went off with her brother, following Samuel and Aaron. That left Callum alone with David and Bronwen, who had been watching the various exchanges with little Catrin on her hip.

Now, Bronwen came over to hug Callum. "I see you have a job. I'm glad."

"You may note that it appears to be the worst one David could think of." But Callum smiled as he said it.

"I'm standing right here," David said. "I speak American too." The three time travelers stood in a little circle. It was as if they'd created their own cone of silence in the center of the bailey while the activity of the castle went on around them.

Bronwen laughed and elbowed David. "Those jobs are the ones he gives to people he trusts the most. Besides, Scotland is a mess and getting more dangerous by the day. You could hardly do worse than King Edward did in the old world."

"King Edward chose John Balliol to be king because he thought Balliol was weaker than Robert Bruce and could be manipulated," David said. "Having never met either man, I can't say which I prefer. Callum will just have to figure it out when he gets there."

"I can't believe I'm going to have to deal with *three* Robert Bruces," Callum said. "How am I to keep them straight, much less keep track of everyone else who claims the throne?"

"Easy," Bronwen said. "The one who's claiming the throne now is Grampa Bruce, his son is Daddy Bruce, and the boy, the one who becomes *the* Robert the Bruce a few decades from now, is Baby Bruce."

"Given that he's fourteen years old," David said, "I suspect he wouldn't take kindly to that nickname. I believe they call him *Robbie*."

"Whatever." Bronwen patted Callum's hand. "Just be grateful they're not all named something unpronounceable like they would be if they were Welsh."

David laughed. "More than anything, I'd like to avoid war. In the old world, King Edward died of dysentery while campaigning in Scotland. That isn't going to be my fate. We're going to figure this out without bloodshed."

Bronwen bit her lip. "You're more worried about this than I expected, David. Do you think it's going to be dangerous for Callum?"

"I hope not," David said.

"We're talking about Scotland, right? We have no idea what's going to happen," Callum said. "And honestly, that's a good thing. If it comes to a fight, I can handle myself."

Bronwen turned on him. "What's with you guys? You come to the Middle Ages and within six months, swinging a sword at an enemy's head is the most fun you can think of."

"Bronwen," David said, "Callum didn't mean anything—"

"Didn't he?" Bronwen glared at David. She was one of three or four people on the planet who could get away with it.

"It's okay, Bronwen." Callum touched her arm with one finger and then moved it up to allow Catrin to wrap her whole hand around it. "I know soldiering. I asked for this job."

"Callum has even learned to curse like a medieval man," David said. "'By St. Gwendolyn's ear', and 'St. Kentigern's bones' are his new favorites. I've heard him myself."

Bronwen tsked under her breath. "We haven't lost any of us yet and I don't want to start with you. Meg feels guilty enough as it is." She abruptly kissed Callum's cheek, and then David's, and left, though not before Callum saw the tears in her eyes.

David looked after her for a long moment and then back at Callum. "Callum—"

"I spoke the truth," Callum said. "When I first arrived here, your mother told me that I had come to the Middle Ages for a reason. I don't know if this is it, or even what she meant, but as long as I'm here, I mean to make something of my life. I think I can make a difference—to you and to the people here."

"I knew I was right to choose you." David stepped closer. "You don't know my father well, but when I first came to Wales, he spoke to me of what it meant to be a man, to lead, and to rule. He talked to me of honor."

Callum gazed into David's eyes, thinking that this king knew far too much about too many things for a boy his age, and that despite Callum's best efforts to see him with clear eyes, David had pulled him under his spell as he had everyone else.

"As did my father," Callum said. "Honor is an easy word to throw around without a true understanding of its meaning."

"And what does it mean to you?" David said.

"To do what is right, regardless of the personal cost," Callum said.

"Most people live only for themselves and thus have no honor," David said. "When a man thinks about feeding his physical wants and not his heart for too long, one day he wakes up with his soul as hollow as his stomach and a lot harder to fill. That's not been your problem, however."

"Do I have a problem?" Callum said, his palms sweating at how close David was to the truth of what was inside him.

"I wasn't there—I don't know what you went through—but my wish for you is that you can find something here, or someone, that can help you fill that hollow space your war carved out of you."

"And you think I might find that in Scotland?" Callum said.

"I don't know," David said, "but it's a place to start."

As Callum watched King David join his wife and family in the hall, it occurred to him that he wasn't the only one who'd come a long way since Chepstow.

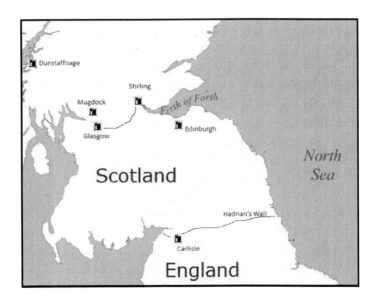

2

Callum

It had taken days longer than Callum had hoped it might to reach the north of England. Edinburgh, located on the east coast of Scotland, was over four hundred miles by road from London. They weren't there yet and wouldn't be for a few more days. They had been forced to ride at a leisurely pace thanks to Kirby, who was a poor horseman and had insisted on riding in a carriage instead of on horseback. It felt to Callum as if they'd plodded their way across England, journeying for ten hours each day just to travel the allotted thirty miles.

Callum's meager consolation was that he was sleeping better than he had at Kings Langley and the weather was pleasant.

Callum had made it his business to find out as much as he could about his traveling companions, most of whom were purely military men, knights with small estates or men-at-arms rather than diplomats. Their job was to protect Kirby, who from his passing comments neither trusted nor liked the Scots. Callum hadn't been an earl long enough to acquire a personal guard himself. Before Callum left Kings Langley, David had promised that when he returned from Scotland, Callum had leave to travel to Shrewsbury and figure out what it meant to be its lord.

Samuel, doing his duty, had made friends with most of the men, including Liam, Kirby's cousin. Liam's mother had married a Scotsman (against the wishes of her family, naturally). While the mother had remained the black sheep of the family, Kirby had brought Liam back into the fold and had included him on this journey because he spoke Gaelic. Samuel, Liam, and Callum had found that the first few evenings of their journey passed more pleasantly in each other's company, even if an earl wouldn't normally be seen hobnobbing with underlings such as they. That was one of the benefits of being an earl, Callum had found. He could do whatever he damn well pleased, not that he wouldn't have anyway.

Four days out of London, they stopped at the royal castle of Skipton. Waiting for them at the castle was twenty-eight-year-old James Stewart, Guardian of Scotland and its Lord High Steward, a title he'd inherited from his father. With him came a company of twenty men and Baby Bruce, otherwise known as Robbie, his fourteen-year-old squire. James had come to greet King David, still thinking he was the leader of the company. He stayed despite the king's absence. He'd been relieved by it, in fact, just as David had hoped.

As they made their way further north, heading for Carlisle, Callum tried to get at James's purpose in joining his little band with theirs, whether to influence the outcome of the mediation (possibly in Grampa Bruce's favor) or merely to scope out the tenor of the delegation. Either way, Kirby welcomed James cordially and took Robbie under his wing. Their conversations tended to be one-sided, however, with Kirby pontificating in French and Robbie listening. From the bits Callum had overheard, Kirby talked mostly about the glories of his recent trip to France—particularly the fine wine he'd had the opportunity to drink—and lectured Robbie on how to be a better squire.

If Kirby was aware of the danger of favoring one claimant to the Scottish throne over another, he didn't show it. He appeared to be so prejudiced against all Scots that he might soon offend them all. Callum wished David had chosen almost anyone else to lead the delegation. Perhaps King David had misread the tenor of Kirby's distrust of the Scots, or the churchman had hidden it better back in London. Callum wondered what Kirby really thought of David, a barbaric Welshman, even if he was England's king.

Then again, maybe David did know exactly who and what Kirby was, and that was why he had included Callum in the company.

Their last stop before entering Scotland was at Carlisle. Taking up nearly ten acres, the castle sat on rising ground at the northern end of the city. David had given Callum the rundown on the castle as part of his briefing, with the added remark—mentioned at the end of their conversation and with amusement—to remember him to Sir John de Falkes, the castellan. A couple of years ago, the man had locked up David and Ieuan. They'd escaped with the help of Falkes's nephew, Thomas. Falkes's soldiers had subsequently chased David and Ieuan to the coast and they'd gotten away only by time traveling to the modern world.

Although Callum was going to do as the king asked, he was pretty sure that David was far more amused by this potential conversation than Falkes would be.

Robbie, riding alongside Callum, waved his hand in the direction of Carlisle, indicating it and the countryside around it. "Our people have raided these lands for centuries. They should be ours." Carlisle had once been a Roman city, standing as one of the last bastions of 'civilization' before the wilds of Scotland. Hadrian's Wall stretched seventy miles east from the city.

Callum glanced at the boy, uncertain if he was boasting or merely stating what he believed to be fact. He opted to respond to Robbie's words as if they were the latter, though the fire in the young Scot's eyes gave Callum pause. "War has been a way of life in these lands since before the Romans came."

Robbie clenched both fists around the reins. "My grandfather would like to avoid war this time."

"But not you?" Callum said. "You would fight?"

James made a calming motion with his hand, but at a nod from Callum, he arrested his movement. Callum wanted to know what Robbie thought. The boy was fourteen, the same age David had been when he'd come to Wales in 1282, and therefore Robbie had reached manhood with the right to a man's opinions. Besides, if history played out here like it had in Callum's old world, Robbie would be King of Scotland someday.

"Of course!" Robbie said.

"King David would like to avoid bloodshed too," Callum said.

"If King David chooses Balliol for the crown, he will be making a mistake," Robbie said. "It might be necessary to show him the error of his ways."

James couldn't keep silent any longer. "Robert."

"My grandfather would make a good king, better than that sop Balliol. He is an old man," Robbie said.

"And you are too hotheaded for your own good." James tipped his head at Callum. "Pardon my squire, my lord. He sees only what is in front of him."

That might be true, but Robbie's outspokenness only made Callum more interested in hearing what he had to say. "What is it about Balliol that you don't like, other than his age?" The fourteen-year-old's perception of age had little to do with reality, since at forty Balliol wasn't exactly decrepit, even for the Middle Ages.

"He wavers," Robbie said.

"Does he?" Callum kept his tone as unconcerned as possible. James didn't attempt to stop his squire from speaking anymore, just gazed stonily ahead. As Guardian of Scotland, it was his role to remain neutral in the current dispute, but his family was closely related to the Bruces. Callum's crash course in Scottish history had told him that in the old world, James had supported his squire's claim to the throne of Scotland in the war against King Edward.

"He lacks fire and thinks the crown is his by right of birth when it is my grandfather's." Robbie pushed out his lower lip, making himself look more like a twelve-year-old than the man he wanted to be. "And Balliol is not a warrior."

That was probably the most damning thing the boy could think to say about a Scottish nobleman, or any nobleman for that matter. Hadn't Callum found acceptance into this society far easier because he knew what it meant to be a soldier? What would he have found if he'd come to the Middle Ages having spent his life as a computer technician? Or if he hadn't been blessed with a tall stature and broad shoulders? How would his mail armor have hung on him then? Callum didn't want to think about that. He was having a hard enough time as it was.

"Your leaders, with King David's help, will make the right decision," Callum said.

Robbie's chin jutted out in defiance. "The people should decide. If they were given a chance they would choose my grandfather." Maybe Robbie really did mean the common folk—the men anyway—when he said 'people', but Callum doubted it. Real democracy for Scotland was centuries away. Regardless, Robbie would have been disappointed to learn that in the old world, the consensus among the barons of Scotland had been for Balliol.

The company finally passed through Carlisle's southern gate following the old Roman road. Once inside, they had to ride the length of the city before they reached the grassy expanse that separated the castle gate from the city walls. A grassed moat that could be flooded by the nearby river protected the inner gatehouse. They crossed it without difficulty and entered the castle's outer bailey, which was the size of a football field. The sight of Carlisle had Callum comparing yet again a living, breathing castle to the ruin that was Chepstow in the twenty-first century. It was like comparing a Ferrari to a Chevy Nova that had been stripped for parts.

Sir John de Falkes himself strode from underneath the inner gatehouse tower. Four men paced behind him. Kirby got down from his carriage and came forward, accompanied by two fellow churchmen and three English noblemen, all of whom David had perceived to be relatively impartial towards the Scottish. Falkes greeted Kirby in French and together the men headed into the inner bailey.

The outrageous snub left Callum laughing to himself. Kirby wasn't obsequious, Callum had to give him that. The bishop, though he had accepted Callum's presence readily enough, hadn't ever given him the attention his title merited as the newly designated Earl of Shrewsbury. At the same time, Callum had endeavored to keep a low profile, not wanting to be viewed as a jumped-up earl even if he was. He found the hierarchy of the medieval world annoying much of the time anyway, and in this case, he wasn't sorry to be 'overlooked'. Callum's job was to snoop around, not sit on display at the high table listening to other men preen and pontificate.

"He didn't wait for either of you." Robbie had dismounted immediately upon entering the bailey in expectation of James being invited into the castle. The boy looked up at Callum. "I might have expected such insolence from an Englishman towards a Scotsman, but doesn't Bishop Kirby know who you are, my Lord Callum?"

"Oh, he does," Callum said.

"Never you mind, Robbie." James dropped to the ground beside his squire.

Callum clapped a hand on Robbie's shoulder. "Listen to your master. It is better to be underestimated. It leaves one's options open."

A stable boy took the horses away. At least Callum wasn't so low as to have to care for his own horse, though he often did because he wanted to. Callum caught Samuel's eye as his friend led his horse towards the enormously long stable built against the curtain wall. Samuel nodded back. They would meet later to discuss anything of interest they'd learned from their respective sources. Callum turned back to his Scottish companions.

"Am I wrong or did King David, your ancestor, take this castle from the English during his reign?" Callum said to Robbie.

James snorted laughter. "Don't—don't get him started again."

Robbie gave James an evil look and stalked on ahead.

"What about you?" Callum asked James. "You don't share our young friend's beliefs or aspirations for his grandfather? Or for yourself, for that matter?"

James stopped walking, allowing Robbie to get another ten paces towards the inner gatehouse. He studied Callum's face for a moment and then said, "If you are to be of service to your king, you need to understand us. Will you come with me now?"

"Of course." Curious, Callum followed James to the steps that led to the battlements above the curtain wall that surrounded the castle. A gatehouse tower allowed them to overlook the whole castle and the city. James gestured towards the north. "This is what I believe in. I would die for Scotland without a second thought."

Callum gazed to where James pointed. On the other side of the River Eden, Scotland stretched before them. Without the A7 highway heading north and a built-up countryside, there was nothing to see but patches of farmland and stands of trees, with hills in the distance. This was good country. No wonder it had been fought over for so long, though even eight hundred years after the Romans had left, the land to the north of Hadrian's Wall had few settlements.

"I believe in Scotland—a Scotland separate from England. It is my hope that your new king believes in it too," said James.

"I don't pretend to know all that goes on in my king's mind. I can't speak for him beyond the matter of the succession," Callum said, "but he has no designs on Scotland for himself."

"But what of his ancestry?" James's hands tightened into fists as they rested on the stones of the battlement. "His claim is as real as many who seek the throne, even if through an illegitimate daughter. He is closer by blood to the throne than either Bruce or Balliol."

Callum sighed. David had told him not to bother denying the documents attesting to Meg's royal blood if they came up. David would deny them himself as many times as it took for people to accept he was telling the truth, but were Callum to do so, it would look like he was trying to undermine David's rule.

"Even if some Scottish lords would accept David as king of Scotland, many would not," Callum said. "He would have to take the throne by force and he doesn't want a war with Scotland any more than you want one with England."

"That is what I'd heard." James gazed straight ahead. "I wasn't sure if I believed it."

Callum shrugged. "Before last year, many wouldn't have believed that the English barons could agree with one another long enough to anoint a prince of Wales as King of England either."

"His rule was better than a civil war," said James. "And again, he carries the blood of King Henry in his veins through his mother. My fear is that some of my peers will fear a claim from him, regardless of what he says openly, and begin the war now rather than wait for it to come to them."

"You know your peers better than I," Callum said, "but I hope you are mistaken."

"Regardless, I would not want to see the two thrones united," said James.

Callum's mouth twitched, but he restrained his laughter out of deference to James who was perfectly serious. Callum's lack of interest in history had dogged him since he'd arrived in the Middle Ages, but he, like virtually every child who spent any time in the British school system, couldn't help but retain one historical tidbit about James: it was his descendants, the Stuarts, who had united the crowns of Scotland and England. James Stewart could become the grandfather of kings.

The evening meal passed as it had in every castle they'd visited so far. Their seventy men were a sizable addition to the population of any castle, but for one night they could be fed and housed without too much inconvenience to the castellan. Falkes and Kirby kept their heads together most of the evening. Watching them, Callum regretted not being included on the dais. Kirby plotted and connived as easily as he breathed. According to David, that wasn't true of Carlisle's castellan. Falkes had crusaded with King Edward and had been rewarded with the honor of Carlisle. He was a military man. It was Callum's thought that he might speak Callum's language more than Kirby's. Callum planned to find out soon if that was true.

Meanwhile, as he had in every place he stayed, he observed the diners in the hall. In the early days, the upside of Callum's ignorance of the language had meant that he'd had to figure out what was going on around him by watching instead of listening. What Callum had seen was people lying to each other. He'd seen smiles that never reached eyes, shoulders that shifted even as a man nodded agreement, and covert glances between diners who were seated at the opposite ends of a table.

Callum had told himself not to be surprised: Shakespeare hadn't concocted his stories out of nothing. And it wasn't that modern people didn't lie, cheat, steal, and commit adultery. It was just that they didn't tend to do it under the noses of a hundred other people who were forced continually into each other's company.

Samuel sat heavily on the bench opposite Callum. "All is quiet."

"You didn't really expect the Scots to march on Carlisle today, did you?" Callum said.

"You can never be too careful."

"What about your lady friend?" Callum said. "Doesn't she live in the town?"

"She does," Samuel said.

Callum eyed him. "And?"

"And what?" Samuel said. "Tonight is not the night for me to slip away from the castle to see her. Besides, her uncle watches her closely these days."

"I would like to see you court her openly," Callum said. "Her uncle will just have to *get over* the fact that you're Jewish."

Samuel's brow furrowed. "Men don't just get over such a thing."

"Well they should," Callum said. "Surely King David will vouch for you. That ought to count for something."

"He has already said he would," Samuel said.

"So what's stopping you?" Callum said. "Life is short, man. How much longer are you going to wait?"

Samuel picked at the food on the trencher in front of him. "I will speak to her in my own time, my lord."

Callum backed off. He'd been speaking casually to Samuel—as a friend—but this was the Middle Ages and the difference in their stations meant that some of what he had said could be interpreted as an order. "I'm sorry," Callum said. "It's none of my business. I won't speak of it again."

Samuel nodded and rose to his feet. "I'll make another circuit."

Callum watched him go. The man was in love and afraid of his feelings. Of course, Callum was hardly one to talk. When was the last time he'd allowed himself to get that close to anyone?

As an agent in the security services, dating had always been fraught with peril. Callum had dated women in pursuit of information more often than in pursuit of a real relationship. Real dates were more challenging. Callum didn't know any coworkers who didn't find the lies exhausting after a few dates. For Callum's part, he had gone back and forth. Sometimes he'd preferred superficial interactions to telling lies. In the months before he'd come to medieval Britain, however, he'd been looking for something more.

Callum had been with his last girlfriend, Emma, only a few weeks before he'd traveled to the Middle Ages. It hadn't been long enough to know how she would have come to view his erratic schedule, less-than-helpful explanations about his job, and lack of forthcomingness in general. Not to mention his demeanor, which other women had occasionally described as 'wooden'. By the time he'd disappeared, she hadn't yet caught on to his obsession with how his hands smelled.

Emma had been expecting Callum for dinner on the night he'd fallen from the balcony at Chepstow Castle. He found it likely that it hadn't taken long for her to move on from him.

Darkness had enclosed the castle and the meal was drawing to a close by the time Callum approached the high table where Falkes sat with the other noblemen. For the meal, James Stewart had found a place among them, with Robbie attending him. Callum had taken a seat near the upper end of one of the long tables, though not below the salt.

Callum came to a halt on the opposite side of the table from Falkes's seat. He didn't put his heels together or bow but only said, "Thank you for your hospitality."

Falkes looked up at Callum and frowned. "Who are you?"

James had watched Callum approach the dais with bright eyes, and now a look of delight crossed his face. He leapt to his feet and came closer. "My Lord Falkes, may I introduce to you the Lord Callum, Earl of Shrewsbury and King David's personal representative to the nation of Scotland."

Falkes had good control because his mouth opened only slightly—and then he was on his feet, bowing. "I apologize, my lord. I did not know who you were. Please—" He gestured to the seat next to him that Kirby had just vacated.

Callum had purposely waited until the bishop left before coming to talk to Falkes. His words were for Falkes's ears alone. While David had entrusted these negotiations to Kirby, Callum wasn't going to trust him with anything else. And certainly not with tidbits of David's history that nobody else needed to know.

Still grinning, James made his way back to his seat at the far end of the table.

Falkes waited until Callum sat before sitting himself, and then he straightened his shoulders. With another bow of his head, he said, "I apologize for not greeting you earlier. I did not know that King David had sent a personal representative of your stature with the company. Bishop Kirby never mentioned that you were here. I would have made a place of honor for you at the high table." Falkes's face flushed. He was very angry, but not at Callum.

"I don't offend easily, and my role is not Kirby's," Callum said. "I was content with where I sat. The beer was just as good."

Falkes allowed himself a wisp of a smile, but he still had a 'v' of concern between his brows. "Nonetheless, I ask your forgiveness." Falkes cleared his throat. "Please give my greetings to the king when you see him next."

Callum was inordinately pleased, now that it came to it, that Kirby had snubbed him so profoundly. Because he'd slighted Callum publically, without a commensurate response on Callum's part, Kirby had given Callum power over him. There might come a time when Callum could take advantage of Kirby's pettiness.

"King David speaks well of you. He sent me with a specific message for your ears alone," Callum said to Falkes.

Falkes was sitting so upright he could have had a steel rod up his spine. "I'm sure I have done nothing to earn the king's attention."

His response told Callum that Falkes truly didn't know who David was and how he knew him. "You are loyal to him, are you not?" Callum said.

"Of course!" Falkes half rose from his seat. "What is this? Who do you take me for?"

"I take you for a man who serves his king with honor," Callum said, willing to appease him now that he had Falkes where he wanted him. It was really too bad David couldn't be here to witness this.

Falkes sat back, mollified. "I have seen with my own eyes what England has suffered these years without a strong hand to guide her. It would be anarchy up here if not for a few good men who hold the north for the crown."

Callum studied Falkes a moment before he enlightened him: "King David asks for confirmation of your loyalty because the last time you and he met, it was under less than ideal circumstances. He wanted to assure himself that you bear him no grudge, as he bears none for you."

Falkes went very still. "I-I'm not sure I understand. What could I have done to arouse King David's ire? I would remember if I'd met him."

"He asked that I prod your memory," Callum said. "Nearly four years ago, you encountered a young Welshman and his companion along Hadrian's Wall. The year before, his mother had rescued your nephew, Thomas, who'd been captured by Scottish marauders. King David spent some hours in the cell at the back of your stables."

David had *so* wanted to be here to see Falkes's reaction to this news, and Falkes didn't disappoint. "I didn't-I didn't—" Falkes's face drained of all color and he swallowed hard.

"The King understands that you meant no disrespect and acknowledges that he didn't tell you at the time that he was the Prince of Wales," Callum said.

Falkes was already recovering from the shock of Callum's revelation, and acceptance of his new reality wasn't far behind. "I must tell you that I would not have treated him better had I known his true identity." Falkes paused. "And yet, even with the history between us, he leaves me as castellan of Carlisle?"

"He has first-hand knowledge of how vigilantly you patrol the north for him," Callum said. "Do you pledge to continue with your task?"

Falkes gave a sharp jerk of his head. "Yes."

Callum was pleased to see no hesitation in Falkes's manner. "King David wanted you to know who he was before you answered his call to come to the Tower of London at midsummer."

"The Tower—what did you say?" said Falkes.

"King David is summoning all his castellans and his sheriffs to him," Callum said. "He met many when he journeyed across England before Christmas, but he wants to consult with you all at the same time, to discuss your views and opinions on the needs of his country."

Falkes swallowed down whatever objections he had been about to voice. "I will be there."

"Good." Callum rose to his feet. "Please bring your nephew with you when you come."

Falkes clenched his teeth. "Of course."

Callum had been about to leave, but the ferocity in Falkes's face had him sitting down again. "The King has no plans to make Thomas hostage to your good behavior, if that is what you fear."

It had been. If David were to go that route, it certainly wouldn't be without precedent. In the past, it was common practice for a king or lord to hold a man's loved ones hostage to ensure that a lord obeyed him in all things. More than one Welsh son had lost his life when his father had found the king's commands untenable.

Falkes leaned forward. "Your news disturbs me. You tell me that King David holds no grudge against me, but I remember him. I remember that my men hunted him through the countryside. One of them wounded his companion. How can he forgive that? If I come to London, he will have my head."

"Is that the man King David is?" Callum said. "You've had an ear to the ground since he took the throne. That's what your spies tell you of his character?"

"William de Valence has fled to France," said Falkes. "He feared the king's wrath."

"Valence plotted against King David's life," Callum said. "He's lucky not to be in the Tower of London with the rest of his co-conspirators—or without his head. The King has forgiven far worse crimes than yours since he took the throne of England. Unlike Valence, you were only doing what you saw as your duty. He knows it."

Falkes sat back in his chair. "What of Scotland?"

"What of it?" Callum said.

"Bishop Kirby tells me that King David seeks a peaceful answer to the question of succession and does not put forth his own claim to the throne. Kirby says that King David does not seek it."

"That's true. He has no desire for the crown of Scotland on his head," Callum said.

Falkes started to scoff his disbelief again but then stopped himself. "You are right that I have no evidence or reason to disbelieve my king. I am loyal to the crown of England. I am loyal to King David if it is my loyalty he wants."

"He wants it," Callum said. "That is as he hoped."

Falkes reached for his cup of wine, though his hand shook as he grasped the stem, and he did not attempt to bring the cup to his mouth. "Margaret."

"Excuse me?"

"The woman, Margaret, who rescued Thomas. She is the Queen of Wales, then?"

"Indeed. She is King David's mother," Callum said.

Falkes put his head in his hands as the delayed realization hit him. Callum could hardly blame him. It was a lot to take in. Then Falkes dropped his hands. He jerked his chin as if to say *okay, moving on*. "While I should have known that he was more than he said, God protected him from my hand. If you say that King David forgives my treatment of him, I believe you." Falkes scooted back his chair and stood. He bowed low. "Please tell the king that I will come to London at midsummer."

Callum stood to match him. "He will be pleased to see you."

"Uncle?"

Callum and Falkes turned to see a teenager approaching. He wore a surcoat with two doves on it.

Falkes held out his hand to the boy. "Thomas, this is Lord Callum, Earl of Shrewsbury. King David sent him to greet both of us."

"My lord." Thomas bowed. "You have honored Carlisle with your presence."

Falkes made an impatient gesture with his hand, though Thomas's greeting had been very professionally done. "Did you want something?" said Falkes.

"Just to tell you that Bishop Kirby has retired for the evening," Thomas said.

Falkes nodded.

"I will retire as well." Callum lifted a hand to Falkes and then stepped off the dais. Thinking it was time to find Samuel again, he headed down the length of the hall towards the great doors.

Thomas fell into step beside Callum. "I heard what you said to my uncle."

Callum glanced at him, surprised. "Did you really? I didn't see you nearby and your uncle and I weren't speaking loudly."

"Robbie Bruce and I sat together a few seats down from my uncle. You didn't see me because I had my back to him. But I have good hearing."

"So you know who King David is?" Callum said.

Thomas shot Callum a grin tinged with satisfaction. "I knew all along he wasn't a simple merchant."

"He has a message for you too," Callum said.

Thomas glanced up, his eyes glinting. Callum could see why David wanted to be remembered to him. Anyone who had the audacity to set Carlisle's stables on fire as a diversion in order to free David and Ieuan from their captivity—against his uncle's express wishes—was worth a second look.

"King David says, 'thank you'."

"I was glad he got away." Thomas grinned again, but then his smile faded and his face fell. "You didn't say anything to my uncle about the manner of the king's escape, did you?"

They'd reached the door to the hall. Before answering, Callum allowed the guard to open the door and let them pass through it. Once at the bottom of the exterior steps, Callum pulled Thomas to one side. "Your uncle still doesn't know who set fire to the stables and freed his prisoners?"

"No. And I'd prefer he never knew," Thomas said.

"Your uncle might thank you now," Callum said.

Thomas looked back towards the hall. "He might." Then he shivered. "I'd be afraid to tell him though."

"Then tell him this," Callum said. "Tell him that he has nothing to fear from King David."

3

Callum

Samuel pushed back his hood and straightened in his saddle. He used his shield like an umbrella to protect himself from the rain and turned this way and that, surveying their surroundings. "This doesn't feel right." His gaze went to Callum and then to Liam, who rode on Callum's other side.

Liam nodded his agreement. "It's too quiet. Where are the birds and the animals? It's raining, but it often rains here. It should affect them little."

While much of Scotland had been denuded of trees, cut down for firewood and prevented from growing back by free roaming cattle and sheep, this was one place where the trees enclosed the road. More trees covered the hills that rose up on either side of the road, marking the border between lowland and highland Scotland.

Callum hunched over his horse, tugging his cloak closer against the rain. The clouds had come in the moment they'd crossed the border into Scotland. They'd spent last night in Glasgow and were headed today for Stirling Castle, one of the ancient royal seats of the Scottish crown, twenty miles away as the crow flies, though longer as they were taking it. One of the Guardians, William Fraser, Bishop of St. Andrews, had so far managed to keep the castle out of the hands of both Balliol and Bruce, for the good of Scotland. All of Scotland's Guardians, along with its Parliament, were to gather there in a few days' time.

Stirling Castle sat at the mouth of the Firth of Forth and was the closest royal castle to the Highlands, which stretched north from the road they were presently on, all the way to the North Sea. In the last six months, Callum had come to understand some of the difficulties involved in ruling Wales, a small country with many petty princes and lords. Though England was larger and richer, it was actually less complicated politically. Scotland, however, was another story entirely. Few kings had ever managed to rule the entire country. Dozens of clans held their own lands, ruled them as mini-kingdoms, and fought among themselves with little interference from the king, as long as the fighting didn't overflow into another lord's domains.

It was an arrangement similar to that which the Marcher barons had enjoyed in their lands on the border of Wales and England—until Wales had gained the upper hand upon the death of King Edward. Now that David was the King of England, he was beginning to reel in the Marcher barons even more and diminish their power in the March. The next Scottish king would want to do the same for the clans he ruled.

At this moment, however, with no ruling king, the balance of power lay between the Bruces and the Balliols. All the other clans lined up on whichever side they owed the greatest loyalty, through family ties or precedence.

A strong breeze caught Callum's hood and swept it off his head. He reached back to pull it up again, half-turning towards Samuel, who was still scanning the hills to the northwest. Callum shielded his eyes so the rain couldn't fall directly into them. "What do you see?" he said.

"Nothing," Samuel said. "That's the problem."

Callum peered upwards, tracing the line of the hill that rose up from the road immediately to the left. It might be May and the sun in the sky for twelve hours a day, but that didn't make Scotland any brighter on the days when clouds covered the sky from horizon to horizon, as they had all that day. The company had made slow progress through the murk, all the more so because of Kirby's carriage.

By now, every man in the company was cursing Kirby's refusal to ride. Ever since Carlisle, they'd had to stop every hour, or multiple times an hour, to unstick Kirby's wheels from the mud. In addition, nobody had told Kirby that most rivers in Scotland weren't crossed by bridges, even on the main roads. Every time they reached a ford, Kirby had fussed about the possibility of getting wet. It was very trying. Yesterday, Samuel had threatened to throw the bishop over his horse's withers and make him ride the rest of the way upside down if he complained one more time. Samuel almost hadn't been joking.

Fortunately, Kirby had been quieter today, huddled in his carriage with his hood up and a blanket wrapped around his shoulders against the rain and cold, so Samuel hadn't gone through with his threat. Still, the delays had continued and it would be dark within the hour.

Callum brushed desultorily at the muck from a carriage wheel that dirtied his cloak. He was pleased at how little he cared about the mud on his hands as he might have if he'd still been living in the modern world. In addition, the further he'd come from Kings Langley, the more surely the mantle of resolution he'd worn as a soldier had settled onto his shoulders. With each day that passed, it wrapped itself around him more tightly than his actual cloak. His ability to focus on the task at hand improved too, along with his mood, allowing him to look at the world with eyes that assessed threat and how to combat it. He'd known that he'd missed this feeling, but back in London or Cardiff, he hadn't admitted how much, not even to himself.

"Do you fear an attack?" Callum said.

"What do I know?" Samuel said. "I always fear it. That's how a man stays alive."

"We've seventy men," Liam said. "That should give even the most passionate Scotsman pause."

"Surely no lord would attack a company sent by King David?" Callum said. "He would be courting war with England."

"Scotsmen aren't always known for their sense, especially Highlanders," said Liam, revealing his prejudices.

The tension in Samuel's face reminded Callum of Afghanistan in other ways, chief among them the constant fear of betrayal. Callum had learned to pass as a normal person in the four years since he'd come home from the war, but the closer he allowed anyone to get to him, the harder it had been to hide his wounds. Callum had borne witness to man's inhumanity to man and had perpetrated it on those weaker than himself. It was a cliché to say that he couldn't wash that away with water and soap, but Callum had wondered sometimes if he hadn't been trying to. He had been one of the lucky ones, too, because even if he'd left part of himself on the battlefield, physically he looked whole.

Callum's hand went to the hilt of his sword. Today if it came to a fight, he'd be using his sword for the first time, killing men up close and personal.

Then Callum straightened his shoulders. If something was truly wrong, he had no time for second thoughts or inner turmoil. He looked around for James Stewart, whom he'd last seen riding near Kirby's carriage, but James was no longer there. Callum did notice that the bishop now sat beside his driver instead of inside the carriage.

Callum didn't know why Kirby had chosen this moment to expose himself to the elements, but he mentally shrugged away the bishop's peculiarities and twisted in his saddle, still looking for James. He spied him and Robbie at the rear of the host of men. Callum directed his horse to the side of the road and caught James's eye. James lifted a hand in acknowledgement and he and

Robbie trotted their horses along the edge of the road, avoiding the columns of riders, in order to reach Callum more quickly.

"Samuel doesn't like the feel of this place," Callum said when they reached him. "There are too many trees and the road is too narrow. His instincts tell him something isn't right."

James sniffed. "We ride on the main road from Glasgow to Stirling. For all that the English believe Scots to be barbarians, I can't believe we're anything but perfectly safe—"

"WAAAAAAAAAAAAAAAAHH—!"

The cry came loud and long, an eerie screech that was cut off suddenly. Horses bucked and skittered, their masters struggling to control them. Robbie's horse reared, almost threw him, and then took off, racing back towards Glasgow, with Robbie hanging on for dear life.

"Robert!" James dug in his heels to go after him, and Callum with him, but the five seconds between Robbie's escape and James's response was too long. The enemy, whoever they were, was upon them.

"Protect the Bishop!"

The call came from one of the men near Kirby's carriage at the front of the company. Callum turned to see the long handle of a spear sticking out of Kirby's back and a bloom of red across his white mantle. He toppled off his seat and ended up face first in the muddy ditch beside the road.

Callum's sword appeared in his hand without him realizing he'd pulled it from its sheath. He looked for James, even as he raised his shield and wheeled his horse, trying to look in all directions at once. "Jesus Christ! Where did they come from?"

James flung himself from his horse and grabbed both his horse's bridle and Callum's. "I'd like to know that too."

Callum looked north and south, holding up his shield to protect himself while trying to find the source of the spears and arrows that flew from the heights on either side. A dozen men had already gone down. The high wail came again.

"Get off that damn horse." James pulled at Callum's cloak and dragged him from the saddle so that Callum might crouch with him in the muck of the road. They used their horses as buffers, though the beasts were panicky enough that Callum didn't think they'd stay still much longer, no matter how well trained. "These men are MacDougalls," said James.

"How do you know?" Callum said. Even he had heard of the MacDougalls. As a clan, they had a colorful and martial history.

But James didn't have time to answer. The spearman and archers had done their work and now a hundred screaming Highlanders descended the hills that rose up on either side of the road. The caterwauling cry blocked out every other sound. A few men even dropped from the tree branches above their heads.

James and Callum fought back to back, slashing and thrusting at their attackers. Their company was outnumbered, though not hopelessly so. They'd been caught unawares, however, so they fought at a terrible disadvantage. Those months of practice paid off for Callum, as his arm seemed to move of its own accord, driving at any man who came against him.

The fighters on both sides gave no quarter. The MacDougalls seemed intent on slaughter and Callum's company just wanted to survive. With war all around, Callum's mouth was dry and gritty with the taste of sand, though it was rain he felt on his face today.

James was chanting in Gaelic what sounded like a poem. With all the chaos around them, Callum couldn't decipher more than one word in three. For his part, Callum kept up a steady stream of profanity in English—and not the medieval profanity that cursed saints and bones. That wasn't meaty enough for Callum today. He didn't care who heard him. By that point, they were going down. Callum had lost sight of Samuel and Liam long since.

"In the name of St. Andrew!" James shouted and leapt at a fiery haired warrior, while Callum blocked an axe destined for James's head. James then gutted a second man who slashed his sword at Callum and with a shout of his own, Callum launched himself at a man just beyond James.

"Hold! Hold I say!"

The order came through a red haze that covered Callum's eyes. A Scottish warrior with a yellow beard and pale eyes planted himself in front of Callum, ignoring his superior's order, and thus, Callum didn't obey him either. With a twist and a shove, Callum upended the man and drove his sword through his midsection. Callum staggered to his feet, his face streaming with a mixture of water and blood, and swung around, looking for James. He'd been beside Callum only a second earlier.

In the moment that he turned, however, someone cannoned into him from behind and knocked him to the ground. Callum's helmet slammed into a rock on the edge of the road, his sight blackened, and he heard nothing more.

* * * * *

Callum's eyes popped open in the instant between unconsciousness and awareness to find darkness all around him. He lay on his side on the ground, though he had no immediate memory as to where he was or how he'd gotten there except that he was pretty sure his vehicle had been blown up by an IED. He had a moment of panic when he couldn't feel his feet, but then he focused harder and shifted them. Relief coursed through him. Callum lifted his head from the ground and blinked. The air didn't smell like the desert. In fact, it was definitely raining.

"Stay still."

The words came from behind him, a woman's voice, and now that he was awake, a faint glow cut through the darkness. Instinctively disobeying, Callum rolled onto his back, towards the shape behind him. As he rolled, he put a hand to his head and his fingers felt for the wound that was giving him a headache. It felt like a sharpened stake had been driven into his skull.

At the sight of the woman, however, Callum dropped his hand, instantly confused not only by her face, but because he wasn't wearing his army-issued combat helmet. The helmet his fingers probed was metal. "Where am I?" he said.

The woman put her hand on Callum's arm to stop him from touching his head again and said, amusement in her voice, "Where do you think you are? You're in a ditch beside the road, just where they left you."

And then Callum remembered ... he remembered and it was as if someone had taken the stake from his head, stabbed it into his gut, and twisted. He tried to sit up but the woman's gentle hands forced him to lie back down.

"It's okay; you're okay."

Callum let the woman ease the helmet from his head. His whole head ached and when he pressed his fingers to his hairline, they came away wet. Because it was still raining, he didn't know if it was water or blood he was feeling. He tasted the moisture on the tip of his finger. *Blood.*

"I asked you not to do that." The woman pressed a hand to Callum's shoulder, forcing him to stay on the ground. Then she shone a light into each of his eyes in turn. "I'm no doctor, but I think you have a concussion."

Callum blinked back the rain that continued to pitter-patter on his face and squinted past the light. Noticing, the woman directed the light away from his eyes.

Callum swallowed, trying to find his voice. The more he looked at the woman, the less he cared if his head hurt or even if he was bleeding out. There was no way he was going to lie still another moment, not when the woman was holding an honest-to-

God modern torch—a flashlight—in her hand. Callum pushed to a sitting position, leaning on one hand, and brought his face to within inches of hers.

A moment ago, Callum had almost mistaken the woman for Anna, but now that he was up close, he could see the differences clearly. The woman's hair was black and straight, not brown like Anna's. Her eyes were also dark and set in a face with a wide forehead and high cheekbones. "Who are you?" Callum said.

"Tell me your name first."

"Callum."

The woman sat back on her heels. Callum reached for the hand that held the torch and brought it between them so that it illumined their faces in a 'v' of light.

"And you're—"

"From the future. Yes," Callum said.

The woman gave a cry that was half laughter, half startled surprise. "When I heard you cursing in English—real English—during the battle, I couldn't believe it. I've searched for so long ..." Her throat closed on the last word, but she didn't look away. Her eyes were very wide and clear as she gazed at Callum.

Callum's hand was still around hers, both of them holding the torch. "If I tell you when I'm from, will you tell me your name, and what you're doing here?"

"Yes." She eased back onto her heels, seeming to want more distance between them.

Callum loosened his hold on her hand without letting her go entirely. The woman was far closer to mastering her emotions than Callum was to his. He needed to get this out of the way right now before his head exploded. "2016," he said.

"Oh God." The woman jerked away.

Callum reached for her, fearing that she wasn't going to keep up her end of the bargain. If she ran away, he couldn't chase her. He didn't even know if he could walk. But then she stopped, breathing hard, having scrambled only four or five feet from Callum. She looked at him, her hands clenched into fists and what he thought might be tear tracks on her dirty cheeks, mixing with the raindrops.

Then as before, her chin firmed. She crawled back to him, her eyes on his. "My name is Cassie. I was born in Oregon."

4

Cassie

Somehow Cassie got Callum upright and walking—or rather stumbling—heading off the road and into the hills to the northwest of the ambush site.

"Where are we going?" Callum said, though it came out more of a mumble, something like *where we?* and Cassie had to infer the rest.

"Some place safe," Cassie said.

It was a wonder he could walk at all, given how long she'd had to leave him lying in the mud until the MacDougalls had marched off. If they'd discovered he wasn't dead and threatened to finish the job, she might have had to pull a Pocahontas and cover his body with her own. Thankfully, it hadn't come to that.

"Is it far?"

"Farther than you want to walk just now, but we can make it," Cassie said.

After that, Callum didn't ask any more questions, just kept walking with his head down, his arm around Cassie's shoulder and hers around his waist, holding him up. Cassie was tall for a woman, almost 5' 9", but he was bigger, easily over six feet. He wore a cloak that weighed twice as much as it should, due to the rain that had waterlogged it. He wore armor, too. She didn't know how he'd come to be a knight in the king's company, but she'd seen him fight and he'd handled himself better than all but a few others, Scot or English.

Cassie had known that Callum was from the twenty-first century from the first time he'd said *you bloody cocked up bastard knob head!* while cutting through two MacDougalls to help one of his fellow soldiers. As they'd walked, and before he became too breathless to talk, Callum had told her about his mission for King David. It had been the first positive news Cassie had heard all day. It meant that King David hadn't been among those killed or captured. The king hadn't come at all.

In the nearly five years that she'd lived in Scotland, Cassie had learned to ignore the rain. As the miles passed, it tapered off, even as the wind picked up. She kept Callum walking higher into the hills, going up and down, heading northwest all the while through scrub and stands of trees.

Finally, as the sky began to lighten towards morning and Callum was stumbling badly, worse with every step he took, they reached Cassie's house. It was set in the middle of a small clearing with a garden next to it. Callum pulled up at the sight of it and spoke his first sentence in hours. "Who lives here?"

"I do."

Though Callum balked like a three-year-old, as if Cassie was dragging him to the dentist instead of entering her home, she eventually got his feet moving again. He was so tired that after his initial protest, he couldn't fight her anymore. Cassie tugged him to the door, lifted the latch, and let them in.

She had built the house herself, for herself, so Cassie hadn't bothered with more than one room. She did have a bed, which she'd also built, and a down mattress, a luxury for which she'd traded labor, rabbit skins, and herbs for three months before she could afford it. Though Callum made straight for the bed, Cassie steered him towards a low stool by the banked fire instead and began stripping him of his clothes.

"You're soaked. I'm not letting you ruin my mattress," Cassie said.

Callum gazed at her blankly. Cassie wanted to fall face first onto her bed too, so she could sympathize with the dullness of his expression. She got his cloak, boots, and mail shirt off him without Callum making much more than a token protest, but as she reached around him to untuck his undershirt, her hand came into contact with something hard and metal at the small of his back.

"No." Callum caught her hand in a strong grip, fully awake for the first time in hours.

Cassie and Callum gazed at each other for five seconds, suspended in a silent tug of war, and then Cassie sat back to allow Callum to pull out the gun himself. He held it loosely in his hand. Cassie was pretty sure his eyes weren't really focusing, even though he'd reacted quickly when she reached for it.

"I'll keep it safe," she said, holding out her hand, palm up, and waiting for him to give it to her.

He studied her for another ten seconds and then nodded. "Okay."

Cassie put the gun on a high shelf behind a box of herbs.

After that, he didn't argue with her anymore. She took his shirt and pants, leaving him only braes—medieval underwear—and refrained from exclaiming *holy crap, the man is cut!* out loud.

"We'll talk when you wake up," she said instead.

Cassie got him off the stool and over to the bed. He lay down and she covered him with a blanket. Within five seconds, he'd closed his eyes and was breathing evenly.

Cassie gazed down at him, glad that he was covered because it seemed unfair to gape at him while he was asleep. He was tall and, to go along with his body, disconcertingly handsome. He had dark brown, close-cropped hair and the most regular features of any man she'd seen outside of television. His hazel eyes were currently hidden, which was a good thing since earlier they'd looked at her with startling frankness. In the old world, women must have been lining up to be with him. Cassie wondered what girl he might have left behind.

She took a last look at him, making sure he was really asleep, though that didn't seem much in doubt. She'd walked through the woods for half the night with him, and if he had been able to argue coherently or had any real ability to move about on his own volition, he wouldn't have accepted her ministrations in the first place. His looks aside, the head wound was the first thing she was worried about. She'd tended it briefly in the ditch beside the road, but even with the flashlight held between her teeth, with the rain and the dark, she hadn't been able to do much for him.

Cassie stirred the fire, which in her absence had died down to a few embers, got it going again, and set a pot of water over it. She didn't have any antibiotic ointment, but at least she could clean and pack his wound. The herbs in the Middle Ages weren't bad for healing and certainly were better than nothing. It was just that they weren't as powerful and didn't work as consistently as many manmade drugs. She'd gotten a good look at Callum's body when she'd undressed him and he was otherwise whole, except for bruises and an old scar that looked like he'd once taken a bullet on his right side, high in his chest.

While she waited for the water to heat, Cassie went through Callum's belongings. As far as she was concerned, they were past worrying about manners or privacy. She wasn't going to wait until he was awake to find out more about him. She had a strange man in her bed. That was rare enough—okay, so rare it had never happened before—that she wasn't going to trust him just because he was from the modern world. She needed to know as much about him as she could, preferably before he woke up and found her going through his clothes.

Cassie dumped the rest of the water out of his boots and set them close to the fire. Then she hung his shirt and pants on her clothesline and laid his armor across the table. It took up half of the space. Callum had been cognizant enough at the ambush site not to sheath his sword while it was still bloody, but Cassie unsheathed it again to make sure he'd dried it completely. The leather wrap for the hilt was butter soft, and gold filigree adorned the crossguard and pommel. Someone had paid a pretty penny for that sword.

She eyed the sleeping man in her bed. Regardless of whether it had been he who'd bought it or King David, Callum appeared to have done very well for himself, despite being from the future. Better than Cassie had, anyway.

The sword would need to be oiled sooner rather than later, but Cassie didn't know exactly the kind of oil it needed so she just polished it again with a clean cloth, resheathed it, and propped it against the wall near the head of the bed. Callum might not be a medieval man, but he acted very much like the few knights she'd met, and that meant his first instinct when he awoke would be to make sure he still had his sword.

And his gun.

Cassie took the gun off the shelf and popped out the magazine. None of the bullets had been fired. That alone was interesting. How long had he been here that he hadn't used the gun at all? Perhaps, for all his ability to hold his own in a medieval battle, this was the first dangerous situation he'd been in. Either that or he was saving the ammunition for absolute need—though she would have thought that the ambush would have qualified as 'need'. Still, bullets couldn't be replaced.

That Callum carried a gun with him, however, meant that the balancing act of living in the Middle Ages was as real for him as it was for Cassie. The gun made him vulnerable to discovery far more than anything else he could have carried. What if the MacDougalls had gone through the bodies of the 'dead' more thoroughly? What if it hadn't been Cassie who had found him? And that didn't even address the real question of the hour: *did King David know who Callum really was?*

Cassie checked for moisture before pushing the magazine, which held the standard fifteen rounds, back into place. The ammunition was military grade and thus sealed. Neither it nor the gun would have been affected by rain and mud that had soaked Callum, but the weapon itself could rust, just as surely as Callum's sword would if he didn't dry and oil it.

Cassie put the gun in its holster—a handmade one that had to have been made here—and placed it back on the shelf where she kept her herbs. Then she poured warm water into a bowl, grabbed a cloth, and sat on the edge of the bed next to Callum. She soaked the cloth, squeezed it out, and patted at his wound, gently at first since she didn't want to wake him and then more thoroughly when he didn't stir. Head wounds were tricky. Earlier, his eyes had told Cassie that he had a concussion. He'd proved her right by throwing up twice on the trek to her house; he was certainly exhausted.

Cassie rubbed the wound with a salve she had made herself, composed mostly of sanicle, but with a few other herbs that added to the healing properties, and left it exposed rather than bandaging it. The sooner the cut scabbed over, the better off Callum would be. Head wounds bled like nobody's business, but since his had stopped bleeding around the time the rain had stopped, and it looked like he would rest for a while, Cassie had hope that he would heal quickly.

Cassie needed to sleep herself, but she spent the next few hours putting her house in order, feeding the fire, and making sure that she had what she needed for whatever tomorrow might bring. All the while, she kept half her mind on the man sleeping in her bed. Callum might have survived the ambush, but if he really was the new English king's emissary, he wasn't safe here or anywhere. The MacDougalls hated the English and their meddling in Scotland. Cassie didn't know what had sent them on the path of war last night, but to attack the king's party meant there was no turning back for them. They had to know that they were committed to see this through. Whatever *this* was.

In fact, Cassie was surprised they'd left Callum alive at all. Even with the dark and the rain, and the bodies of fifty dead men littering the road, it was still sloppy work and very unlike them. They'd taken only those who could walk, killed those who couldn't, and departed. Callum had been lucky to have fallen face down and out of his senses under two other men.

By noon, Cassie was ready to sleep, but she didn't know if she dared, in case someone came looking for him. In that event, Callum wasn't going to be of any help, but Cassie couldn't stay up for another day and night either. Ultimately, Cassie barred the door and slipped into the bed, wrapped in her own blanket. She rested a hand on Callum's chest so she would know the instant he awoke, giving her time to leap from the bed before he saw that she was in it with him.

It was breaking all sorts of her personal rules to have him there at all, but Cassie tried to ignore the uneasy feeling it gave her to be so close to another person. To sleep beside Callum was breaking medieval rules too, but Cassie didn't care much about them. She'd learned how to adapt and survive, not fit in. She hadn't ever wanted to fit in.

The difference between the modern world and the medieval one was more than the absence of plastics or that peasants had to bow to their overlords. It had to do not only with what to eat but how to eat it; not only what to say but how to say it. Living out here on her own, Cassie had managed to sidestep most of the differences, even as she concocted rules for herself, which included what she allowed herself to think about, how much alcohol she allowed herself to drink (essentially, none), and the fact that she'd never let a man into her house before, not even once.

More important than all of these was how close she allowed any person to come to her before she eased away so as not to risk revealing her secrets.

Cassie slept through until dark and woke just as Callum began to stir. She climbed out of bed, and he opened his eyes long enough to accept a drink of water but then closed them after four or five sips and lay back down. He was asleep again in an instant. In those few moments of consciousness, Cassie hadn't seen recognition in his eyes. Perhaps his body had acknowledged his need for liquid while his mind still slept.

She used to do that when she was a little girl. Cassie hadn't actually sleepwalked, but according to her grandfather, she could hold whole conversations with people and have no memory of it in the morning.

It had been a long time since Cassie had allowed herself to think of her childhood—a long time since she'd allowed herself to think about anything but her own survival. She'd been twenty-four years old when she'd found herself in medieval Scotland. Her grandfather and she had been bow hunting high up in the Wallowa Mountains of Oregon when she'd crossed through that pit of blackness to come here.

Her grandfather hadn't been intent on killing a deer as much as finding time and space to talk to Cassie. She'd been away from home most of the last six years, at college and then graduate school, and her grandfather was trying to convince her to come home, that her place was with her family and that she should use her education and skills for the benefit of her tribe.

For Cassie's part, she'd spent her life half-in and half-out of the tribal community and had never been sure she fit into either. Maybe that had turned out to be for the best, since she didn't fit into the medieval world and had learned not to expect it.

Not that she had tried. Cassie couldn't be a medieval woman—couldn't even pretend very well. She'd spent that first year traveling Scotland—even venturing as far south as Hadrian's Wall—looking for answers, looking for a passage through time. She'd thought maybe if she found a cave or a ring of standing stones like in some of those romance novels, she could find her way back home.

But real life wasn't like life in a romance novel, and while Cassie never gave up trying, she had eventually chosen to make the best of it, to live here as well as she could. She'd survived by living as her ancestors once did, using all the old skills her grandfather had taught her as a girl. If only he could see her now. Cassie hoped that he would be proud.

5

Callum

When Callum awoke, Cassie was sitting beside him, checking his head wound again. Her long rope of braided black hair had fallen over her left shoulder and it swung towards him. She still wore men's clothes—breeches, shirt, a thick knitted sweater, hiking boots—which would have kept her warmer than Callum had been as they'd trekked across the wilds of Scotland.

At the moment, however, he was warm and comfortable. For the first time in months, he'd slept without dreaming of Afghanistan. That thought brought him upright with a jerk. He put a hand out to his sword, which leaned against the wall by the head of the bed, and then he glanced upwards to the shelf. "I need my gun."

Cassie didn't say a word, just reached above her head and handed the gun to Callum.

"How long have I been out?" Callum said.

"Two days," she said. "You woke only enough to drink and eat a little."

"I don't remember." Callum put a hand to his head, which hurt less than it had, though he still felt like he'd been run over by a lorry. "Thank you for saving me."

"They left you for dead," Cassie said. "That was sloppy of them, but that close to Kilsyth, they knew they had to get out of there quickly."

The way she spoke was music to Callum's ears. Her words flowed. He understood her without having to think about it.

"James Stewart said something about MacDougalls," Callum said.

Cassie tsked through her teeth. "He was right to assume the worst. It was the MacDougalls."

Callum tried to conjure up a map of Scotland in his head. "I thought their lands were far to the west. What were they doing so close to Stirling and Glasgow?"

"They were attacking your company, obviously. They're allies of the MacGregors and the Grahams, who have lands around here. They hate the Stewarts."

"So their target was James Stewart and not to influence the succession?" Callum said. All these names and alliances were muddling his already aching head.

"Everything is about the succession," Cassie said. "The MacDougalls support the Comyns, who support Balliol. They hate the Stewarts so they hate the Bruces too. In Scotland, you're either on one side or the other."

"King David warned me about that," Callum said. "He won't be happy that it's already come to open war."

"This isn't open war," Cassie said. "If you'd seen open war between clans, you'd know that this isn't it. This was a raid."

Callum shook his head in disbelief, but the motion made his head hurt and he moaned before he could stop himself. He put a hand to the cut at his hairline, probing with his fingers, but Cassie brushed them away.

"Don't touch it. It's healing."

"They killed Bishop Kirby," Callum said.

"I saw a man in white robes go down at the beginning of the fight," Cassie said. "Is that who he was?"

"Why would they do this?" Callum said. "What do the MacDougalls hope to gain by slaughtering the king's men?"

"The rumor among the clans had it that King David should have been in your company," Cassie said. "I don't care about the guy one way or the other, but killing the king of England is a great way to start a war."

"He didn't come," Callum said. "His wife's about to have a baby and he wanted to be there when she did. He sent Bishop Kirby and me to talk to the Scots for him."

Cassie chewed on her lower lip. "Would the MacDougalls have known about the king's change of plans?"

"I don't know," Callum said. "Perhaps they wouldn't unless a spy sent word ahead of us, either by coming himself or by pigeon." Since becoming King of England, David had taken over and improved upon King Edward's well-established communication network. That included a man in Edinburgh and a second in Stirling, both with the ability to get word to him by carrier pigeon. Callum had their names and was to have found his contact as soon as he arrived in Stirling.

"Rumors have been racing around the north country for weeks," Cassie said. "They say that if King David isn't going to take the throne himself, he has already decided to give it to the Bruces. The MacDougalls, obviously, decided not to wait to find out if the rumor was true."

Callum struggled to sit up and Cassie didn't force him back. Instead, she handed him a cup from which he drank thirstily. It was Callum's first real look at his surroundings. "What is this place?"

"My home."

"I guessed that," Callum said, "but it's—it's—" He couldn't find the words. It could have been the cabin in rural Virginia where his family had gone on holiday when he was a boy.

"It's nice, isn't it?" Cassie looked around at her house. "I built it myself."

Cassie's home was an old-fashioned log cabin, like the ones the pioneers had constructed in the American West. The room had a fireplace built into a side wall, which drew out the smoke remarkably well. Most medieval fireplaces hardly worked at all, but a fire in the center of a room could be much worse.

"How did you do all this?" Callum said.

Cassie's brow furrowed. "The same way houses like this have always been built—by hand, with time. It's not that hard."

"It would have been hard for me."

Cassie turned to a line that she'd strung from the fireplace to a hook beside the door and felt at the clothes hanging on it. She took down Callum's pants and shirt and tossed them to him. "Here. I dried the chain mail as best I could, but I think you need a special brush to get rid of the rust. I don't have one."

Callum grabbed the clothes out of the air and dressed while Cassie bent to the fire and stirred a pot that hung over it. By the time she handed him a bowl of porridge, he was looking and feeling more like himself.

But now that Callum was conscious and getting used to being upright, he started to focus on how strange this all was. The ambush, certainly, was unexpected. That the MacDougalls might have wanted to kill or capture David was going to give the king a headache in the weeks ahead, once he found out about it. But it was Cassie's very existence that was the most troubling.

"How did you get here, Cassie?" Callum said.

"I walked with you. Don't you remember?"

"I don't mean that. I mean *how did you get here?* To Scotland."

Cassie lifted one shoulder. "I can't even tell you. I've thought over those last moments in Oregon again and again and come up with precisely nothing. I can't fix any of it in my mind for long enough to trace the path I followed."

"What do you remember?"

"I had been visiting my grandfather on a quick vacation from my job in California, working for the Bureau of Land

Management. My grandfather and I had been hunting, working with my new bow—" She drew Callum's attention to the bow hanging over her front door.

Callum's jaw dropped. It was a modern recurve bow. A quiver of arrows hung on a hook beside it.

"—when a storm blew up out of nowhere. Storms are pretty rare in the summer in Eastern Oregon. We had been just about to turn for home, since neither hunting nor talk was much fun in a thunderstorm, when I heard the whine of an airplane engine, growing closer until it was almost on top of us. My grandfather was fifty yards away when the plane came in. He shouted at me to run, and I did, but with the storm and the driving rain, I couldn't see which way to go. Suddenly, an enormous black hole opened beneath me and sucked me into it. And then I was here."

"Here, as in, right here?" Callum said.

Cassie shrugged. "It was a few miles further west, near the sea. Between one instant and the next, I went from my forest to this one, though I didn't know until later that I was in Scotland. All I knew was that I was on my knees in the dirt in an unfamiliar woods, surrounded by a fog, with the sound of the airplane fading into the distance."

Throughout Cassie's narration, a coldness had seeped through Callum and his stomach had fallen into his boots. He knew with a certainty that Cassie's story was Meg's story, but told from the ground. Callum rubbed at his forehead with his fingers. He didn't know what to say. How was he to tell Cassie that her presence here was a mistake, just like his, and she'd been caught up in the wake of a miracle? How was he going to tell her that even if it was theoretically possible, there was no going back?

Goronwy had made that clear on Callum's first night in the Middle Ages. Callum had been unable to sleep, to face lying on his pallet in his cold room with Meg and Llywelyn asleep in the room next to his. He'd understood that he was privileged to have a room at all, that he could have been sleeping on a bench in the great hall or with soldiers in the barracks. But his head had been spinning with all that had happened to him and he couldn't sleep just yet. He'd climbed the battlements at Windsor Castle and found Goronwy beside him.

"What are your plans?" Goronwy had said.

Callum tipped his head as he looked at him, unsure if he'd heard him correctly, given how monumentally weak his French had been at the time. *Plans?* "I don't understand."

Goronwy's brow had furrowed. "Is it your intent to serve King Llywelyn? You are not Welsh. You do not have ties to him or our country."

It had been a delicate moment. Callum had thought through what he was going to say before he said it, so Goronwy couldn't misunderstand. "I have no plans. I have no allegiance to anyone else in this world but your king."

In truth, Callum's big plan had been to stand in the gentle rain and stare out at the medieval world for a while longer and then to find more of the beer they'd served earlier in the hall. Beyond that, he hadn't had a clue.

Goronwy had leaned over the battlement and looked down on the soldiers who paced the lower wall-walk above the Thames River. "Meg could jump from here and return you to your world."

Callum hadn't replied. That had been just a bit too close to what he had been thinking when he first looked over the wall himself.

Goronwy had nodded. "You think to wait. You think you can be patient and she will eventually give you what you want. You are mistaken." He'd gripped Callum's upper arm so tightly it hurt, but Callum hadn't wrenched away.

Goronwy looked into Callum's eyes. "If you do anything to hurt her, I will stop you."

"I would never harm Meg. Never," Callum said.

Goronwy released Callum's arm. "You did no more than your duty in coming here, in trying to stop us. I might have done the same had I been wearing your boots. But you will not ask for what she should not give. She would help you out of guilt or pity."

Callum cleared his throat.

"You do not want that, no?" Goronwy had said.

"No."

Goronwy had nodded and as Callum met his eyes, he understood that Goronwy would kill him if he perceived that Callum posed even a hint of a threat to Meg. And he would do it without a single twinge of conscience.

Now, Callum gazed at Cassie, wishing that he could tell her anything but the truth. "How did you survive, Cassie?"

"I had my bow and wire for snares in my backpack. I had a water bottle. It was summer, so I could feed myself with meat and plants I recognized. These aren't my mountains but what is natural here was sometimes an invasive species at home." Cassie shrugged. "Blackberries grow in Scotland too. Mostly I walked and slept rough, until after a week I got up the courage to approach a village—well, really it was a castle associated with a village."

"It must have been a shock to realize where you were."

Cassie made a sound of dismissal. "Even then, I didn't know where I was. I made a fool of myself, talking American, thinking I could get help. My saving grace was that my hair was short then, boyish, and I wore a jacket and a hat against the rain. They thought I was a boy, a stranger, even English. The Scots blame everything on the English, you know, from a change in the weather to poor crops. The people in the village shut their doors in my face and fortunately, I had the sense to retreat to the woods. It was only later that they hunted me."

Callum didn't like the sound of that. In fact, he didn't like the sound of any of this. His stomach clenched as he pictured her—a girl alone—in the middle of medieval Scotland. "So you hid?"

"I hid; I ran; I never slept. And then I made a friend."

"Who was that?"

"The clan chief, Patrick Graham. His seat is at Mugdock."

Callum sputtered into his drink. "Did you say Mugdock?"

Cassie laughed. "I was squatting on his land and he knew it, but he hadn't forced me out, for reasons he has never shared with me. By then, the villagers knew I was a woman, though a very strange kind of woman. I'd gotten a reputation as a hermit, which was far better than a witch. They didn't shun me anymore and let me warm myself every once in a while over a drink in the only tavern in the district. Maybe they began to accept me because their crops were really good the year I arrived.

"Then, about six months after I settled here, I spotted a band of Stewarts riding across Graham land. I'd learned some Gaelic by then and knew of the rivalries and feuds among many of the clans. I took the opportunity to tell Lord Graham they were coming. He repaid me by speaking to his people on my behalf."

"And you've lived here alone ever since?" Callum said.

"It's not so bad most of the time," Cassie said. "It's better than being stranded on a desert island. I'm rarely hungry now ..." Her voice trailed off, probably in reaction to Callum's expression. He couldn't hide either his horror at what she'd experienced or the realization that she'd been here so long. He'd lived in the Middle Ages for six months and had tried very hard not to look that far into the future.

"I don't know if I would have had your strength," Callum said, and meant it.

"Why? How did you get here?" Cassie said. When Callum didn't answer right away, she moved closer, her expression intent. "You know something. Tell me."

Callum had to tell her. It wasn't fair not to, not when she'd come so far all by herself. "It's a terrible thing that was done to you, Cassie." He took in a deep breath and let it out. "Let me say first that you and I are not the only ones from the future who have made their way here."

Cassie pressed her fingers to her cheeks. "What do you mean? It's obvious that you've done very well for yourself, given that you serve the King of England, but ..." She clenched her teeth together.

"I came the same way you did, hitching a ride," Callum said. "In my case, however, I was trying to stop them."

"Stop who?" Cassie said.

That was the real question, wasn't it? Callum cleared his throat and leaned forward resting his elbows on his thighs and looking straight into Cassie's face. She knelt in front of him, focused on his face and gripping her knees with her hands.

"Let me ask you this first: I know you're an American, but did you ever learn enough about British history to recognize that what is happening now in Great Britain isn't what happened in our world?" Callum said.

Hesitantly, Cassie shook her head. "I studied biology in college. A little anthropology. If you knew my background, you'd understand why British history before Columbus held no interest for me."

"You're Native American?" Callum said.

Cassie nodded. "One-quarter."

"Okay, so ... departing from history into the realm of science fiction, from what we've been able to piece together, we're in an alternate universe that has followed a different path from the history of our world. I don't know if it always was different or if it became different after travelers came from our world to this one."

"Who are *we*?" Cassie said.

"I worked for MI-5, the British internal security service," Callum said. "We learned about travelers between these two worlds when the brother-in-law of one of them told one of our people about it."

Cassie coughed a laugh and then stopped herself when Callum didn't laugh with her. She studied him with her head tilted to one side. "You're serious."

"I'm here, aren't I?"

"And who are these *travelers*?" she said.

"Well, for one, our new King of England."

6

Cassie

"That's not possible." Cassie eased away from Callum, a wariness filling her that she hadn't felt up until now. It was as if he'd become the lunatic the Scots had thought her to be.

"I know it sounds crazy," Callum said, "but it's true. I came here six months ago, on the coattails of the King of Wales and his wife, Meg. Meg was born in Pennsylvania and our new King of England is their son, David."

"You are out of your mind," Cassie said, trying to stave off the hysterical laughter that was brewing in her chest. She'd been taught to swallow down her emotions, but she couldn't swallow this. "You have to be."

"Meg has traveled back and forth to this world three times," Callum said. "The first time was in 1268 when she met and married Llywelyn. She returned to our world later that year before David's birth. The second time was in August of 1284 when she was flying in a commuter plane from Pasco, Washington to Boise, Idaho." Callum paused.

Cassie's mocking laughter dissipated in an instant. Her breath caught in her throat and she could barely speak around it. "What?"

"The pilot lost control of his plane in a storm that shorted out his instruments. Instead of crashing into a mountain, he brought Meg to the Middle Ages. They came through somewhere on the west coast of Scotland, though they didn't land there. The pilot, Marty, immediately flew south. He dumped Meg off at Hadrian's Wall and then came north, never to be heard from again."

Cassie had both hands to her mouth, trying to calm her breathing which was coming in quick bursts. "So ... so you're saying ... can you really be saying that he brought me?"

"To be fair, it wasn't the pilot who had the ability to travel between worlds, but Meg. She has no real control of it. It isn't conscious, but seems to happen when world shifting will save her life."

"And the third time?" Cassie said.

Callum's voice dropped to a whisper. "Six months ago. That was my turn."

In Cassie's family, white Englishmen didn't engender a lot of sympathy, no matter how difficult their struggles, but her heart stirred for Callum now. "How did that come about?"

"I was trying to stop her from coming back," Callum said. "It's my own fault I'm here."

Cassie eased back from him, realizing that as they'd been speaking, she'd moved so close to him that their faces were only a foot apart. "Then Meg could take us back, Callum. Back home. Couldn't she?"

Callum had been leaning forward too, but now he straightened. "Who's to say?"

His tone struck Cassie as *off*. As if they'd been revealing truths to each other and now he was hiding something. "But she's done it three times. Why couldn't she again?"

Callum let out a sharp breath. "The problem is the way she does it. I've spent far too much time considering the possibilities myself, believe me. What's she supposed to do to help us? Fly an airplane into a mountain? Deliberately cause a car crash? Jump off a cliff?"

Cassie pursed her lips as she studied him. "I didn't really catch it the first time, but you meant that her *traveling* happens only when she's in danger, is that right?"

"When we fell through time most recently, when I came here with her, she jumped off the balcony at Chepstow Castle. It's a four story drop into the Wye River."

Cassie sat back on her heels, her enthusiasm squashed. She felt reality condensing around her again. "Oh. That's a problem." Then she got to her feet and turned towards the fire so Callum couldn't see her face as she composed herself.

"Just because you can't get back to our world doesn't mean you have to stay here, in this place," Callum said.

Cassie stopped in the act of stirring the pot over the fire, the spoon suspended over the porridge. "What do you mean?" she said without turning around.

"David is the King of England," Callum said. "He grew up in Oregon, like you, until he was fourteen. He would welcome you to London or to any of his castles in Wales, any time you wanted to come. You don't have to live alone anymore."

Cassie held very still. Callum's words had frozen her feet to the floor. *Not live here?* One hand went to her long braid. Cassie caught the end in her fist and she tugged on it. "Let's—let's leave that for another day." She tossed the braid over her shoulder and turned to look at Callum. "We have more important things to worry about right now."

"Like getting word to King David about what has happened?" Callum said.

Cassie laughed. "Not hardly. That can wait. Aren't you concerned about what the MacDougalls have done with the rest of the men in your party?"

Callum's mouth dropped open. Cassie had surprised him. "You mean there were survivors?"

"About a dozen," Cassie said. "The MacDougalls gathered them up and marched them away, heading west."

"Do you know where they took them?"

"My guess is Mugdock Castle, or close to it," Cassie said. "I'm surprised that Lord Patrick is openly involved, but even if your friends aren't there, he'll know where they went. This is his land. The MacDougalls are his allies and they wouldn't have marched across it without telling him they were coming, even if they didn't tell him why."

"Where's the MacDougall stronghold?" Callum said.

"Dunstaffnage. Fifty miles from here." Cassie had been there. The castle had been built on a prominent rock and was surrounded on three sides by the sea. Meg and Marty, admittedly unbeknownst to them, had dumped Cassie in a forest a mile to the east of the castle when they'd shifted worlds.

"Too far." Callum's chin was set as he thought.

It looked like Callum was starting to think like a soldier again. Just as long as he didn't think he could act like one too soon: that concussion was going to give him trouble for at least a week.

"There's too much daylight between here and there," Callum said.

"I think you're right," Cassie said. "They had wounded of their own and would have had to go to ground closer than Dunstaffnage, at least for what was left of the night."

Callum looked hard at Cassie. "Do you really think they hoped to capture—or kill—King David? How could they possibly have thought that would end well for them?"

Cassie shrugged. She'd heard about the Battle in the Severn Estuary nearly a year ago. The traitor, William de Valence, was famous up here too, though more because his daughter had just married a Scotsman than because of his plot to kill King David. Perhaps Alexander MacDougall thought he was a better man than

Valence. Until now, the ins and outs of Scottish politics had concerned her only when they threatened her survival.

"I can't tell you," Cassie said, "except that the MacDougalls have never been known for their timidity."

"Did you see what happened to the prisoners?" Callum said. "Did you see who they were?"

Cassie shook her head. "I don't know faces. It's not like the rulers here traipse around to charity auctions and get their picture taken. I saw twelve bedraggled, blood-spattered, defeated men."

"What were you doing there in the first place?" Callum said.

He had finally asked the question Cassie had been waiting for since he woke up, before they got side-tracked by the time travel thing. "I told you about warning the clan chief about marauders on his land?" Cassie said.

Callum nodded.

"Lord Patrick and I have an understanding: I let him know if I see something that might concern him and he makes sure that nobody bothers me."

"So you spotted the MacDougalls—when?"

"I trailed them all afternoon," Cassie said. "Since the MacDougalls are allied with the Grahams, I would've let them go once I found out who they were, but then they went to ground at the ambush site and didn't advertise themselves in the way that they sometimes do. I decided I'd better stay and see what they were up to—for my own protection if for no other reason."

"You saved my life," Callum said.

"Maybe ..." Cassie said. "You would have woken on your own. What would have been bad is if you'd looked for help from the wrong people and blurted out what happened without knowing who *their* friends were. My guess is that once the MacDougalls realized that King David wasn't leading the company, they got out of there as quickly as they could. Do you remember a man shouting for everyone to stop?"

Callum nodded.

"That was Alexander MacDougall himself."

"If they're smart, they'll keep the prisoners until they can trade them for immunity from prosecution," Callum said.

"Good luck with that," Cassie said. "Scots aren't known for their forgiveness."

"At least Robbie got away," Callum said.

"Who?" Cassie said.

"Robbie Bruce is James Stewart's squire," Callum said. "It was his horse that bolted right before the MacDougalls attacked."

"I saw that," Cassie said. "I'm glad. He looked awfully young."

"So ... Lord Patrick," Callum said, switching topics without warning. "He never objected to your way of life or your clothing?"

"He objects, but he doesn't stop me," Cassie said. "You have to understand that up here, everyone who isn't a lord lives in remote hamlets or isolated huts. People are vulnerable to raiding parties. My information saved him a herd of cattle. He repays me by ignoring me."

Callum made a gesture that took in the whole of the room. "And by the loan of some tools?"

"That too."

"He's not going to like it that this time you're coming in on the other side," Callum said.

Cassie gave him a long look. "Is that what I'm doing? Has King David already decided in favor of Bruce?"

"He hadn't when I left," Callum said.

"Then I'm on the side of peace," Cassie said. "The MacDougalls killed a bishop. They captured your friends. It may be that Lord Graham doesn't know what really happened."

"And if he does and condones what the MacDougalls have done?" Callum said.

"Then we'll see," Cassie said.

7

Callum

Callum got off the bed and didn't immediately feel like falling over, which was a good sign. "How far do we have to walk to get to Mugdock Castle?"

"Three miles," Cassie said.

"I can handle three miles," Callum said. "My only injury is to my head, along with some bangs and bruises from the fight."

Cassie looked at him, skepticism written on her face. "You have a concussion."

"I've had one before," Callum said. "I'll feel terrible for a few days and then I'll start to feel better."

"From what I saw at the ambush, you fought well. Have you been in battle before?" Cassie said.

"Not here," Callum said. "In Afghanistan."

"I didn't know you guys—Brits, right?—fought there too," she said.

"Our forces fought there especially," Callum said.

Cassie picked up the padded shirt that Callum wore under his mail and held it out. "I know you need help getting dressed so don't bother to pretend you don't."

Cassie had taken the mail off him by brute force, but putting it on again correctly was more difficult. Together, they managed it. While nobody was going to confuse Callum for a Highlander, he once again resembled a knight in the service of the King of England. The men who'd attacked his company had worn armor over shirts and pants, though of a different style than Callum was used to: shorter pants, longer shirts which were more like tunics, and no kilts like he might have expected. Instead, they had worn blankets wrapped around their shoulders and torsos like cloaks, and pinned.

While Callum belted his sword around his waist and slung his cloak over his shoulders, Cassie pulled off her sweater and stepped into a dress, tugging it up over her shirt and pants. Cassie saw Callum watching her and she wrinkled her nose at him. "The lord prefers it."

She put the sweater back on, a cloak over the sweater, and then snapped her quiver onto a heavy backpack, the contents of which she didn't share with Callum. She slipped the straps of the backpack through slits in her cloak before buckling them across her front. Callum pulled an arrow from the quiver. It was shorter than the yard-long Welsh longbow arrows, but then her bow was shorter too.

"Why were you hunting with a recurve bow instead of a compound one, a crossbow, or even a gun?" Callum said.

"My grandfather is a traditionalist," Cassie said.

She picked up her bow and Callum picked up his gun from where he'd left it on the bed. He slid it into its holster at the small of his back.

Cassie watched him, her lips pressed together. "You haven't fired it."

Callum turned around. "You checked?"

Cassie nodded but didn't ask forgiveness for meddling with his things. Callum gazed at her for a few seconds before he realized she wasn't going to.

He shook his head. "Too many complications would ensue if I used the gun. It's not worth it."

"Not even during the ambush?" Cassie said.

"Especially not during the ambush," Callum said. At Cassie's raised eyebrows, he added, "David and I talked about this. He's been here since 1282, and while I've only lived in the Middle Ages for six months, I can see that what he says is true: you can't fix everything, even if David is going to try. If I'd opened fire on the MacDougalls when they attacked us—what then?"

They both thought about that for a moment. "The noise alone would've brought everyone up short," Cassie said. "You could have given your company time to sort themselves out."

"True," Callum said, "but after my clip was empty? The MacDougalls would have seen I was out of bullets and attacked. And then, if I survived, just by its very existence the gun would have called attention to me, to King David, and to everything that we are."

"Saving the bullets wouldn't have done you much good if you were dead," Cassie said.

"That is the weak point in this argument," Callum admitted. "My death isn't the worst thing that could happen, though. And I didn't feel like I was going to die. Not on that road."

"What if using the gun was the only way to save someone else?" Cassie said.

Callum sighed. "I don't know. I guess I'll decide what to do when the time comes. If it comes."

They left Cassie's cabin with darkness falling, but a warmer breeze filled the air and the rain had stopped completely. It was May, after all. It couldn't rain all the time. *Or could it?* After they'd traveled a mile, a pitter-patter started on the leaves above their heads. Callum tried not to groan. Cassie's lips twitched, but she said nothing.

In fact, she said nothing about anything, even when Callum tried to draw her out with questions. She wouldn't elaborate on her life in Scotland or the possibility of leaving it behind. In fact, she didn't say more than three words the entire walk to Mugdock. She appeared completely comfortable with no communication at all, didn't ask him anything about himself, and held her face so still, Callum couldn't begin to discern what she was thinking.

After a while, he let it go. He didn't know her or her circumstances, other than that she'd done pretty well for herself, considering that she'd been dumped here with no warning and with no one to help her. By rights, she should be dead, or at the very least, should have had to sell herself to survive. But she hadn't, and that meant it wasn't his place to press her.

Callum took Cassie to be somewhere in her twenties, which meant she'd been less than twenty-five when she'd come to the Middle Ages. At twenty-five, all of Callum's needs had been taken care of by the army and his personal life had alternated between nonexistent and screwed up.

He glanced at Cassie, wondering if anything he'd said or done so far was right. He was out of practice with women, having spent most of his time with men since he'd come to the Middle Ages. Peasants and whores aside, no unmarried girl was ever allowed to spend time alone with a man, so he hadn't yet figured out how to get to know one. Until now, he'd had no land or money of his own to offer anyway. While Cassie seemed unconcerned about her reputation, they were violating all sorts of medieval rules by spending so much time alone together. Callum hadn't yet figured out what, if anything, he was going to do about it.

The rain squall didn't last long, stopping by the time Callum and Cassie came out of the woods onto lower ground. Cassie pulled up before they reached the small village, above which rose Mugdock Castle, which was situated on a rocky outcrop on the western end of Mugdock Loch. Towers lit by torches shone above a stone curtain wall. A wooden palisade extended around the whole of the mound, encompassing a much larger space below it. The sneer forming on Callum's lips told him that he'd spent too much time in English castles. He'd already adopted the English prejudice against the primitiveness of Scottish settlements.

Cassie hadn't seen his expression so Callum quickly rearranged his face before she could. "Do you think the MacDougalls are here?" he said.

Cassie studied the castle. "See how many men patrol the battlements?" And then she answered her own question. "Dozens. It's too many compared to other times I've been here."

"Is it safe for you to be here?" Callum said. "For us?"

"I'm wearing a dress today. Lord Graham won't turn me away," she said.

Callum couldn't tell if she was deliberately misunderstanding his question or really thought that a dress would take care of any threat.

"Let me do the talking," Cassie said. "You're dressed all wrong. They'll know you for English just by looking at you."

Callum opted not to mention the bow along her back, which surely showed her for being out of the ordinary too. "I speak Gaelic and medieval English," he said.

"Oh." Cassie looked Callum up and down, as if seeing him for the first time. "I've been treating you as if you were a child. I'm sorry."

Callum laughed. "I didn't notice. Up until a month or so ago, everyone treated me that way. It's easy to confuse ignorance with stupidity, especially when a man can't speak the language. People have a tendency to talk louder, as if I were deaf or a difficult three-year-old."

"It's more than that. You don't project yourself," Cassie said. "I'm not used to it."

"I don't understand."

"Men in Scotland are taught to fill up every room they're in," she said. "They're forceful and loud. You'll have to be careful that they don't confuse your lack of bravado with weakness."

"I don't mind if they do," Callum said. "A man viewed as weak is a man underestimated. Currently, I'd prefer to come across as your companion rather than as a threat to Lord Patrick."

Cassie actually laughed. "You want him to see you as my sidekick?"

"I'd choose to be your protector, but I don't think you need one," Callum said.

Cassie ignored that. "How much do you want me to tell him about you?"

"What if you were to say that I'm a Mackay, from the far north, and that I'm sympathetic to the Scottish cause, whomever they choose as king? Would he believe it?"

"Only if you could name your ancestors," she said.

"Donald," Callum said. "Every single Mackay is named Donald or Hugh."

She pursed her lips. "That you speak Gaelic will help, but I wouldn't mention how or why, or where you come from in Scotland. If King David really doesn't care who gets crowned king of Scotland, it would be better just to say so. You're here as his representative, not your own."

Callum nodded. He would rather not lie, but he happened to be good at it, a product of working for MI-5 for four years after he came home from the war.

Cassie led Callum through Mugdock's village, no more than a cluster of huts that huddled at the base of the mound upon which the castle was built. With darkness nearly complete, except for some stars that blinked in and out from behind the clouds, the only light came from a few open doorways and the torches at the castle gate.

Cassie marched right up to the doors. "I'm here to see Lord Patrick," she said in Gaelic.

"Nobody in or out after nightfall, those are our orders," the man said.

"I'm not nobody," Cassie said, rendering the double negative even in Gaelic, completely flummoxing the man.

"Lord Patrick will want to see us." Callum stepped closer to Cassie and into the light. "I guarantee it."

Whatever Cassie thought about the conceptual space Callum took up, he did have size to his advantage. The guard at the gate was eight inches shorter and had to look up at Callum. They exchanged a long look before the guard took a step back, pushing with his shoulder at the door behind him to open it.

Inside the palisade, the bailey showed evidence of night coming on. A few people trotted here and there, but the blacksmith works were dark, with just a dim glow from a banked fire. The door to the inner bailey was open, revealing bright lights within. From the sound of voices beyond it, the evening meal was in progress.

"What is this? You were told to let nobody in tonight." A man of obviously higher rank and authority stalked towards Cassie and Callum.

"They insisted—"

The second man cuffed the first man upside the head. "Get back to your post."

"Yes, sir." The underling obeyed, though not without shooting a glare at his superior from behind his back.

Cassie watched the guard go and then said, "Hello, John."

John grunted. He seemed to accept that Cassie wasn't going to call him 'sir' or 'my lord' or whatever the man might be used to from other people. "What do you want, Cassie? You shouldn't be here."

"I brought someone to whom Lord Patrick will want to speak," she said.

"He's busy."

"With the same business as this, I think," Cassie said. "When he finds out that you sent me away, which he will eventually, he's not going to be happy with you."

That sounded good, but Callum was feeling more nervous by the second about how easily Cassie sashayed in here and said what was on her mind. He hadn't heard anyone—much less a woman—make such bold statements about what she wanted since he'd come to the Middle Ages. Well—apart from David, who could say whatever he pleased. Though even he could take lessons in assertiveness from Cassie.

While Callum wore a sword and Cassie held her bow (a goddamned recurve—Callum still couldn't believe it), neither of them could hold off the dozens—maybe multiple dozens—of men currently filling Mugdock Castle. Callum made sure he didn't reveal his uncertainty by shifting from one foot to another and instead stood staunchly beside Cassie as she gazed steadily into John's face.

John, however, didn't blink. "All right, then. But not in the hall. You can wait in the south tower."

John led the way up the hill to the inner gate, set in a stone curtain wall with four towers that protected the keep. They climbed the stairs to the main floor of the tower to the left of the gatehouse. John pushed open the door, revealing a single square room. A stairway went around the exterior of the tower, rather than around the interior. Once John closed the door on them, if he chose to bar it, Cassie and Callum would have no way out. Callum glanced at Cassie, but she seemed unperturbed by their accommodations and entered the room.

Mistrusting where trust didn't seem warranted, Callum didn't follow her. Instead, he leaned against the frame of the door and folded his arms across his chest. John opened his mouth to speak, closed it, and then said, "You might have a long wait."

"Fine," Callum said.

John shot a look at Cassie, who had unslung her backpack from her back and was inspecting the arrows in her quiver. Then he looked at Callum. He didn't speak, just gave a quick jerk of his head and departed. Callum had the sense that what he would have said, if he'd said anything, was *better you than me.*

Damn straight.

Cassie moved to stand in the doorway with Callum and they looked out on the activity in the inner bailey. "The MacDougalls were here but I'm not sure they still are, and I don't get the sense the prisoners are here either."

"Why would you say that?" Callum said.

"I recognize that man." She lifted her chin to point at someone just entering the great hall. He looked an awful lot like the last soldier Callum had fought at the ambush site, before he'd been felled by that unseen assailant. "The other men are all from Graham lands. It looks as if Lord Patrick called them here as a precaution, to help fortify Mugdock."

Callum and Cassie waited a long time, maybe because Lord Patrick really was busy, or maybe because he was reluctant to meet them. In that time, nobody who went in or out of the keep looked at them. It was as though they were invisible, and maybe they were, since the candle that had lit the little room had gone out within five minutes of their arrival. Callum took the wait as an opportunity to ask his new friend a bit more about herself.

"You haven't told me the truth, Cassie," Callum said.

"What do you mean?" she said. "The truth about what?"

"Yourself."

"I have no idea what you're talking about."

"You pretend that you're a simple girl, raised in the woods," Callum said, "but you're not. You're well-educated; you speak elegantly and with a sophisticated vocabulary. And how does a simple girl learn Gaelic and medieval English so fluently, even if she's had nearly five years to do it?"

Cassie looked out at the bailey, not answering. Callum thought she wasn't going to answer, but then she said, "Indians aren't savages, Callum. Or stupid. I told you that I went to college."

"I-I-I didn't mean that. I meant—I just—"

"Really?" Her chin jutted out and her eyes flashed. "Maybe you should stop talking now."

Callum snapped his mouth shut, knowing he'd bolloxed that up beyond measure. To his regret, Cassie went quiet and Callum didn't restart the conversation. If he had his way, she was coming with him wherever he went next, no matter how low her opinion of him. That meant he'd have plenty of time to drag her story out of her.

"I don't like this plan anymore," Callum said. "I think it's time we made a new one."

"Give him a few more minutes," Cassie said.

Half of Cassie's face was in shadow, but Callum could see enough of it to know that she remained relaxed. "You seem very sure of him. Why?"

"He's—" she stopped.

"What?"

But then Cassie didn't have to answer because at that moment, John came out of one of the lesser structures built into the curtain wall and hurried towards them. Another man strode beside him on longer legs, dressed in mail and cloak like the other soldiers. Lord Patrick Graham. Callum knew it without having to ask. Given his grey hair but relatively young face and well-muscled stature, Callum put him in his late forties.

"Christ on the cross, Cassie!" Lord Patrick said, even before he'd come halfway up the stairs to the tower room. "What are you doing here?"

Cassie bowed her head about three millimeters. "We need to talk."

Lord Patrick let out a sharp burst of air and then transferred his gaze to Callum. "Who is this?"

"The personal emissary of King David of England," Callum said, not giving Cassie time to answer first.

Lord Patrick's lips thinned into a line. "You shouldn't be here."

Cassie leaned in. "Do you realize that King David was supposed to be in that party the MacDougalls ambushed, and that Bishop Kirby, the former regent of England, is dead? Do you understand what the MacDougalls have done and how much danger you're in? What are the chances that their sins will spill over to you?"

"I have no idea what you're talking about. I sheltered my kinsmen. That is all." But Lord Patrick's nostrils flared and Callum saw something that looked like fear in his eyes.

"What about the survivors of the ambush?" Callum said. "You're saying that the MacDougalls didn't bring them here?"

"We know they kept some men alive. I watched them march away," Cassie said. "Please say Alexander MacDougall didn't order their deaths after all?"

Lord Patrick clenched his teeth. "I had nothing to do with any of this."

"How are you going to prove that?" Cassie said.

"To whom should I have to prove it?" Lord Patrick said.

"How about the King of England?" Callum said.

"You have called in every able-bodied man from your lands," Cassie said. "You're saying that's for no reason?"

By way of an answer, Lord Patrick grabbed Cassie's arm and pulled her into the darkness of the tower room. Callum followed. "Rumor has it that if King David decides not to take the throne for himself, he will choose Robert Bruce to be king."

"That's where you're wrong," Callum said. "King David had decided no such thing. With this act, however, with the MacDougalls seeking his head—"

"I know." Lord Patrick ran a hand through his hair. "They have forced King David's hand. He will come with an army. He cannot let this act go unpunished."

"Your own Guardians promised safe travel for the king's party," Cassie said. "If this can't be resolved quickly, Scotland may find itself at war with England."

A shout came from the battlements. "They're coming!"

"You need to leave. Now." The words came out in a whispered hiss, though the only member of the garrison who could have heard him was John.

"If you tell me what's going on, I can plead your case to King David," Callum said. "I can tell him you helped us."

That was exactly the wrong thing to say. Lord Patrick pulled away from Cassie with a jerk and put his nose into Callum's face. "The day I need the King of England's assistance is the day I lose my honor."

He strode to the door. Cassie and Callum followed and turned to look as Lord Patrick headed up the stairs to the wall-walk above the inner bailey. He stopped before he reached the top, however, and although he pointed back at Cassie, his words were for Callum. "Get her out of here."

Callum took a step towards him. "Who comes? Who's *they*?"

Lord Patrick cursed and trotted back down the steps so he didn't have to shout. "James Stewart was in your company. There must have been someone else, someone who supported Robert Bruce."

"Why would you say that?" Callum said.

"Who else of importance traveled with you? You say the bishop is dead. Who else?" Lord Patrick said.

"King David sent a dozen noblemen with Kirby, along with members of his own household," Callum said.

"Robbie Bruce was there, too, as his squire," Cassie said. "His horse panicked and got him away before the MacDougalls descended upon the English."

Lord Patrick nodded. "So that's it, then."

"What is it?" Cassie said.

"Of all the luck." Lord Patrick looked up to the battlements as he spoke, not actually talking to Callum or Cassie anymore. Then he glared at Callum again. "It's too late for regrets. You don't know the Bruce as I do. It is he who comes against me now and we're all dead."

"My lord—" John said from the walkway above. Such was the tenseness in his voice that he didn't have to say more than that.

Lord Patrick looked at Cassie and Callum. "If you knew Robert Bruce as I do, you'd know that the King of England is the least of my concerns tonight."

8

Cassie

Callum and Cassie trotted up the steps after Lord Patrick, with no need to discuss the fact that they weren't going to heed his admonition to flee. Not yet. Cassie didn't feel any more than Callum did that she could run away without finding out what had happened to Callum's friends. Even if Lord Patrick was telling the truth—that the survivors of the ambush weren't at Mugdock—someone here would know where they'd gone.

They came out on the top of the wall to find that Lord Patrick had been entirely correct about what he faced and the immediacy of the danger. The Bruces had indeed come. Their banner rippled from a pole driven into the ground just out of arrow range, not that Lord Patrick had more than a half-dozen archers in his garrison. Bruce seemed to have a few more—enough anyway to loose the first rain of fire arrows at the castle. Meanwhile, other soldiers set fire to the thatched huts outside the palisade. Cassie hoped the villagers had sought shelter inside the castle before the Bruces had arrived. Not that ultimate safety lay there either.

Robbie Bruce had roused his family. It seemed impossible to think that they could have gathered hundreds of men in the few days since the ambush on the road, but if the torches they carried were any indication, their numbers neared a thousand. This had become more than a clan war. It was a kingdom they were fighting for.

"Those Bruces don't screw around, do they?" Callum said.

"Not much." Cassie took in a breath. "We need to make sure the prisoners aren't inside Mugdock."

"You don't think Lord Patrick was telling the truth?" Callum said.

"Do you?" Cassie really wanted to know what Callum thought. He wasn't a medieval man, not by a long shot, but he seemed to understand the medieval mind far better than she did. Even weirder, he seemed to want to understand *her*.

"I didn't say that," Callum said. "You did see a MacDougall."

"He could have been injured and left behind or been chosen to stay behind to keep an eye on Lord Patrick." Cassie paused. "You saw Lord Patrick's face. He didn't know that Robbie Bruce had been in your company."

"And yet he feared retaliation from someone—enough to call in his men from the surrounding countryside," Callum said. "He was prepared for something bad to happen."

"But do you think he was prepared for this?" Cassie said.

Callum faced the inner bailey and didn't answer. "Would this castle have a dungeon?"

"No," Cassie said, "at least not like you might see in the movies. Prisoners would be housed in a shallow basement like the one below the south tower. Mugdock Castle is built on solid rock."

Cassie gazed around at the sudden burst of activity wrought by the arrival of the Bruces. She and Callum were the only people in the entire castle not moving.

"We'll have to check each of the towers. I don't think anyone is going to stop us today." Callum shot a glare at Cassie. "And don't even suggest that we should split up."

Cassie hadn't been going to suggest it. She had her bow, still in its sling on her back, but she wasn't planning to take on the Grahams and the Bruces at the same time. When she'd first come to Scotland, that bow had been all that stood between her and starvation. Or rape. Growing up as she had, half on the reservation and half off it, Cassie understood the importance of family. Here, she was clanless, and that meant she was fair game to anyone who could catch her. Until Lord Patrick had taken her under his wing.

Cassie had seen the look that Callum had given her when she'd talked to Lord Patrick. Like everyone else, he thought that Cassie was, or perhaps had been at one time, his mistress. She hadn't been, however. Stereotypes of medieval men aside, Lord Patrick was loyal to his wife. All the man wanted was someone with a brain (which, sadly, his wife didn't appear to have) to whom he could speak freely.

Cassie didn't mind. He was old enough to be her father, a man Cassie had never met, and reminded her of her grandfather, who'd helped raise her. Cassie missed her grandfather every day, and it had been nice to have Lord Patrick on the margins of her life.

"Come on. I have a better idea." Cassie headed down the stairs and across the courtyard without waiting to see if Callum followed her. After a few seconds, he caught up and fell into step beside her. Nobody stopped them. Nobody even looked twice at them. It gave Cassie hope that they might be able to complete their search quickly, though no matter how fast they moved, she didn't yet have a plan for getting out of Mugdock in one piece.

Cassie didn't head straight for one of the towers but led Callum to the kitchen, a squat building separated from the keep by a walkway and from the other buildings by a good thirty feet. It had been built that way so if the kitchen caught fire (not an uncommon event), the flames might not spread to the rest of the castle. Cassie had a friend of a sort, Isobel, who worked there as undercook to Heck, the master of the kitchen. As they entered, Cassie traded the smell of smoke and manure for wet wool and baking bread.

"Cassie! What are you doing? You shouldn't be here!" Isobel, her blonde hair swept back from her face in a messy bun and her thick figure swathed in a giant apron, kneaded a humongous mound of bread dough.

"So I've been told," Cassie said, "but I could say the same to you. What are you doing here, making bread? The castle is under attack!"

"Men still have to eat," Isobel said. "Have you seen who comes against us?"

"The Bruces, we know," Cassie said.

Cassie lost Isobel's attention as she broke off to shout at a kitchen boy stirring a large pot over the fire.

"The village is already on fire," Callum said.

Isobel took in Callum with a glance and then looked again at Cassie. "I heard. What do you want, Cassie? This is no time for talking."

"Where are the prisoners?" Cassie said.

Isobel bit her lip. She started to shake her head but then stopped herself and said instead, "I shouldn't tell you, but since this is why the Bruce is here, it's not as if it's a secret. They've all gone—the MacDougalls, that is, and their prisoners too, though—" She paused as she thought some more. "They left one prisoner behind, a Scotsman not from around here, along with one MacDougall to keep an eye on him."

Callum turned his face away from Isobel and whispered in Cassie's ear, "That isn't exactly what Lord Patrick said." Then he straightened and said to the cook, "Where were the MacDougalls headed?"

"North to Dunstaffnage Castle."

"What about the prisoner who's still here?" Cassie was disappointed to learn that Lord Patrick could lie so convincingly. "Why was he left behind?"

"He couldn't be moved," Isobel said. "He was just a soldier anyway, not like some of the others. Not like the Stewart."

Callum drew in an audible breath. "James Stewart is alive?"

"To judge by his cursing all MacDougalls and Grahams for eternity, he's well too," Isobel said.

"They'll use him as leverage. That's why they're keeping him alive," Cassie said to Callum in modern English. "If they can't have King David, they'll take what they can get."

"Perhaps Bruce knows that the prisoners aren't here, and that's why he's so quick to burn Graham out rather than negotiate," Callum said in the same language.

Isobel's brow furrowed and she glared at Cassie. "You brought an Englishman here?"

Callum put out a hand in a gesture of appeasement and said in Gaelic, "I'm a Mackay, from up north. I have no dog in this hunt."

But Isobel lifted her chin. "I won't say more. You should go."

"We're going, Isobel," Cassie said, sorry to have their relationship marred because of Callum, but she couldn't fix it now. "Can you tell me where the soldier is being kept?"

Isobel was still looking sullen. "Donella has him with her."

"Thank you. Thank you for helping us." Cassie touched Isobel's shoulder. "Take care of yourself."

Isobel was already back to her kneading. "Go on with you. Until the Bruce burns us out, I have men to feed. I'll stop when Lord Patrick himself tells me to and not before."

Cassie backed away towards the door. "Let's go, Callum."

Callum put his heels together and bowed, prompting Isobel to pinch her lips together as she held back a smile. "Go on with you!" She shooed him away with one hand.

With a smile himself, Callum followed Cassie into the courtyard again, but this time it wouldn't be so easy to get across it. The thatched roof of the barracks was on fire and men had formed a line from the well, passing buckets of water from hand to hand. More fire arrows flew towards them, more than a dozen every minute.

"We don't have time to help," Callum said.

"I know. Come with me." Cassie led the way around the far side of the keep, which hadn't yet been touched by the battle.

"Which way to the postern gate?" Callum said.

"That's what I'm showing you." Cassie held up her skirt with one hand as she sprinted towards the inner gatehouse, which was still open, though it wouldn't be open for long if the Bruces breached the outer palisade. Once through the inner gate, they skidded down the slope from the castle into the outer bailey, which the palisade protected.

"We're running out of time," Callum said.

Cassie put a hand to her chest. It had been too long since she'd sprinted. "Donella is the herbalist and lives just there." She pointed to a cluster of buildings built against the southern wall. "She would have wanted the soldier close to her if he was very ill, though since he's a prisoner, I'm surprised Lord Patrick allowed it."

"Maybe he didn't want to be a party to the murder of a member of the king's company more than he already was," Callum said.

"It depends on whether or not he sheltered the MacDougalls by choice." Cassie picked up the pace again, jogging past the blacksmith works. John was among a group of soldiers huddled nearby, but he didn't look up as they passed. "I can't see him condoning the murder of King David."

"Would he believe that King David could be King Alexander II's grandson?" Callum said.

"Everyone else does," Cassie said. "It was the talk of the countryside last Christmas. So it's true, about his mother?" Her brow furrowed. "I thought you said she was from our time?"

"She is," Callum said. "So no, it isn't true. But David's denials haven't made any headway in England. True or not, the people believe it. What clan did King Alexander belong to?"

Cassie was silent a moment as she tried to recall it. "The House of Dunkeld."

"Then that is the clan upon which Graham and MacDougall have just begun a war, isn't it?" Callum said. "Isn't that the fear we saw in Lord Patrick's eyes?"

"You may be right," Cassie said.

They reached the six-foot-high wall that surrounded the kitchen garden. It had been built in stone to protect the plants from the wind that swirled through the courtyard year round, though it wasn't blowing tonight. The garden lay on a slight south-facing slope to make the most of whatever sun peeked through the clouds.

Cassie pushed open the door in the wall and came face to face with the end of a pike. Her hands came up and she froze. Donella crouched six feet away with her weapon at the ready.

"Whoa." Callum had come through the door right behind Cassie. He pulled up too, so close to Cassie that she could feel the warmth of his breath on her neck.

"Donella, it's me. Cassie."

Donella hesitated for another three seconds and then lowered her pike. "The Bruce is here."

"We heard," Cassie said. "We want to talk to the prisoner."

Donella narrowed her eyes and looked past Cassie to Callum. "Who's he?"

Cassie suspected that Callum was going to get that a lot, as long as he was with her and in Scotland. "Callum. A friend."

"He a Bruce?"

"Mackay," Cassie said.

Donella harrumphed at that, though what she meant by it, Cassie didn't know. Every Scot knew something about every clan, good and bad, but the Mackays were from the far north and Cassie didn't know how much contact the Grahams would have had with them. "Come with me," Donella said.

This time of year, the plantings were well under way, though still small enough that if a fire arrow came down among them there wasn't much to burn. So far the Bruces seemed to be focusing on getting through the palisade. That was on the north and northwest sides of the castle, not here to the south where the approach was steeper and the ground fell away to an elevation several hundred feet lower than the hill on which the castle rested.

Donella brought Cassie and Callum to her hut, ten feet wide and fifteen feet long. Its southern wall was the palisade itself. The hut had a thatched roof with a hole in the center to let out the smoke from the glowing brazier. Thick candles set in plates lit the interior.

Callum bounded towards the man lying on a pallet in the far corner but then pulled up, moderating his enthusiasm at the sight of the man's wounds. He crouched to the floor. "Hello, Liam."

"A tough one, he is," Donella said. "They walked him here, but by the time he arrived, he was out of his mind, raving. Alexander MacDougall wanted to kill him rather than leave him, but Lord Patrick wouldn't let him. I gave him a potion that put him to sleep. The MacDougall said that there was no point in killing a man so near death—though after the MacDougalls left, Lord Patrick said hastening it might have been a mercy."

Callum took Liam's hand in his. "I see a lot of blood."

"The blood isn't his," Donella said. "He took a blow to the head and it looks like he used his forearm as a shield. I've splinted the arm and bound it. We'll see about the head when he wakes."

"We need to go now," Callum said.

Men shouted outside the hut, calling for reinforcements on the palisade. Callum glanced up at Cassie and she nodded that she'd heard them too. It didn't seem as if the palisade had been breached, but it had to happen soon.

"What if we waited for the Bruces to come to us?" Cassie said.

"I don't trust them to stop long enough to listen," Callum said. "They're fired up, more so by the minute. No—" He shook his head. "I'm getting both of you out of here."

"How?" Cassie said.

"I'll carry him," Callum said. "We can go over the wall."

Cassie might have scoffed, but Callum's intensity was such that she believed he really would. "He's almost as big as you are, Callum."

"You couldn't carry him to Cassie's house, much less all the way to Dundochill," Donella said.

"I can walk," Liam said and at Donella's gasp added, "I've been awake on and off for a while now."

Donella poked at Callum's shoulder to move him out of the way and then crouched beside Liam. "Tricky, aren't you?" She felt his forehead.

Liam brushed away her ministrations with his good hand and reached out to Callum. "Help me up." His left forearm was tightly wrapped, and he held it gingerly to his chest. "I didn't know where I was and thought it might be better for my health if I played I was asleep."

Callum grasped Liam's hand and levered him to a sitting position. "What happened to the rest of our company?" Callum said.

"Dead or captured," Liam said.

"I realize that, but how many survivors were there?" Callum said.

"A dozen," Liam said, which was what both Cassie and Donella had told Callum too. "Your friend, Samuel, was among them."

Callum let out a sharp breath. "Thank the Lord. I was afraid to ask."

"We heard in the kitchen that they're being taken to Dunstaffnage Castle," Cassie said.

Donella began to shake her head, but then she turned it into a shrug and reached for one of the salves on the table in the center of her hut.

Cassie turned to Donella, a questioning look on her face. Callum had noticed the healer's odd movement too. "What was that?" he said. "Do you know something we don't?"

"Plenty," Donella said, with a wary look. "But that I didn't hear."

Cassie eyed her for a second, feeling that Donella wasn't being honest, but gestured to Callum to stop him from questioning her more forcefully. "We'll find them," Cassie said.

"We will," he said.

Cassie acknowledged that Callum was going to go after the prisoners, no matter the consequences, all the way to Dunstaffnage if need be. Cassie's next decision was going to be whether or not she was going with him.

Liam gestured to Callum's temple. "Looks like you've had your share of trouble as well."

"Oh, this?" Callum's hand went to his head and came away with a pinpoint of blood. "It doesn't hurt much anymore."

"Let me see that." Donella ordered Callum to a low stool, patted at his wound with a cloth, and then brought an oil lamp from her table so she could see better. She turned to Cassie. "What did you put on it?"

"Sanicle and comfrey," Cassie said.

Donella nodded grudgingly. She could hardly complain. Cassie had gotten the herbs from her in the first place. "I will treat them both again and then you should leave," Donella said.

"How?" Cassie said.

Callum peered up at Donella. "You have a way out, don't you? A secret way. I can tell from your voice."

Donella sucked on her teeth. "You know so much, do you? Donella knows some things too."

"I imagine you do," Callum said, "but if you could hurry …"

Moving steadily, though at a faster pace than Cassie had ever seen her use, Donella patched up Callum and helped Liam put his arm into a sling. Then she asked Callum to pull Liam's pallet aside. Muttering to herself, she knocked on the south wall of her hut and then swung open a four by four section of it. Freedom lay beyond the wall.

"I trust you not to tell the Bruce of this," she said to Cassie. "Lord Patrick trusts you."

"We have nothing against your lord." Callum grunted as he helped Liam through the opening. Liam was having an awkward time of it since he had only one usable arm on which to crawl.

Cassie turned to go too, but Donella caught her arm. "There's no going back if you follow him."

Cassie froze. "What—what do you mean?"

"You've lived cozy the last few years, but your little shell is cracked now and no amount of daub is going to mend it," Donella said.

Cassie leaned in closer. Donella's voice had taken on a singsong tone. Others had spoken of her as having the *sight*, but her eyes looked clear to Cassie. "Donella. What are you talking about?"

Callum poked his head back through the hole. "You coming?"

"Yes!" Cassie squeezed Donella's hand. "Thank you for your help."

Cassie's show of affection seemed to surprise Donella as much as she had surprised Cassie with her warning. "Bring me a rabbit sometime." Donella nodded to Cassie's bow. "You're good about not damaging the fur."

"I will." Cassie ducked through the hole, waited a moment for Donella to set the panel back in place, and then ran at a crouch from the palisade to the edge of the plateau some thirty yards away. The trees had been cut down along its rim, but a few remained below the level of the field as the hill fell away. Callum crouched with Liam behind some bushes. Liam had his head down and was breathing hard.

"I'm not entirely sure what to do next," Callum said. "Do we go to Stirling, or should we try to do something about this little war the MacDougalls have started?"

"Do you think Robert Bruce would listen to you?" Liam knelt in the grass, holding his wounded arm with his good hand

"He might," Callum said, "but can we really walk up to the rear of the Bruce force and introduce ourselves? They'll attack us on sight."

"If it's really the Bruces who've come, then Robbie could be with them," Cassie said.

"That's a good point," Callum said. "I'd like to think that he would listen to me."

"Whatever we do, we can't stay here." Cassie glanced back to Mugdock Castle. What had Donella meant about Cassie following Callum?

A great shout came up from the outer bailey. "Sounds like they've breached the palisade," Callum said. "That'll keep both sides busy for a while."

"We can follow the cliff around the edge of the loch," Cassie said. "Once we're away from the castle, then we can decide what to do."

"Lead on," Callum said.

So Cassie did. The going was rough: Lord Patrick had deliberately encouraged the growth of vegetation around the loch so as to discourage an army from trying to do exactly what they were doing. Fortunately, the moon had risen and the clouds had cleared, so they had light to see by. Even so, ruts and holes in the ground that lay in shadow tripped them up. They had to walk nearly a mile, which was a good half hour of effort and more than Liam could afford. Callum was holding up well, considering he'd spent the day in bed too, but Liam was more seriously injured than he. He held onto Callum's shoulder with his good hand and winced painfully every few steps as the movement jarred both his arm and his head.

They reached a point within a hundred yards of the outer pickets of the Bruce camp before they stopped to regroup. Cassie was in favor of walking right up to the soldiers guarding the perimeter, but neither Callum nor Liam thought that was a good idea.

"Why don't I just talk to them?" Cassie said.

Callum moved to one side, a step away from Liam, and lowered his voice. "No."

"I pose no threat." She spoke in modern English.

Callum scoffed at her. "There's no way I'm letting you walk up to those men all by yourself."

Cassie glared at him. "I've lived on my own here for years. Don't you think I've learned how to handle myself around soldiers by now?"

"Maybe you have," Callum said, "and maybe you've learned not to fear, but we would fear for you and we'd be too far away to help you if the men were to capture you and bring you into their camp."

"That's what we want though, right?" Cassie said. "We need to find Robbie Bruce, or at the very least, his father."

Callum shook his head. "No. We should all go together." He switched back to Gaelic, turning away from Cassie so as to include Liam in their conversation. "You and I will help Liam to walk between us and he can hobble and moan and pretend to be more ill than he is."

"I don't think I will have to pretend much," Liam said.

Cassie agreed, albeit reluctantly, and they did as Callum suggested. Four men guarded the entrance to the camp and spotted the trio the moment they stepped from the trees. Two came forward to meet the three companions before they'd crossed half the cleared space that separated the camp from the trees.

"Halt!" One of the soldiers barked the order. "Put your hands where I can see them!"

Liam, of course, had only one hand to raise. Cassie and Callum compromised by propping Liam between them and holding up one hand each.

The second soldier stepped closer. "Who are you?"

"My name is Callum. I was one of the men who rode with Bishop Kirby, Robbie Bruce, and James Stewart. I am King David's emissary to the throne of Scotland."

Callum still wore his mail and sword, of course, and was obviously well-turned out, which was why Cassie had agree that he should do the talking. The soldier lifted his torch so he could see Callum more clearly and then shifted from one foot to the other as he acknowledged that he faced a knight. "Donald—"

"Hush, Rory," the first soldier said. "Run and get the lord."

Rory obeyed, hustling towards the camp. Cassie, Callum, and Liam waited with Donald, though Liam looked like he was about to fall over. Cassie slowly lowered her hand so she could hold him up with both arms around his waist. Although Cassie still wore her bow and quiver, and she'd seen Donald's eyes go to them and then move away before he'd spoken to Rory, she hardly posed a threat against so many men.

Rory came hurrying back with a middle-aged man of medium height. He was dressed in a fine tunic that fell to his knees and a wool cloak, but wore no sword.

"My apologies, my apologies!" The man waved a hand. At the sight of him, Callum leaned Liam further into Cassie and stepped one pace forward. The man came to a halt in front of Callum.

"So it is you," the man said.

"So it is," Callum said. "I thought you were dead. I saw you fall."

"A necessary illusion." The man's eyes went to Liam, widened, and then he moved towards him with arms outstretched. He took Liam from Cassie and enveloped him in an embrace. "My boy. I'm so glad to see you alive."

"Thank you, Uncle," Liam said. "It pleases me to be alive too."

Cassie might be slow on the uptake, but she'd caught on by now. This was Bishop Kirby.

"Come with me," Kirby said.

"Of course," Callum said, but he let Bishop Kirby and Liam get ahead of them, the Bishop assisting his nephew on one side while Donald took the other. Rory followed, leaving Callum rubbing at his temples with his fingers and still not moving. "He was dead. I swear it."

"I saw him fall, too," Cassie said. "I saw the blood."

"So if he didn't die, who did?" Callum said. "Why the deception?"

"Could he have known about the ambush in advance and left before it started?" Cassie said.

Callum glanced at her. "You have a suspicious mind." Before Cassie could protest, he added, "I like that." The two of them took a couple of steps towards the camp, but then Callum stopped again and shook his head. "Men died. Good men."

"You will find the answers." Cassie had spent three days with Callum, two of them with him asleep, but from what she'd learned of him so far, there was no way he was letting this go. If Cassie was sure of anything, she was sure of that.

9

Callum

This situation stunk so high to heaven, Callum was having trouble not holding his nose in the bishop's presence. Callum had seen the look in Kirby's eyes as he'd recognized Callum and Liam. He'd thought they were dead. More to the point, he'd *wanted* them dead. Callum hadn't seen that look since Afghanistan, and even then it had been in the eyes of one of his own men who hadn't known when to stop firing his rounds.

Callum's biggest concern at this point was the welfare of Cassie and Liam. Just after that came the fear that if Kirby would have preferred Callum dead, was that true of Daddy and Grampa Bruce too? And if so, were any of them going to get out of here alive?

A healer's tent had been set up near the center of the camp. Kirby dropped Liam off there and after a quick check on him, Cassie and Callum followed Kirby to another tent of similar size, twenty by twenty, with the Bruce banner planted in front of it. The door flaps were pulled back and the soldier who guarded the entrance gestured them inside.

"Lord Callum!"

At Callum's entrance, Robbie Bruce leapt towards him, grabbed his arms, and then forsook decorum to hug him. Callum patted Robbie on the back, happy to see him alive and that his greeting appeared genuine. Murderous intrigue was an unlikely thing with which to have entrusted a fourteen-year-old, but family politics being what they were—and Callum had heard plenty from David about what had gone on over the years in Wales—one never knew.

The four men already in the tent looked up at Robbie's exclamation. A man in his middle forties, with black hair receding at the temples, came around from behind the table. "I'm Robert Bruce. Robbie has told me much about you." Daddy Bruce (Callum couldn't decide if he should throttle Bronwen when he saw her again or thank her for putting these nicknames in his head) didn't hide his examination of Callum, openly looking him up and down. Callum stood six inches taller and broader, but Daddy Bruce had a presence about him that seemed to fill the tent.

Daddy Bruce's eyes then went past Callum to Cassie, so Callum gestured Cassie forward. "My lord, this is ... Cassandra. She is under my protection." Callum made the comment knowing that it would cause Cassie to grind her teeth, but he needed everyone to know that she was with him and not fair game for any other man.

Daddy Bruce nodded, but Callum could see him instantly dismiss Cassie from his mind. Such an attitude towards women, even one with a bow across her back, was typical of medieval noblemen. Callum had seen Meg and Bronwen use that disregard to their advantage, as a way to disarm a man and find out information they wanted to know. Daddy Bruce underestimated Cassie at his peril.

In this case, Daddy Bruce had a task before him and thus a clear focus on those whom he considered important, further winnowed down to those he could use. Likely, Daddy Bruce hadn't yet decided whether or not he could use Callum. Callum, for his part, was happy to keep him guessing. Staying alive might depend on it. David had never been further away.

"I'm glad to see that you're alive," Robbie said. And then his face fell. "All the others ... James ... he's dead."

"No, Robbie." Callum lifted his hand to gain Daddy Bruce's attention. "My lord, he isn't."

Daddy Bruce had been turning away, having lost interest in Callum, but now spun back. "What did you say? Bishop Kirby told me that he was the only survivor of the ambush."

Kirby cleared his throat. He had entered the tent before Callum and Cassie, but had sidled to the side and come to stand near a tent pole in the far corner. "I awoke after the battle having been left for dead. I assumed I was the only one to survive."

"Liam and I survived," Callum said.

Cassie put a hand on the back of Callum's cloak and gave a slight tug. She had her cheek near Callum's left shoulder blade and said in low voice in their English, "I looked into every face. *Every face*. Nobody was alive on that road but you."

Callum turned his head and spoke softly, "Did you see Kirby?"

"If that man is Kirby, he wasn't there. The one who died wore the white robes of a bishop, but he only faintly resembled this man."

As Cassie and Callum spoke, identical annoyed expressions crossed the faces of Daddy Bruce and Kirby. "What language are you two speaking?" Daddy Bruce said.

Callum hesitated for half a second before answering. "English. A dialect from the place where Cassie and I grew up."

Kirby's face flushed red. "I can tell from your demeanor that you doubt my word. I am offended."

"King David relies upon me to doubt," Callum said. "I doubt everyone. What I can tell you is that we have just come from Mugdock Castle. Alexander MacDougall did not murder everyone. He marched the survivors north this morning. James Stewart was among them."

Daddy Bruce slammed a hand onto the table in front of him. "They were here, then! We are correct in thinking that Lord Patrick was a party to the ambush!"

"No." Cassie stepped out from behind Callum. "He was unaware of what had transpired until the perpetrators arrived at his doorstep. Your ire is misplaced."

"He could have sent word to me! He could have denied them hospitality," Daddy Bruce said.

"From what I saw, he was caught between his honor and his loyalty," Callum said. "You ask too much of him to turn aside Alexander MacDougall."

"John Balliol, you mean," Daddy Bruce said.

"No, I don't—" Callum began, but Kirby cut him off.

"MacDougall was acting on Balliol's orders. We know it for a fact."

Callum pursed his lips. "How can you know—?"

But again Kirby overrode him. "Without honor, a man is nothing, and Alexander MacDougall has no honor."

"Regardless of who's at fault, anger towards Lord Patrick is misplaced," Cassie said.

"Lord Patrick did not know of the ambush in advance," Callum said, determined to back Cassie up. Kirby's disrespect was starting to irritate him. "He bears no grudge against Lord Stewart or your son."

Bruce's face was still flushed with anger, but he gave a jerk of his head in acknowledgement of Callum's reasoning. It was just Patrick Graham's bad luck to be the laird of a lesser clan caught between Balliol and Bruce. In Scottish history, that was never a good place to be.

"MacDougall will be taking them to Dunstaffnage Castle," Kirby said.

"I don't—" Callum was about to tell him that this might not be true, but Daddy Bruce cut him off with a bark.

"I will waste Mugdock and then turn my attention to Dunstaffnage." Daddy Bruce placed his hands on his hips, gazed at

Callum for a count of five, and then turned to Kirby. "I want MacDougall's head for what he's done. He has conspired against my family for the last time."

"My lord—please. A private vendetta is the last thing Scotland needs right now," Callum said. "We must find the prisoners, but Alexander MacDougall's punishment ... surely that is the king's responsibility."

"We have no king," Daddy Bruce said. "Thus, those who have the strength must act in his stead."

"The Guardians of Scotland act as king until one is approved," Callum said. "You must inform them and leave MacDougall's punishment to them."

"The Black Comyn is one of the Guardians!" Daddy Bruce said. "As John Balliol's brother-in-law, he had to have known of this plot!"

Cassie started beside Callum. "I don't think—" she said, but not loud enough for Daddy Bruce to hear. Callum wasn't following the reasoning either.

The Comyns were a powerful clan in their own right with their own strong claim to the Scottish throne, though the elder Comyn had forgone his claim in favor of his brother-in-law, John Balliol. Like the Bruces, the Comyns insisted on giving every son the same name, but history had done the nicknaming for Callum, dubbing the elder John Comyn, 'Black'; and his son, 'Red'.

"I would see the proof of that before I condemn him," Callum said.

"You have no authority here either to condone or to condemn." Daddy Bruce's chin came up. "You are King David's pet, not my liege lord."

"Lord Bruce—" Even Kirby knew this was going too far. To call a man a 'pet' was one of the most insulting things you could say in the Middle Ages. It outranked even 'bastard'. Given that Kirby had neglected to mention that Callum was the Earl of Shrewsbury to Falkes, he probably hadn't informed Daddy Bruce of it either, but 'pet' was still an insult. Suddenly, Callum didn't feel bad about calling him 'Daddy Bruce' in his head.

"So that means—what?" Callum said. "Do you rebel against the Guardians just as MacDougall does? Do you seek a war with England?"

"King David should have no say in Scotland. The Guardians should never have gone to him," Daddy Bruce said.

Callum found it interesting that Kirby stood by and let Daddy Bruce express this dissent openly without making even a token protest. As a governing body, the Guardians of Scotland *were* the king, which had been Callum's whole point. It didn't matter which individuals were involved. Kirby had accused the Black Comyn of conspiring with Balliol and MacDougall, but Comyn was still a Guardian. As a body, they would move heaven and earth to rescue one of their own.

"King David did not interject himself until the Guardians asked for his help," Callum said. "It is well that you pursue those who murdered the king's men. King David would have no quarrel with that. But if your real aim is to destroy Balliol's claim to the throne of Scotland, with that he would have issue."

"Besides, what is your resentment against King David?" Cassie said. "Everyone in Mugdock thinks that he has already decided the throne in your father's favor. That's why the MacDougalls ambushed the company in the first place."

Callum had to suppress a laugh at the surprised look on Bruce's face.

"You hadn't heard those rumors?" Cassie said.

What surprised Callum was that Cassie hadn't interjected herself into the conversation more. She wore a dress, as a sop to Lord Patrick's sensibilities, but that was about as far as her patience with the role of women in the Middle Ages went.

Meg, Anna, and Bronwen had worked hard to fit into the Middle Ages. They'd compromised their independence because the alternative was to call attention to themselves and the way they had arrived here. David had done the same, so it wasn't just because they were women. As far as Callum could tell, Cassie had bought into none of it.

Daddy Bruce peered at Cassie. "Who are you?"

"Her point is valid," Callum said, seeking to distract him. "Call off this fight with Lord Patrick and seek the prisoners elsewhere."

Daddy Bruce had been leaning on his hands on the table and now straightened. "Are you giving me an order?"

Callum didn't back down. He'd had enough of Daddy Bruce's attitude. "I will if I have to. You may view it as a suggestion if you prefer, if only because James Stewart was alive this morning. King David would prefer he stay that way."

At least Daddy Bruce didn't argue with Callum's ability to speak for King David. It was how things were done here. It wasn't like Callum could pick up his mobile phone and call him to confirm a given course of action.

Daddy Bruce took in a deep breath and let it out. His brow furrowed as he gazed down at the table and then he nodded. "I will put up the white flag and see if Lord Patrick says the same as you." Daddy Bruce glared past Callum to the world outside the tent. "I'd prefer to know if Lord Stewart is still alive before I burn either Mugdock or Dunstaffnage to the ground. I wouldn't want him killed by mistake."

Callum nodded and stepped to one side with Cassie to allow Daddy Bruce, Kirby, and Robbie to leave the tent. As he passed Callum, Daddy Bruce didn't look at him and his color remained high. In the end, it had been Daddy Bruce who had backed down a moment ago. Callum hoped he wouldn't pay for it later.

Daddy Bruce ducked through the doorway and was immediately distracted by one of his men, who gave him a rundown of the current state of the assault on Mugdock.

Callum took the opportunity to head out of the tent and over to one side, out of the firelight. Cassie came with him. "We have to get out of here," she said.

"I know."

Side by side, they hustled back to the healer's tent. Not for the first time since he'd come to this world, Callum was struck by the power a single man could wield. Kirby's influence arose from his status as a bishop and the leader of the English delegation to Scotland. He answered only to King David, and because the king was far away, effectively that meant Kirby answered to no one. Daddy Bruce, as far as Callum could tell, believed himself to be above the law and that he could do whatever he wanted as long as he thought it was right. Callum, as David's representative, had power too, though without a company of soldiers behind him, that meant considerably less than it had three days ago. Still, he'd had enough to influence Daddy Bruce.

Liam had been sitting on a low stool as they entered the tent, but at their approach, he stood.

"How are you?" Callum said.

"Well enough." Liam nodded at the other man in the tent, who was folding bandages into piles. "He saw no reason to add to what Donella had already done."

Callum turned to the healer. "Excuse us, please."

The man looked from Liam to Callum, bowed at the waist, and departed. Here, and everywhere, there were worse things than being an earl. Liam had color in his face again and seemed sturdier than before.

"Can you walk?" Callum said.

"Are we going somewhere?" Liam said.

"Anywhere but here, I think," Cassie said.

Liam's expression lightened. "I was just trying to figure out how I was going to convince you that it wasn't safe to stay."

"I'm glad you agree," Callum said. "What made you decide we had to leave? Your uncle is here—"

"My uncle was singularly unhappy to see me. I haven't seen that look on his face since he came to visit my mother, to offer to bring me up in his household. He'd hoped that my father would be overcome by his generosity."

Cassie smiled. "I gather he wasn't?"

"My father didn't exactly throw Kirby out of the house, but he did tell him that if he crossed our threshold before ten years had passed, he would have his head. It was only at that point that I would be old enough to make my own decision about my future."

"And yet ten years later you decided to go with Kirby," Cassie said. "Why?"

Liam lifted one shoulder. "My father had died, we'd had a few bad growing seasons, and my older brother didn't manage the lands as well as my father had. It seemed the expedient thing to do."

"What I want to know is how Kirby teamed up with Bruce," Callum said.

"How well do you know your uncle, Liam?" Cassie said.

"Obviously, not well enough," Liam said.

"It's odd, isn't it?" Callum said. "I don't understand the play either side is making here, not at all."

"Alexander MacDougall is a hothead," Cassie said. "When he gets fired up, his warriors will do anything for him."

"That I understand," Callum said, "but is he really working for John Balliol?"

"And if so, to what end?" Cassie said. "Surely Balliol wouldn't condone the capture, or murder, of the King of England?"

"It does seem to be a mare's nest of intrigue," Callum said. "Balliol supporters think King David has decided in Bruce's favor, and Bruce seems to think that King David had already decided in favor of Balliol. Neither side is going to stand for losing. It's as if they both *want* a war."

"We already know the real fear is that King David wants the crown for himself," Cassie said. "That's the information you need to include for this to add up. Nobody truly believes the king means what he says."

"So each side is making a preemptive strike for the throne?" Callum said.

"My father thinks that since MacDougall failed to capture or kill King David, he will use James Stewart to negotiate himself out of punishment, or to put Balliol on the throne."

Cassie and Callum turned at the voice. Robbie Bruce had ducked through a door in the rear corner of the tent.

"We think so too," Callum said, "but MacDougall has to know Scotland can't choose a king this way. There are more families in Scotland than the Bruces and the Balliols. Fourteen men claim the throne."

Robbie shrugged. "Either way, you need to leave. Now."

Cassie took a step closer to him. "So we were just saying. What is it you fear?"

"I don't know. It's just …" Robbie shrugged again. "When my horse fled the battle, I went to my father's lands at Kilmarnock, south of Glasgow, for help."

"I know of the place," Callum said.

Robbie's voice dropped lower, as if he was afraid to speak his next words out loud, even when nobody but Cassie, Liam, and Callum were listening. "My father and his men were already prepared for battle because Bishop Kirby had arrived ahead of me."

"How is that possible?" Callum said.

"I-I-I don't know," Robbie said.

"Or maybe you don't want to know," Callum said.

Cassie shot Callum a quelling look and put a hand on Robbie's arm. "You think Kirby knew about the ambush in advance and left the company before the MacDougalls attacked? That's the only way he could have reached your father before you did."

Robbie swallowed hard. "Maybe."

Cassie moved with Callum to one side and spoke in modern English. "What I don't understand is if Kirby knew about the ambush in advance—enough to arrange for a decoy for the MacDougalls to murder instead of him—how could he not have warned Robbie's father that the king was absent and Robbie present?"

"He wanted Daddy Bruce filled with righteous anger so that he would do exactly as he did," Callum said, "which was to go on the offensive."

Cassie stared at Callum. "What did you just call him?"

Callum tsked through his teeth. "It was Bronwen's way of keeping the three Bruces straight: Grampa Bruce, who is striving for the throne; Daddy Bruce, his son and Robbie's father; and Baby Bruce—our Robbie—who becomes *the* Robert the Bruce later in history."

Cassie turned on her heel and spoke to Robbie in Gaelic. "What about you? You're your father's heir and yet in conspiring with Kirby, your father left your survival or death at the hands of the MacDougalls up to fate?"

"No! No!" Robbie said. "He didn't know that I was in the company, or about the ambush, until Kirby told him of it. He mourned my death and his joy at my resurrection was real."

"Unlike Kirby's reaction to seeing Liam alive," Callum said.

Robbie nodded. "I know my father well. He was *very* angry, first to have lost me, and then at how close he'd come to losing me."

"No wonder he seeks vengeance," Liam said.

"I need to tell you one more thing so you understand how urgent it is that you leave," Robbie said. "My father hates the Black Comyn and was adamantly opposed to him being appointed as one of Scotland's Guardians."

"So I gathered," Callum said.

Robbie looked down at his feet. "Kirby told my father that he saw Andrew Moray and Red Comyn among the raiders. Andrew Moray's stepmother is the Black Comyn's sister, and of course, Red Comyn is the Black Comyn's son."

Cassie lifted her chin and gazed at a point above Robbie's right shoulder. She held that pose for ten seconds and then shook her head.

"You don't remember seeing either of them?" Callum said.

"I've never encountered Andrew Moray. I've seen Red Comyn only once, and not up close," she said. "I didn't notice him among the assailants but that's not to say he wasn't there. If what Kirby says is true, then the Guardians are corrupted too."

"That's what I've been trying to tell you. That's why you have to leave," Robbie said. "Because of Kirby's information, my father's forces attacked the Comyns' Castle at Kilbride before riding on Mugdock."

This was getting worse and worse with each minute that passed. "Another few days and all of Scotland will be at war, and nobody will know the why of it," Callum said.

"You are taking a great risk telling us all this," Cassie said, "especially if your father is implicated in wrongdoing."

"James Stewart is my friend and master," Robbie said. "I would do anything for him."

"I didn't know him long, but I would call him a friend," Callum said. "We need horses. And a way out."

Robbie nodded. "I can arrange for both for you. That's why I came to find you. Come with me." It was only then that Callum noticed that Robbie had a bag slung over his shoulder. "I brought you some supplies."

Cassie, Callum, and Liam hurried out of the tent after Robbie. "Where is your father now?" Callum said.

"He is arranging to speak with Lord Graham, as you suggested," Robbie said.

"Will he miss you?" Cassie said.

"No."

The finality in his voice stopped Callum from asking any more of him, or pressing as to why he was helping them. Families were complicated at the best of times. It could only be made worse when a kingdom was involved. "If anyone asks, you didn't see us," Callum said.

"You don't need to worry about me," Robbie said.

From the healer's tent, they scuttled around the northern perimeter of the camp, heading east through the no man's land between the firelight and the men posted to watch Daddy Bruce's flank. The pickets surrounded the camp in a human wall, but the space between the watchers allowed Callum and the others to slip through without raising an alarm. The further they went from the main activity centered on Daddy Bruce's tent, the more permeable the perimeter became. Daddy Bruce was giving lip service to the idea that another enemy could come behind him, but he wasn't worried about it.

Robbie pulled up at the end of a long fence that enclosed over a hundred horses, picketed in a field adjacent to the camp.

"Go," Callum said to Robbie. "Your father may not miss you, but one of his men might. Kirby might."

"I'll say I was at the latrine," Robbie said. "No one will gainsay me."

Callum held out his hand to Robbie and they grasped forearms, man to man. "Thank you," Callum said.

"I'm not helping you because I don't believe my grandfather should be the king of Scotland," Robbie said.

"It may still happen," Callum said.

"I intend to be king of Scotland myself one day," Robbie said, "but I don't believe in this. I don't want our rule to come about this way or for people to say we murdered our way to the throne like Macbeth. I won't take the throne over your dead body. Or James's. I will fight the MacDougalls, and the Comyns, and Balliol, but I don't believe that King David means us ill."

Callum held his arm a second longer. "Why don't you?"

"Because you don't." Robbie released Callum, sketched a wave, and ran off into the darkness, leaving Callum looking after him, speechless.

"I never saw myself as a horse thief," Liam said as he climbed over the split rail fence into the field.

Cassie ducked between the top and bottom rails. "I've done worse."

Callum believed her, if only because there was so much about her he didn't yet know. But he thought he understood more about her than she knew. The two of them shared a past and an old world. If Callum had arrived here as she had, he might have done worse too.

When Callum had first come to the Middle Ages, the shock of it had left him reeling for weeks. Slowly, he'd come to himself and resolved to make the best of the life that was left to him. At the same time, with nothing to tie him in one place and no way to get home, it was as if he'd died and been reborn. Callum saw that same attitude in Cassie. Without a past other than what was in her own head, the freedom from it had turned to recklessness, as if she didn't care whether she lived or died. Callum had seen that before too, in Afghanistan.

Cassie moved among the horses, patting a nose here and there. Callum didn't know what she was looking for, but when she found it, she waved him over. "This one is for you," she said as Callum reached her. "Some of the others are too much like ponies. You're too big for them to carry as far as we might need to go."

The horse was black against a black night and wore a blanket, saddle, and bridle, though it carried no saddle bags. About a third of the horses were still kitted out with their gear. As Callum took the reins, he glanced around, looking for the boys whose job it was to watch the horses. He didn't see them.

Liam wasn't as large as Callum, so Cassie had less trouble finding a mount for him. Then she picked out one for herself. "You've ridden a lot, have you?" Callum said.

"I grew up in Eastern Oregon," she said. At his quizzical look, she added, "I realize that means nothing to you, but suffice to say, it's cowboy country."

Callum almost laughed, not at what she'd said, but at her choice of words: *suffice to say* coupled with *cowboy*. She was speaking American and her vocabulary told him yet again that if she was a cowgirl, she was an educated one. "Cowboys—as in cattle ranches?" Callum said. "Like the wild west?"

"Exactly like the wild west." Cassie smiled. "Although with fewer saloons and brothels these days."

"I thought Oregon was all rain and trees," Callum said.

"That's only on the west side of the state," Cassie said.

She led her horse towards a far gate and Liam and Callum followed. The horse boys had finally appeared. They blocked the gap in the fence as Cassie approached.

Liam spoke in a low voice from just behind Callum. "How are we doing this?"

"Just follow my lead," Callum said, with every intention of bluffing his way out of the paddock, but it was Cassie who had it well in hand.

"Hello." She spoke in a tone Callum had never heard her use before. Lower, a little sexy, and definitely out of the boys' league. "It's a beautiful night."

The two boys straightened and stepped back as Cassie and her horse crowded them out of the exit. Neither of them could have been more than sixteen and both were shorter than Cassie. Even so, keeping her attention was all they could think about. Liam and Callum kept on going, past Cassie's horse and into the woods that bordered the camp to the north. They were out of earshot by the time she came hurrying up, leading her horse.

"They won't forget you," Callum said.

"Being memorable was worth it to get away with no trouble. Daddy Bruce is busy." Cassie shot Callum an amused glance and then swung up onto her horse. The move revealed the pants beneath her dress and she made a half-hearted attempt to pull down her skirt. "It will be a while before he remembers us, and then longer still until those boys are questioned."

"How are you doing, Liam?" Callum said, after boosting him onto his horse. With a damaged arm, Liam couldn't have managed it without help.

"Well enough," he said.

Cassie tsked through her teeth. "Both of you are suffering the aftereffects of a concussion. If either of you feel like you're going to fall off your horse, let me know before it happens. You're both too big for me to catch or lift."

"Deal," Callum said.

They headed east. At a junction, they could have turned south and connected with the Glasgow-Stirling road, but Callum turned his horse's nose resolutely north. He couldn't abandon the captives. At Killearn, six miles north of Mugdock Castle, he would have passed up another opportunity to turn east, but Liam hesitated at the crossroads.

"What is it?" Callum said.

Liam still hesitated and Cassie said, "He didn't say anything earlier, but he's wondering if we shouldn't ride to Stirling Castle and warn William Fraser and the other Guardians what is afoot."

"Perhaps that would be the best course, but I feel an obligation to James," Callum said, "and to Samuel if he's alive. However much Bruce might admire James, I don't trust him to care about the hostages when he catches up with the MacDougalls."

"I'm not asking you to change course," Liam said. "I will go alone."

Cassie and Callum exchanged a look. That wasn't a good idea either.

"I have family in the area," Liam said. "I won't be alone once I reach their holdings to the west of Stirling."

"What is your clan?" Callum said.

"MacLaren," Liam said, and then he grinned. "We support the claim of Bruce and hate the MacGregors, MacDougalls, and Grahams."

"I can see why you didn't mention that earlier," Callum said.

"I didn't want to muddy the waters," Liam said. "Besides, my uncle knows my father's family. He would have told Bruce my allegiance if he thought it was important."

"Maybe he didn't think your loyalties mattered," Cassie said, and then spoke the hard truth they couldn't deny: "He meant for you to die along with everyone else."

Callum nodded. "She's right. Liam, we do need you to ride to Stirling and make sure that the remaining Guardians know what's happening. Presumably, someone will have reported the massacre on the road, but they won't know who led it until you tell them."

Cassie put a hand out to Liam. "Don't say a word about your uncle, though, or Bruce and Kirby's accusation against John Balliol for that matter. We don't know who to trust or who else might be involved in this plot."

"I won't," Liam said.

Callum held out his hand to him. "May God go with you."

"It's only ten miles to safety," Liam said, clasping Callum's forearm with his good hand. "I won't stop until I reach help, no matter the cost. Where should I tell Bishop Fraser you're going?"

"North—but don't have him try to track us down," Callum said. "We'll come to him when we can. The Black Comyn should have been headed to Stirling Castle already for the gathering with Parliament. Now he will have his burned castle on his mind. Hopefully, he hasn't already started his own war against Bruce in the south."

Callum longed for a fast car and a good road. Ten miles was nothing in the modern world—ten minutes of your time, no matter how heart-stopping the danger. But here in the Middle Ages, the twenty miles from Glasgow to Stirling had proved their undoing.

He consoled himself with the knowledge that Liam, as a lone rider, could travel the distance in less than three hours—two if the roads were good and his body didn't fail him. For the thousandth time, Callum wished for a mobile phone.

"Good luck," Cassie said.

Liam rode away, heading east into the lightening sky. Callum and Cassie watched until he disappeared into the morning mist.

10

Cassie

"Do you know where you're going?" Cassie said to Callum after Liam had ridden out of sight.

"No idea," Callum said. "I was hoping you did."

That was another thing that was different about Callum: his ability to admit he didn't have an answer to every question. It spoke of a deep and abiding confidence in himself and what he was that he didn't feel threatened by his own ignorance.

"I ranged all over this area at one time," Cassie said. "My memory isn't perfect, and sadly, what I can't tell you is where the MacDougalls would have hidden their captives. The problem, as I see it, is that much of this land is hostile territory. The Grahams and MacGregors exist in little pockets between here and MacDougall land in the west."

"In the course of my work, I memorized maps of Britain on the off chance that I would ever be stuck somewhere without one," Callum said. "I traveled this part of Scotland by car a few years ago, but the world looks completely different from the back of a horse. Most of the main roads don't even follow the medieval roads anymore." He shook his head. "I've even been near Dunstaffnage, to that castle that juts out into the water at Loch Awe. Do you know it?"

"Maybe." Cassie wrinkled her nose at him. "I think I know where you're talking about. If you search for 'Scottish castle' on the internet—or at least if you searched back when I could—it's the most photographed one ever. But I don't remember seeing it when I passed by the loch. I don't think it's been built yet."

"I thought you didn't know anything about Scottish history," Callum said.

Cassie stuck out her chin in an attempt not to blush. "It doesn't mean I don't like castles."

Callum laughed. "I'm not touching that one." Cassie glared at him, but he just shrugged. "Regardless, if we're going anywhere, you're going to have to lead us."

"I wouldn't have said growing up as I did in Oregon would better prepare me for living here than growing up in England," Cassie said. "It's *your* history."

"I actually spent a lot of years in Washington D.C., since my father worked for the U.S. State Department. After my parents' divorce, my mother and I lived in London, and then I went to university at Cambridge," Callum said. "There's not a lot of call for trapping rabbits there."

Cassie couldn't help but laugh. Callum smiled too, with a flash of white teeth. His eyes glinted at her as she met his gaze, and she realized that this wasn't the first time he'd made her laugh—far from it. Cassie looked away, her insides churning.

"How far could the MacDougalls have marched the prisoners in one day?" Callum said.

Cassie was thankful that he'd changed the subject. "If everyone was healthy? Thirty miles? Much more and they'd not walk another step the next day."

"They went in daylight," Callum said, "so they must not have been worried about being seen."

"Or they didn't have far to go." Cassie tapped a finger to her lips as she thought. "You know, Callum ... do you remember Donella saying something about Dundochill?"

"No," Callum said.

"She said it when we first found Liam, something about you carrying him all the way to Dundochill." Cassie said. "It's an island in Loch Ard, ten miles north of here."

"I know that loch. Doesn't it belong to the Earl of Lennox?"

"I think so," Cassie said.

"He supports Grampa Bruce," Callum said.

"He does." Cassie gazed north, not that there was much to see but the dark shape of the hill in front of them and mountains beyond that. "I was up there once. Nobody lives there. It would be a good hiding place."

"It might be worth checking out," Callum said. "Donella *was* holding something back."

"I think you're right. If the prisoners aren't there, we can always ride on to Dunstaffnage," Cassie said. "You can have another go at Daddy Bruce."

Callum chewed on his lower lip. Cassie had said it as a joke, but he took it seriously. "It might be better if we stayed off his radar for now."

"You got him to talk to Lord Patrick. It was better than what he was doing." Cassie paused. "Thank you for that. Lord Patrick is a friend."

"We should have waited to leave," Callum said. "I would have liked to know the outcome of their conversation."

"I feel bad about leaving Lord Patrick too. I owe him a lot," Cassie said, "but Robbie told us we needed to go and he knows his own father. Daddy Bruce is either going to Dunstaffnage or he's not; the prisoners are there, or they're not."

"I know," Callum said.

"I don't think we could have helped Lord Patrick more than you did by getting Daddy Bruce to talk to him," Cassie said.

"Robbie was very convincing in his urgency," Callum said, "though it would have been nice to understand Kirby's end game. What's he up to?"

"No good," Cassie said, "but that, too, is out of our hands for the time being."

"You're right, of course," Callum said.

Cassie was glad Callum saw that. She liked being right. She was also finding that she liked having something important to do.

It had been too long since she'd made a difference in anyone's life but her own.

A mile out of Killearn, Cassie and Callum forded the river that flowed east out of Loch Lomond and rode northeast for several more miles, before turning north again. If they kept going as they were, they would reach the river that flowed from Loch Ard and could follow it west to the loch. Cassie yawned. With the rising of the sun, a glorious May day was creeping across the hills and valleys. Now that the excitement had abated, she was feeling her lack of sleep.

Callum looked over at her. "Stay alert, Cassie. We have a ways to go."

"I know." Cassie shook herself and looked at her companion. He swept his hood off his head and allowed the sun to bathe his face. He looked tired too, but in better shape than he could have been, given what he'd been through in the last few days. "So, how did you learn Gaelic?" Cassie said.

"My mother is Scottish," he said. "I missed her every day before I came to the Middle Ages."

"She's gone, then?"

Callum nodded. "My father too. They both died of cancer two years ago, within six weeks of each other."

"I'm sorry," Cassie said. And then she asked him—despite herself and even though it was so unlike her—"did you have a girlfriend or a wife, back in the old world?"

"I was dating a girl, Emma. We hadn't been together long." He paused. "She would have no idea why I stopped calling."

"I'm sorry," Cassie said again, and meant it.

Callum shrugged. "I had a job to do and I did it. I can't be sorry, since it's who I am. It's because of the army and then MI-5 that I was at all prepared for this life." He shot Cassie a wicked grin. "Being a spy is all fun and games until a man ends up in the Middle Ages."

Cassie snorted a laugh, which she tried to swallow back. "You seem to have done all right for yourself. You're an emissary from the King of England."

"That's only because he's a twenty-year-old kid from Oregon," Callum said, "though the more time I spend with him, the less I remember that."

"I don't like that there are kings at all," Cassie said. "Why hasn't he instituted a democracy already? What about letting women vote?"

"What about letting men vote?" Callum said. "England has its own Parliament, as does Wales, but democracy depends on education. David's building printing presses all over Britain, and since he became the Prince of Wales, he has been encouraging children to go to school—both girls and boys. It's coming, but he's only been King of England for six months. These things take time."

"Too much time, if you ask me," Cassie said and then managed to curb her irritation. "But I get it. Change is going to take place over generations, not overnight."

"With your attitude, why haven't you ever been accused of being a witch?" Callum said.

Cassie almost laughed again. "Who says I haven't?"

"Have you?"

"You're not one to let anything go, are you?"

"No," he said.

Cassie sighed. "My neighbors have been suspicious of me, but nobody has ever accused me of being a witch. You do realize that being an Englishman is far worse, right?"

Callum was back to laughing. "You have me there."

"At the same time, I'm not quite English—I'm not quite anything—and for a long time that was my biggest problem." Cassie looked at Callum sideways. The sun had come out from behind a cloud again and it shone full on her face. It felt good. She could use some warmth. "When I first got here, I didn't even know if I was on planet Earth, much less Scotland."

"You had it much worse than Meg," Callum said. "She arrived as you did and at much the same age, alone and friendless. But Llywelyn took her under his wing right away."

"I had Lord Patrick's help, after a fashion." Cassie patted her bow. "And I had this."

"Did you ever tell Lord Patrick where you were from?"

"God, no!" Cassie shivered at the thought. "Did Meg?"

"Her closest companions know," Callum said, "and of course, Llywelyn."

"Sometimes I've been tempted," Cassie said, "but it would be stupid to do so. It would ruin everything."

"That's why you need to come to England with me when I return there," Callum said, very sure of himself. "You need to talk to David."

Cassie didn't say anything. She could admit to herself that she was tempted by that too, but she'd made a home here. From what Callum had described, the English court didn't sound very inviting. Here, she was in charge of her own life and knew the world well enough to lead Callum through it. She would be lost in England.

One of the things Cassie liked about Scotland was how wild it was. It had few towns and most people lived scattered among the hills, herding sheep and cattle. It was unusual to find a woman living alone like she did, but not unheard of. What could she do in England but find a husband and pop out one baby after another like every other medieval woman? Even if King David believed in equal rights for women, this world had generations to go before that could become a reality. Cassie didn't have that kind of time. This was the only life she was going to have and whiling it away at the English court was the last thing she wanted to do with it.

In addition, the Scots understood something that Cassie hadn't known any non-Indians to ever really *get* before: family lands were sacred and if you lost them, you lost a part of yourself. Cassie didn't know how long some of these people had lived here, but for many it was countless generations, the same as for her family back in Oregon. Even if some of their ancestors came from the south, or from France originally, Highlanders couldn't breathe if too many people were around. Open space and the natural world were in their blood, as they were in Cassie's. No wonder they fought so hard and for so long against the English who wanted to take their land from them.

Cassie and Callum lapsed into silence until the sun was well up and they reached the river that sprang from the northwestern lochs. They turned to follow it as it wound sinuously west. The terrain was rougher until they found a trail that led to a ford across a tributary. Loch Ard was three miles long, if one included the narrows, and roughly half a mile wide.

"We're getting close," Cassie said. "We should walk from here."

Both travelers dismounted stiffly. Callum put a hand to the small of his back and bent forward and back. "I'm getting old, Cassie."

Oh, he was so annoying! He'd made her laugh again. "You're what? Thirty-four or five?"

"That's old for here," Callum said.

"I've probably led us on a wild goose chase anyway," Cassie said.

"Even if the prisoners aren't here, I don't regret this journey," Callum said.

"We're out of Daddy Bruce's hands—or Kirby's for that matter—Liam is on his way to warn William Fraser of what has happened, and we can ask at a village if the MacDougalls have come through recently."

"They wouldn't tell us," Cassie said. "Or rather, they wouldn't tell you. I might get an answer if they liked the look of me."

It was no trouble to keep to the trees that lined the loch's shore, walking silently along a narrow path, leading the horses.

The day was actually getting hot. Cassie stripped off several layers of clothes, including her cloak, dress, and sweater, and stuffed them into her pack. Birds sang in the trees, most of which were pine, but the deciduous trees were finally fully leafed after a long cold spring.

"So few people live here. Why?" Callum said.

"It's not like someone's going to build a vacation home on the lochshore," Cassie said. "There's nothing up here. The grazing isn't even good—"

"Ssh!" Callum put out his hand and they both stilled.

Cassie didn't hear anything at first, but as they waited, listening, the sound of an axe against a tree echoed through the woods, followed by the smell of smoke. "Someone's close," Cassie said. "What should we do next?"

"Let's tie the horses here and continue without them," he said.

Cassie didn't like to leave them, but Callum was right. They were hunting men today rather than game. In such thick trees, the horses would get in the way, or worse, give Cassie and Callum away with an untimely whicker. Leaving the leading reins long, they picketed the horses near a brook that gurgled as it ran into the loch. Immediately, the beasts began to crop the patches of grass growing in the cleared spaces between the trees. Both would need a real rest and more and better food soon, but they would be all right for now.

Cassie let Callum lead, not because he was a man but because he seemed to know what he was doing. Cassie had brought them to the loch, but he was the soldier. Although she'd spent many days alone in the woods, she'd never fought in a battle or scouted an enemy camp. He had experience with both from Afghanistan, even if the ambush had been his first battle here.

Callum took Cassie up a hill to the south, still tree-covered but more sparsely so. It rose fifty feet above the path on which they'd been walking. Cassie kept looking back, hoping to see something that would clarify what they faced, but she couldn't see anything until Callum found an open space that allowed them to directly overlook the loch.

Callum let out a *whuf* of air. "I don't like the look of that."

"What is it exactly?" Cassie stood on her tiptoes and tried to see what he saw.

He glanced at her. "Come on. That rock should give us a better view."

A flat piece of granite jutted out from the hill farther down the slope. They crawled up onto it and peered over the edge. A palisaded hunting lodge, built on the edge of the loch, lay below them a quarter of a mile to the north of their position.

"Can you see how many men defend it?" Callum squinted ahead. "Maybe it belongs to the local lord and has nothing to do with the MacDougalls."

"I bet it belongs to the Earl of Lennox," Cassie said. "I remember hearing that he'd built a hunting lodge up here."

"It's a fine day for a hunt," Callum said.

"Yup." Cassie reached for the pack on her back, pulled out her scope, and peered through it. "I see—" She paused as she counted, "—a dozen soldiers, some on the wall-walk on the palisade, some in the courtyard of the fort."

Callum had been looking down at the fort, his hands shading his eyes from the bright sunlight. Now he glanced over at Cassie. "My God! How many more gadgets do you have? First the torch and now this?"

Cassie smiled at his appreciation and handed him the scope. "Do you want to see?"

"Yes, I want to see." He took the scope, checking the location of the lodge and then the sun, which by now was almost directly overhead. Callum studied the lodge for a full minute while Cassie studied him. She looked away just as he put down the scope so he wouldn't catch her looking. "The sun's pretty bright. I'm worried they'll see the flash from the sun's reflection and come to investigate."

Cassie's hands were itching to take back the scope, but she let him keep it for a bit longer. "Can you see any sign of the prisoners?"

"No."

"There wouldn't be, though, would there?" Cassie said. "If they're in the lodge, they're nicely locked up, maybe in that smaller building against the eastern fence."

"I'm sure you're right," Callum said. "I'm worried that one or more of them are badly injured. If that's the case, their chance of escaping would be pretty slim."

"What chance do we have of getting them out?" Cassie said. "For sure, a direct assault isn't going to work."

Callum continued examining the lodge through the scope. "I think I remember seeing several of these men at the fight on the road. It's hard to tell since they're not wearing helmets today." He handed the scope back to Cassie. "How about you? Do you recognize anyone?"

Cassie put the scope to her eye. "Maybe. I would say at least one. And … I think one of them is a MacDougall cousin."

"Brilliant." Callum rolled onto his back and threw his hand across his eyes. "We need to talk through this."

"Talk through what?"

"I'm just trying to get straight what we think is happening here." Callum shaded his eyes as Cassie took off her backpack and scooted down to lie beside him, with her bow resting on her stomach. Their closeness wasn't wise—she was way more attracted to him than she wanted to be—but the rock wasn't big enough for her to put more than an inch between them. "It makes no sense for the MacDougalls to hide their captives in a lodge belonging to the Earl of Lennox, who is loyal to Grampa Bruce."

"The Earl is rabidly anti-English," Cassie said.

"Up until now, clan loyalties have trumped national ones every time," Callum said.

"What I want to know," Cassie said, "is why Alexander MacDougall took captives at all once he realized that King David wasn't part of your company?"

"As leverage, like Robbie said," Callum said.

"No." Cassie shook her head. "MacDougall has to know that Balliol can't win the crown through blackmail. It can't happen."

"Okay," Callum said. "Let's start at the beginning: our company was making its way from Glasgow to Stirling, to help adjudicate the succession for the crown of Scotland. First of all, who knew about that journey and when did they know it?"

"Everyone knew about it," Cassie said, "except they all thought King David was leading the embassage, not Kirby."

"Second, Kirby disguised one of his underlings in his own robes and set him on the carriage," Callum said. "How cold must his blood be to sacrifice not only his nephew, but his own man, an entire company of the king's men, and James Stewart and Robbie Bruce for this cause."

"Bad luck for him that Robbie escaped and could tell us the truth," Cassie said. "So that leads us to a third question: Why?"

Callum's eyes narrowed as he thought. "Kirby gets MacDougall to attack my company, but intends for him to leave no survivors, no proof left behind of what they've done."

"Then Kirby goes to Daddy Bruce and gets him to attack the Comyns followed by the MacDougalls, and—" Cassie stopped. "I've got nothing."

"Um ... all of Scotland rises up against both Bruce and Balliol when the atrocities committed on both sides exceed their tolerance," Callum said. "How about that?"

"What does Kirby get out of it?" Cassie said.

"I have no idea," Callum said.

"What if Kirby is up to his old tricks again?" Cassie sat up straight. "Isn't this what you said Kirby tried to do for England? Clear David's way to the throne? What if Kirby wants a similar outcome here?"

"Cassie!" Callum reached for Cassie's arm to pull her down beside him again, but she evaded his hand and lay back on her own. She'd forgotten where she was for a second in her enthusiasm for her theory.

"If that hypothesis is true, then if David had come north as he'd initially planned, none of this would have happened," Callum said.

"If I'm right," Cassie said, "then Kirby may have thought he had a good chance of manipulating him into taking the throne without bloodshed."

"As it is, if David doesn't take the throne, how many possible outcomes of this dispute are there?" Callum said. "I see war, war, and more war."

"How much better would it be if David became the King of Scotland as the compromise choice," Cassie said. "I'd vote for that."

"Kirby is taking a huge risk. He might find himself in the Tower of London," Callum said. "Not that he doesn't deserve it. So many men died ..."

"Regardless of the details, he has to fear that we'll tell King David what we know," Cassie said.

"He should fear it," Callum said, "because we will tell him."

"Now I'm really glad we came up here," Cassie said.

Callum shook himself. "We're getting ahead of ourselves thinking about Kirby. Let's deal with today and let tomorrow take care of itself."

"Right," Cassie said. "Prisoners who need rescue."

"Prisoners Alexander MacDougall took without clearing it with Kirby," Callum said. "Good for him."

Cassie flipped onto her stomach again and looked through her scope. "How do we get them out?"

"What are our assets?" Callum said.

"I have a bow; you have a sword," Cassie said. "That's it."

"No wheelbarrow?" Callum said.

Cassie laughed. "*The Princess Bride*. A quote for every occasion, even this one."

"Especially this one." Callum smirked and pointed towards the trees. Cassie scooted off the rock and they ran back to the woods at a crouch.

Cassie pulled up. "What about going for help?"

"I've been thinking the same thing," Callum said. "But to whom? We don't know who we can trust. Grampa Bruce has allies in this area but so do the MacDougalls and the Balliols for that matter. Nobody is neutral but us. We'd have to go all the way to Stirling and by the time we returned with an army, they might have moved the prisoners again. Or killed them."

"I don't suppose you have a plan?" Cassie said.

Callum eyed her. "Have you ever killed a man?"

Cassie almost didn't want to answer him because it was a way in which they couldn't be equals. "No."

Callum nodded. "Let's not have you start now if we can help it."

"How are we going to get the captives out without killing anyone?" Cassie said.

"How about we at least try. I'm working on some ideas." Callum touched Cassie's quiver. "Those arrows are precious, but could you stand losing a few for a good cause?"

"The arrows I brought with me from our world are long gone." Cassie pulled out a shaft and held it up. "One of the first things I learned was how to fill my quiver."

Callum fingered the fletching on the arrow. "How many do you have with you now?"

"Twenty."

"Then twenty will have to do." Callum let out a quick breath. "Here's my plan: you're going to create a series of diversions and while the men inside that lodge are worrying about the havoc you're wreaking out here, I'm going to get inside and see what's what."

"How are you going to do that?" Cassie said.

Callum pointed at the fort. "The palisade was built to protect a hunting lodge from wild animals, not humans. It's not a fortress. Did you see how the fence protects the front and sides but ends at the water's edge?"

Cassie nodded. She had noticed that.

"We need to find me a boat."

"Where are we going to find a boat big enough to fit a dozen men?" Cassie said. "You don't want that. They'll spot you coming in. You'll never even reach the shore."

"I just need a boat big enough for me," Callum said. "On the way out, we'll probably just have to get wet."

11

Callum

Cassie and Callum spent the next hour hiking along the loch, looking for a boat Callum could borrow. They found one that would suit him, finally, a mile along the shore to the west. It had been pulled up among the trees and looked very much like a Native American canoe, complete with two paddles. Cassie eyed it, her mouth working in amusement. "Great minds think alike, I guess," she said.

They carried it back along the shore in preference to getting in it and paddling right away. They both agreed that the sound of their movements on the water would carry to the fort more easily than if they traveled most of the way there on land. Eventually, however, they reached a patch of thicker undergrowth and were forced to get into the canoe.

Hugging the shore, they paddled to a point a few hundred yards shy of the fort, though around a point of land so that anyone standing on the shore within the palisade would have no chance of seeing them. There, they left the canoe. Next, they checked on the horses, moving them deeper into the woods to a spot where they hoped they'd be safe. They'd forsaken the trail from the start, thinking it too open, and on the return journey reached a point fifty yards above it. It was only then, near the overlooking piece of granite, that they encountered a patrol from the fort.

Cassie spotted them first. "Get down!" She tugged on the back of his surcoat. Since the day had remained hot, he'd left his cloak with the horses. He wished it made sense to take off his armor too, since it was like wearing a personal sauna. At times, Callum wondered why it hadn't fused to his skin yet since he wore it constantly. The water in the loch had looked inviting, but despite his offhand comment to Cassie about swimming, the last thing he wanted was another fully-clothed soaking in a medieval body of water.

Cassie and Callum hustled behind some bracken. Three men strolled below them, one in front, hacking at the underbrush desultorily with a stick, and two behind. They chatted with one another, apparently unconcerned about being spotted. If this was a patrol, they weren't doing a very professional job of it. They seemed to be headed back to the fort.

"The MacDougall is not going to be happy when he hears of this," the man in the lead said.

"How is he going to hear of it unless you tell him?" one of other men said. "You're the one who saw the flash. We aren't going to say anything if you don't."

Cassie looked at Callum and nodded. She didn't need to say—*the scope*—for both of them to know what flash the man had seen. The patrol moved on, their footsteps plodding away down the hill towards the fort. Cassie and Callum let the sound of their movements fade completely before they moved again.

"We're going to have to be more careful," she said. "Right now, they have nothing. If they get another hint of something not quite right, they'll be on alert."

"So we take it slow," Callum said.

More wary than they'd been before, and more glad than Callum could say that nobody on the fort's ramparts had their own scope, they set to work fabricating the diversions. Callum's grand plan was a matter of building a half-dozen piles of brush and debris for Cassie to light, one after another, before she directed her attention to the fort itself. They decided that she should start her attack on the fort with ten fire arrows. Ideally, between the bonfires and the arrows, the men inside would be so busy putting out the fires and worrying about how many men were coming at them, that they wouldn't leave the fort.

What Callum was asking Cassie to do would require as much effort as what his job entailed, but hopefully it would be less dangerous. When she'd told him that she'd never killed a man—and why would she have? She wasn't a soldier—he'd gone a bit cold. He needed a soldier today and was sorry if she was going to have to become one because of him.

Cassie checked the sky. "The afternoon is moving on. It won't get dark until nearly nine o'clock. We should eat something and maybe get some sleep."

Right away, Callum wished she hadn't mentioned sleep. He'd been holding his exhaustion at bay the whole day. Granted, he'd slept a long time in her hut, but he'd awoken nearly twenty-four hours ago and they'd come a long way since then. They both needed to sleep.

They returned to where they'd left the horses, and Callum settled into a hollow at the base of a tree with the sack that Robbie had given him. They'd eaten during the journey and refilled the water skins along the way, but now was the time to fill up while they could. Callum had learned to close his mind to whatever contaminants might be in the water he drank: not chemicals or heavy metals like in the modern world, but if an animal had died upstream and polluted the water, they could be in trouble. Callum took a long drink anyway and held out the water skin to Cassie.

She gave him an assessing look.

"After all we've been through together, you still think I bite?" Callum said.

"Of course not." She walked to him and took the water. "I could sleep, except for the fact that we're so exposed out here."

Callum scooted over so she could sit beside him in a cradle created by the tree roots. She sat stiffly at first, and then scrunched down so she reclined against the tree and their shoulders were only a few inches apart, rather than the two feet Cassie usually kept between them. Except when she tended his wound, Cassie hadn't ever touched him. Not even once. Because of it, he was trying not to touch her either, though he really wanted to. She maintained a cushion of space around her that he didn't feel he could violate. As an Englishman—and a veteran of the military at that—he had a reputation for being reserved and undemonstrative, but his coolness had nothing on Cassie's.

"In Afghanistan, I learned to sleep with one eye open. I haven't lost the skill." Callum reclined a bit more and Cassie followed suit, using her cloak as a pillow rather than his chest, which he certainly would have preferred. They both closed their eyes.

"My grandfather used to tell me stories to get me to go to sleep," Cassie said. "I had a teddy bear the same size I was; I would rest my head on its belly and fall asleep while my grandfather talked."

Callum smiled. "Neither of my parents went in much for bedtime stories."

"Maybe that was a good thing—Coyote stories can sometimes keep you awake," Cassie said. "He's the trickster in our legends."

"Like Loki in the Norse tales?" Callum said.

"Uh ... sort of ... but not really." Cassie gave a low chuckle deep in her belly. "I was really looking forward to *Thor II*. I miss movies."

"I miss stories in general," Callum said. "Many nights in Afghanistan, I would read myself to sleep."

Cassie glanced at him. "Me too! When I first came to Scotland, I didn't sleep except in bits and snatches, if at all. I'd tell myself stories like my grandfather used to as the only way to lull myself to sleep."

"I don't like to think of you surviving by yourself," Callum said. "I can't imagine what you went through." Already, his muscles were relaxing, listening to Cassie talk. This was the most open she'd been with him since they'd met. He set an internal alarm for sunset; they had fewer than six hours.

"I know I don't have to tell you how hard it is to sleep when you're afraid," she said. "And when I did sleep, I had nightmares, and not of Coyote."

Callum's hands tightened into fists. "I wish you hadn't gotten caught up in this. For me to be here is one thing. For you ...."

"Bad things happen sometimes." Cassie curved onto her side, rubbing her cheek against her cloak.

"I'm sorry." He didn't know what else to say.

Now she shook her head. "I would go home if I could, but even if Meg were to take me back to our time, it wouldn't be the same as when I left. I'm not the same person I was then." She paused. "But you probably already understand that, too, don't you?"

"Yes."

Her breathing became soft and even. Callum took the risk of sweeping a stray hair out of her face without touching her cheek. She didn't move so he didn't add to his answer. He'd gone to Afghanistan with what he thought were realistic expectations. He hadn't joined the military because he loved war or shooting people. He had wanted to make a difference, and by the end, had become good at what he did. But he'd come home bruised on the inside. What made his return so much harder was the fact that except for the one scar on his chest, he looked much the same on the outside as when he'd left, and therefore people expected him to *be* the same.

Listening to Cassie talk, he'd had another thought: that she was the loneliest person he'd ever met other than himself. Like him, she'd lost everyone she'd ever loved. Like him, she struggled for control and had created a world for herself that kept her safe, and that included keeping everyone at arm's length—literally. She was as traumatized by her past as he was by his. He just hoped he wasn't about to make it worse.

Callum woke Cassie at sunset as he'd promised, both having slept solidly. "Are you ready for this?" he said.

"I don't know," she said. "We're risking our lives for something neither of us believes in. Do I care who takes the Scottish throne?"

"We believe in justice, both of us," Callum said, "and in doing what is right."

Cassie rested her chin in the palm of her hand. "Sadly, I still do, despite the fact that so few people around us seem to."

"Besides, this is about rescuing friends, not about Scotland."

"Okay." Cassie sat up straight. "If I'm going to risk my life to save a Guardian of Scotland, we might as well get started." She shot Callum a laughing look. "This James Stewart had better be worth it."

"They may have Samuel too," Callum said.

"And he's a true friend, I know. I'm sorry. I shouldn't joke about something like that."

They stood and shared a moment's hesitation. Callum looked at Cassie, she looked at him, and just as Callum was telling himself *to hell with it*, she stepped towards him and wrapped her arms around his waist, squeezing him tightly. "You take care."

Callum clutched her to him, his lips to her temple. He wanted to hold her all night, but instead he said, "You need to do exactly as we planned."

"I will."

They released each other and stepped back. "Let's go," Callum said.

Cassie nodded, turned on her heel, and walked off, heading up the hill to the lookout post they'd designated. Callum watched her go, still feeling the warmth of her body against his. *God*—not only had she touched him, she'd *hugged* him. He swallowed hard, shook himself, and resolved not to presume to know what she meant by it.

For now, he needed to put away his emotions and focus on what lay before him. He had to trust Cassie to do her job just as he would do his. Callum circled around the hill that she'd climbed. He briefly crossed the trail that led to the fort, scuttling across it as quickly as he could, and then moved into the woods on the other side.

The canoe was where they'd left it—he hadn't allowed himself to consider what he'd do if it wasn't—and he got into it. He pushed off from the bank and used the paddle without any real expertise—though Cassie had tried to instruct him earlier—first on one side of the boat and then the other. He tried not to make even a single splash that could call attention to his progress.

Darkness had fallen at last, bringing a night as clear as the day had been. Stars peppered the sky and the starry band of the Milky Way hung above Callum's head. He hugged the shoreline, barely putting his oar in the water at all, just enough to keep the boat away from the tree roots, branches, and debris that lined the shore. Several rivers fed the eastward flowing loch. Thus, the natural movement of the water carried him towards the fort even though his overall progress was slow.

It wasn't a dark night, so what most worried Callum was the moment he came around the bend in the shoreline that had kept him hidden from any watchers at the fort. If someone was keeping an eye on the water, looking for movement, he would see Callum. For once, Callum wished for cloud cover and rain, even if it would have made it hard for him to see until he reached the fort. His only consolation was that the torches that lit the fort would hamper the guards' night vision.

Callum eased closer to the shore, hardly daring to breathe, and suddenly had to fight against the current which was making the boat go faster than he wanted. Soon he reached the point on the shoreline where the trees ended. The Earl of Lennox had cleared the vegetation around the lodge, leaving fifty yards of no man's land between the trees and the palisade. Since no trees grew down to the shore either, Callum would be exposed the whole of that distance.

He hesitated in the darkness, waiting and watching. Men patrolled the wall-walk, though like the men he and Cassie had seen on the trail earlier that afternoon, they seemed half-hearted about it. Callum was all in favor of bored men when they were his adversaries. He and Cassie had agreed that she should give him half an hour to get into position before she lit the first bonfire. Neither of them wore watches, of course, and Callum's internal clock told him that it had been a bit longer than they'd planned.

But then Cassie got to work: a flare of light went up from the first bonfire and they were in business.

They didn't actually want to burn the forest down, just distract the defenders of the fort long enough for Callum to get inside. A second fire started, a hundred yards from the first one. Even at this distance, Callum could smell the smoke, but the alarm coming from the fort drowned out all other sounds including the slap of water against the boat. Only two men had patrolled the palisade before Cassie lit the first bonfire, but a shout from them had brought other men running. A dozen now stood above the gatehouse, pointing at the fires.

It was time to go. Callum put his head down and paddled as fast as he could for the end of the western wall of the palisade.

The lodge had been built on an almost flat, grassy expanse that ended with a three-foot drop to where the water lapped at eroded rock and dirt. With the fort essentially open to the loch, the Earl of Lennox had given lip service to defense. He'd built a fence to keep animals and raiders out but never thought about a determined man like Callum.

Callum pulled the boat next to a relatively flat rock and climbed onto it without even getting his feet wet. Lifting his head above the level of the grass, he could see into the interior of the fort. Three boats rested side by side a foot from his nose. All to the good. He could leave his boat where it was, partially pulled onto the rock so it wouldn't float away, and no one would be the wiser. Perhaps Callum could escape with the prisoners this way after all.

He crouched between the boats, still keeping his head down. He'd put his cloak back on before he left Cassie, hoping its dark color and hood would disguise him long enough to confuse any MacDougall who gave Callum a second look. What Callum really wanted was for everyone to be distracted by the fire arrows—

Thwtt!

Cassie's first arrow hit the steep roof of the lodge. It had been built primarily in stone, mortared and two stories high, but had a thatched roof like most medieval houses in Scotland. Her assault came almost too soon. Callum barely had time to reach the back wall of the building before four men raced past him heading for the loch, buckets swinging from their hands. Before they wondered why Callum wasn't helping, he ducked through the rear door.

Just inside, he stopped short. He was in a large room that ran unbroken by walls all the way to the front of the house. The door opposite him was open, and he could see into the courtyard beyond it and to the front gate. The room itself was empty of people, though from the remains of a meal on the long table by the hearth, men had been eating here before Cassie had lit her fires. To Callum's left, a stairway ran up the interior wall of the building to a second floor loft that took up the front half of the lodge. It was open at the back, without even a railing to prevent a wayward sleeper from falling to the floor below.

Callum peered upwards into the darkness of the loft. "Stewart!" *Nothing.* And then, "Is anyone there?"

Still nothing. Unless the prisoners were gagged or unconscious, they weren't there. Given that nobody guarded this building, Callum thought his conclusion likely. He backed out of the door he'd come in. The men fighting the fires had formed a line that curved around to the front of the lodge. They passed water buckets from hand to hand.

Callum flipped up the hood of his cloak and dashed to his right towards the smaller building that he and Cassie had seen from the hill. It was attached to the wooden palisade and made of loosely fitted wooden planks. It also had a thatched roof that the fire hadn't reached, which explained the lack of attention currently being paid to it. Callum held his knife in his fist, ready to slash at anyone he met coming through the door. During hand-to-hand combat in tight quarters like the hut, his sword would only get in the way.

Unsure if it would be better to sneak in or burst in, Callum opted for a combination of the two. He quietly lifted the latch to release the lock and then put his shoulder into the door with a quick thrust. Whether those inside had been alerted by the shouts and simply wanted to check on their companions' progress, or if Callum hadn't been as quiet as he intended, the door slammed into the forehead of a man coming to open it. He fell against the northern wall of the hut, momentarily stunned.

A second man had been standing to the right of the first, waiting for the door to open. He reached for the hilt of his sword as Callum pushed through the door. Callum took a step and jammed the palm of his left hand underneath the man's chin. His teeth snapped together, his head fell back, and he collapsed to the floor. The back of his head hit the ground with a nauseating thud, but because the floor of the hut was made of dirt not stone, Callum didn't think he'd killed him, even if he'd knocked him out.

Callum turned to look at the first man, who was struggling to his feet. Callum recognized him as one of the men who'd dropped out of a tree at the ambush on the road. Even with that knowledge, Callum didn't want to kill him if he didn't have too. He took one step and then directed a kick at the man's jaw with such force that the man fell back and lay still.

Callum spun on his heel, looking for someone else to fight. James and Samuel gaped at him from the floor by the south wall. A third man Callum didn't recognize lay beside them. His friends were bound at their wrists and ankles and tied to iron stakes that had been driven into the ground. Both James and Samuel strained against their bonds, but the third man—more of a boy, really—remained slumped on the floor.

"Praise be to God," said James as Callum took the fighting axe of one of the downed soldiers and tried to hack through the links that attached James to his stake. "The dead one has the key to our shackles."

Callum found the keys and freed his friends. Then he clasped Samuel's forearm and helped him to his feet. "I am glad to find you here." That was the understatement of the year.

"I'm glad to be found," Samuel said.

Callum glanced at Samuel's face. Despite what had to have been a desperate few days, Samuel's eyes remained bright, and at the moment, full of humor.

"Who is he?" Callum put his hand to the boy's neck, feeling for a pulse.

"We don't know," Samuel said. "He hasn't woken since they brought him in."

Callum frowned. "He wasn't a member our company?"

"No," Samuel said.

James went to the entrance and peered through the crack between the frame and the door. "How many men do you have?"

"Ah ... it's just me and a woman friend."

James turned to look at him. "You're jesting."

"No," Callum said. "You'll see."

Callum picked up the axe again. His experience at Mugdock had given him an idea. "I don't think we can risk leaving by boat as I'd hoped."

"Then how—" said James, just as Callum took a huge swing with the axe, directing the blow at the side wall of the hut. The boards splintered.

"Looks like freedom to me." Callum swung the axe again. Three more blows and he could put his boot through the remaining boards to create a hole in the palisade.

After his initial open-mouthed astonishment, James helped Callum clear away the last of the splinters. Then Samuel lifted the mystery boy onto his shoulder in a fireman's carry. James went through the opening first, followed by Samuel, who needed Callum's help to maneuver his burden through the three foot wide opening. Callum was taking a last look back, one foot already on the ground outside the palisade, when the door to the hut opened. The man in the doorway hadn't been expecting anything untoward. He stared at Callum for half a second, and then opened his mouth to shout: "The prisoners—!"

"I've got this, Callum." Cassie thrust her bow past Callum's shoulder and loosed an arrow.

The man fell backwards, the arrow through his throat.

12

Cassie

Cassie closed her mind. She'd gotten good at it over the years, and really, what was there to think about? The man was dead and she'd had no choice but to shoot him if they were going to get away.

When that axe head had come through the side of the palisade with the force of an oncoming train, Cassie hadn't been looking for it. She'd been staying to the woods on the eastern side of the fort, waiting for Callum to come around the wall, either by slogging through the water on foot or in his little boat. She'd been too busy lighting fires to follow his progress initially, but from brief glances through her scope when she'd had the chance, she'd seen the line of men with buckets start near the western palisade wall. She'd known then that if Callum found the prisoners, there was no way he was leaving in that direction.

The fires she'd lit in the hills around the fort had been designed to keep the defenders guessing and afraid of the army that had been brought up to attack them. Overall, Callum's plan had worked better than Cassie had hoped or imagined it could. While a half-dozen men fought the fire in the main building, the rest watched the perimeter from the wall-walk. Earlier, a group of four had charged out of the gate and ... well ... Cassie had been waiting for that. She'd put arrows in two of them without killing them and narrowly missed a third before all of them scrambled back inside.

Personally, if she had to choose between going down in flames in a lodge that didn't belong to her and charging out of it to do battle, she would have chosen the latter too. Too bad for them that she'd been waiting.

"It would have been smarter for the defenders to evacuate into the water," Callum said as they raced for the trees. "They have the boats for it."

Cassie figured that Callum was just making conversation to distract her, but she was grateful to him nonetheless. She feared an arrow would strike her in the middle of the back at any second in repayment for what she'd done. "Maybe they view it as a path of last resort," Cassie said.

Callum sniffed. "Likely, none of them can swim and they fear the deep waters of the loch."

As they reached the trees, Cassie whipped out her last arrow, set it into her bow, and looked back. A man standing above the eastern palisade shouted and pointed towards her. Cassie hesitated, gauging the distance and the angle of the shot. She didn't want to waste her last arrow on someone she could barely see, when more men might be coming any second.

"Leave him, Cassie," Callum said. "We need to go."

Cassie nodded. She turned and ran after Callum, deeper into the trees. "Where are the other prisoners?" Cassie said. The two able-bodied former prisoners loped ahead of them, holding a steady place despite the burden one of them carried. Cassie checked behind her. She couldn't see the lodge anymore, but she could smell the smoke.

"I didn't have time to ask." Callum said.

"I moved the horses back to the first spot, just off the trail," Cassie said. "They may be a bit spooked from all the smoke."

"You're amazing."

Cassie blinked away a vision of Callum wrapping an arm around her shoulders, pulling her close, and kissing her. He did none of those things and it was probably just as well.

Instead, Callum added, "I'm going to thank God every day for the rest of my life for putting me in your path."

Callum kept on going through the trees, leaving Cassie shaken. He'd done nothing but tell her how great she was. He probably had no idea that he was the first person she'd hugged in five years. It was as if she hadn't known she was starving until presented with food.

The two men Callum had rescued finally came to a halt. One of them bent over, his hands on his knees, breathing hard, while the larger of the two rested his shoulder against a tree. Cassie couldn't believe he'd managed to carry his burden that far.

Callum took a moment to wave a hand. "James, Samuel, this is Cassie."

They all nodded at each other, took a deep breath, and were off again, this time with Cassie leading the way along the trail and Callum bringing up the rear. "I never wanted to burn this forest down, but it seems it can't be helped," Callum said, loud enough for Cassie to hear.

"The rain that's coming should take care of the fires," Cassie said.

"How do you know that it's going to rain?" said James. Even with Cassie's limited experience with noblemen, she could tell he spoke Gaelic with a very upper-crust accent.

"I can smell it in the air," Cassie said.

"Cassie's a better woodsman than all of us combined," Callum said. "She knows what she's talking about."

Cassie was glad that it was too dark for the men to see her blush.

They reached the horses without any obvious pursuit, so Callum helped Samuel ease the unconscious prisoner off his shoulder and onto the ground. Samuel straightened his spine with a *snap, crackle, pop*.

"We should hurry," Cassie said. "That guard on the palisade raised the alarm and the soldiers will be on us in no time."

"Come here, Cassie," Callum said. "Do you recognize him?"

Cassie crouched beside the injured prisoner and brushed the hair back from his face. "Oh no!" she said.

"Who is it?" Callum said.

"This is Lord Patrick Graham's son, John," she said. "He's fifteen."

Callum bent to feel the pulse at John's throat and then said to James and Samuel, "Did you say, back at the lodge, that your captors brought him in later?"

James nodded. "That is correct."

"Where are the rest of the prisoners?" Cassie said. "I watched the MacDougalls lead you away from the ambush site. There must have been at least a dozen of you."

"They separated us from the main group after the first night we spent at Mugdock," said James. "You were watching the ambush?"

Cassie nodded but didn't feel the need to elaborate. "Why did they keep the two of you together?"

"I've asked myself that many times in the last few days," Samuel said. "It can only be because of Lord Callum, though how Alexander MacDougall knew about our relationship, I don't know."

Callum exchanged a look with Cassie. "Kirby," she said.

Callum stood. "We have no time for this riddle. We need to move. Listen."

Cassie had been patting at John, looking for wounds, but her head came up at Callum's warning. Sound traveled more easily in the dark. Now that he'd mentioned it, it was easy to make out the shouts of men in the distance.

"James—you ride with the boy on my horse," Callum said. "Samuel, you take Cassie's."

"My lord, there's no need—" Samuel began.

"You've been hiding a long gash down your leg," Callum said. "It may no longer be bleeding, but you're still lame. Get up there!"

James and Samuel didn't argue further. Both mounted the horses, and then Callum and Cassie struggled to get John's unconscious body in front of James. He held John's waist and allowed the boy to rest his head against his collar bone. The ride would be awkward, but worse would be throwing John across the horse's withers and letting him hang there upside down.

Callum set off with James and John, holding the reins of his horse and trotting beside it. Cassie followed with Samuel. It was dark under the trees, but the horses maintained a sure-footed pace. They could see better than humans in the dark, and the path was well-used and free of obstacles. While he trotted beside James, Callum gave him the rundown on what had been happening since the ambush.

"As I said, *Kirby*," Cassie said.

As the tale wound down, Samuel, who'd been listening too, said to Cassie, "I never liked him. He was always slippery, even for a bishop."

"Well, now we know him to be a traitor," Cassie said.

Samuel turned in the saddle to look behind them. "I don't see our pursuers yet."

"I should have shot that man on the wall-walk," Cassie said. "I choked."

"You got everyone out of the fort," Samuel said. "That was the important thing."

"It was dark and I thought the soldier was too far away to make a viable target," Cassie said. "I didn't want to waste my last arrow, but if I'd at least tried, he might not have been able to tell anyone what he saw."

Samuel shrugged. "It might have delayed the pursuit but all they would have had to do was check the hut. Lord Callum cut a hole in the wall, Cassie. There was no disguising the direction we went."

"Maybe we should double back?" Cassie said.

Callum overheard her question. "Better to cross the river and head north," he said.

"We should continue east, my lord," said James. "The Priory at Inchmahome will shelter us."

"The MacDougalls will know that you know it's there," Callum said. "If they don't catch us, that will be the first place they'll look."

The trees thickened, indicating they'd reached the Narrows, the stretch of water before the loch became a river.

"Then I offer my castle at Doune as an alternative," said James.

Cassie tsked through her teeth. "That's twenty miles away. And again, it's east. If we go just a little further, we'll reach a ford and we can cross the river as Callum suggested."

"No direction is going to be safe," said James.

They reached the ford and stopped. The trail continued to the east, while another began on the other side of the ford. Cassie looked back, listening for the sound of the pursuit. Callum ran a hand through his hair. "We can't split up. We must choose now."

"I fear for John's life if we don't find shelter soon, my lord." James wasn't willing to defer to Callum. He was a Guardian of Scotland and not used to resistance to his plans any more than Callum seemed to be.

"I fear it too," Cassie said. "I hate that John was caught up in the fighting and has been mistreated, but if we go to the priory, can we protect him and all the monks once we're there?"

None of the men said anything, and that was answer enough. *No.*

Callum turned to Cassie. "Can you tell what's wrong with John?"

She shook her head. "He has no open wounds. Perhaps a closed wound has turned septic?"

"He hasn't woken up even once," Samuel said.

"A blow to the head might have put him in this state," Cassie said.

"He needs help, Cassie," Callum said, in modern English. "Am I making the wrong choice not going to the monks?"

"I don't know," Cassie said, "but I trust you and I trust your instincts. Just decide. They're coming, Callum."

"I hear them." Callum grabbed the bridle of James's horse and pulled the horse down the bank and across the ford. Cassie followed, trotting through the water next to Samuel's horse. She could smell the sweat and the blood on Samuel's clothes and was glad that the horses weren't spooked by the fear in all of them.

By now their pursuers were close enough that Cassie could see the light from their torches. "How many do you think there are?" Cassie said to Samuel. "We never pinned down their exact numbers."

"Only ten escorted us here, but more came after they locked us up," Samuel said.

"They lost three in the hut," Cassie said, "and two at the entrance to the fort."

"How did that happen?" Samuel said.

"I shot them."

Samuel merely nodded. "They don't have horses or they might have caught us by now."

"Come to think of it, I didn't see any horses in the fort," Cassie said. "How did you get to the lodge, Samuel?"

"We walked."

Cassie didn't know a lot about the nobility of the Middle Ages, but she knew enough to know that noblemen didn't walk. Lucky for James, he didn't have to walk now, though he might as well have been for all the progress they were making. In the last fifteen minutes, clouds had come up, sweeping across the moon and making it more difficult to see the path ahead. They needed torches to see properly, but darkness was preferable to giving away their position.

On the north side of the river, the terrain forced the horses east, even though Callum didn't want to go in that direction. His head swiveled constantly to the left, searching for a pathway that would take them up and over the hills to the north. After a hundred yards, the trail broadened, which made the going easier, and then they reached a fork in the road that looked familiar to Cassie.

"Wait a minute!" Cassie left Samuel's side and hurried to catch up to Callum. "I know where we can go. I've been on this path. It climbs steeply but then descends into a little village that sits between two lochs to the north of here. It's a five mile walk, so it's not close, but it's closer than Doune Castle. I can't promise that we'll be safe, but a healer lived there four years ago. Plus, we'll be nearer to Stewart lands."

"It seems quite a chance to take on a four-year-old memory," said James. "I'd prefer to try somewhere else—"

A man shouted behind them. James snapped his mouth shut and everyone looked back. Lights from the oncoming torches bobbed and weaved in the distance. They were still a good quarter mile away.

"Surely they can't see us," Samuel said. "It's too dark."

"They're at the ford," Callum said. "We can't wait for them to decide to cross it. If they look for our footprints on this side of the ford, they'll know where we are and they'll be coming fast, unburdened by a wounded man as we are."

"Lead James and Samuel to the village, Callum," Cassie said. "I'll keep following this path. We need them to think we're still headed for the priory."

Callum grimaced but gave the order. "Go, James. Do as she says." Callum slapped the rump of James's horse and it headed up the path. Samuel's horse followed, but Callum stayed where he was, looking down at Cassie. "It would be better to stay together."

"I know what I'm doing," Cassie said, even though she didn't, quite. "We need to divert them. Though he would never say so, Samuel is barely holding onto that horse."

"I should be the one to lead our pursuers away," Callum said.

"No," Cassie said. "It's your protection James and the others need if this trick doesn't work. I have only one arrow and am no good with a sword."

Callum leaned in close. With just moonlight to see by, the only part of his expression Cassie could make out was the glint in his eye, but that was enough to know how much he didn't like this plan. "I'm trusting you to take care of yourself. Be careful."

"I will."

She didn't hug him this time. There was no time anyway, and she hadn't yet decided if the first one had been a good idea or not. Then Callum was gone, racing up the path after James and Samuel. Cassie pulled her cloak from her backpack and followed him a few steps up the trail. The voices of the pursuers echoed along the river. It sounded as if some of them were arguing, just as

Callum and James had argued. They were giving Cassie a chance to put more distance between them and her.

Cassie needed to convince the men who followed them that they'd continued east. She swept her cloak through the dirt and smoothed out the few foot and hoof prints the others had left. Fortunately, the warm sun of today had dried what had already been hard-packed earth. She'd come down this trail from the village four years ago; it looked as if the people in this region still used this avenue often.

Cassie couldn't recreate hoof prints, but she ran forward and back along the ten yards of trail immediately to the east of the turnoff, trying to simulate the passage of several people. To judge by the torchlight, the pursuers had finally decided to split up, with a portion of them heading east along the south side of the river, and others following Cassie and her friends across the ford.

As a last deception, Cassie rammed the edge of her cloak down onto a branch of a gorse bush that grew beside the trail. The cloth caught and she jerked at it, mimicking what could have happened if she were really fleeing down this path. Her breath caught in her throat when it wouldn't tear. She'd allowed their pursuers to come closer than she intended—a matter of a few dozen yards. Finally, the corner ripped, leaving a square of fabric behind on a thorn.

As Cassie ran down the trail, she risked another glance back. By the sound of tramping feet and loud voices, at least a dozen men had crossed the ford. The path continued straight on and Cassie followed it to a point where the trees grew so close together on either side that they formed an arching canopy overhead. It was pitch dark underneath them, made worse by the clouds that had increased in number and played hide and seek with the moon. The lack of light forced Cassie to slow even more.

She squinted into the darkness, trotting twenty yards down the trail by feel until an unseen tree root tripped her. She fell forward, stinging her hands and knees, and decided it was time to change tactics. She reached for a low branch above her head and swung herself off the trail and onto the hill that rose up beside her to her left at a sixty degree angle from the path.

Cassie crouched in the leaves at what would be head height for someone on the trail, listening for the men who pursued her. She couldn't see a thing. After a minute, she realized they weren't coming.

Crap!

Cassie climbed straight up the hill on her feet and hands like a monkey, heedless of the brambles and bracken that scratched her face. She found a vantage point that allowed her to see where the pursuers had stopped. They'd passed the turnoff Callum and the others had taken, but they hadn't continued down the trail to the east more than twenty feet.

Thanks to the torches they carried, Cassie could see the men clearly as they conferred. They seemed to be arguing again; then one of the men threw up his hands and turned away. With a broad sweep of his arm, he gestured the men to follow him back the way they'd come. Almost gagging at how badly she had failed Callum, Cassie pulled out her bow. She took a deep breath, trying to calm her pounding heart, aimed carefully at the leader, and loosed her last arrow.

    And then she ran.

13

Callum

Callum spent the first ten minutes of his hike up the trail cursing himself. He should have been the one to decoy their pursuers. Why had he let Cassie do it?

"She's quite a woman," Samuel said once Callum caught up with the horses. Callum didn't think he'd ever heard him use quite so dry a tone.

"Don't I know it," Callum said. "I can't believe I let her talk me into this."

"She seems to know what she's doing," Samuel said. "Where'd you find her?"

"She found me," Callum said. "She rescued me from the pile of bodies in the road after the MacDougalls left me for dead."

Samuel shook his head. "Scotland will feel the repercussions of this week for years to come."

"It's not over yet, either," Callum said.

"Thank you for the rescue," Samuel said softly.

Callum glanced up. He couldn't see much of Samuel's face, but it looked more drawn than it had been earlier, even in his prison cell. His wound was hurting more than he let on. "You're welcome. You would have done the same for me."

Samuel put his lips together, seemingly pleased at Callum's expression of confidence in him, but Callum knew it to be true.

"While I am delighted to know that Robert Bruce believed his duty was to come after me, I wish he had solicited the support of the other Guardians before he acted—and certainly before he burned out the Black Comyn," said James, from just ahead of them.

"Who happens to be another Guardian of Scotland," Callum said.

"Exactly," said James. "I have supported Robert Bruce's claim to the throne. What is his son doing?"

"The father might not know, or if he does know, might not have approved his son's actions," Callum said, not using Grampa Bruce's nickname in polite company. "To be fair, we have no proof that the eldest Bruce is involved in any of this, and only Kirby's word of the involvement of John Balliol."

"I am very disappointed in Kirby," said James. "I feel as though I should have known something wasn't right about him when he snubbed you at Carlisle."

"He snubbed you too," Callum said.

James shifted in the saddle and didn't answer, so Callum didn't continue the conversation. The man had a lot on his mind, perhaps the most minor of which was the fact that he was fleeing for his life over a mountain.

The road continued to climb, but the trail was good and the horses navigated it without difficulty. Callum had to trot to keep up, and he was glad for all those hours he'd spent training in the winter and spring. The soldier's mentality in this world was remarkably similar to that in the old one: a man trained constantly, hoping his skills would never be used, but was prepared to use them if he needed to. Callum's training had saved his life many times, even before the ambush on the road.

Callum hoped that Cassie's experience would save her now. He cursed under his breath again. Where was she?

After approximately two miles, the path leveled out. They'd reached the heights above the river and the loch. With the rise in elevation, the wind picked up and even Callum could smell the change in the weather of which Cassie had spoken. They continued as best they could for another mile, though more clouds blew in every minute and it was becoming difficult to see anything at all when the moon wasn't showing. After another mile, the path started to descend.

"Callum!" Samuel said. "Someone's coming!"

Callum swung around.

"I hear running feet," Samuel said.

"Go! Go on!" Callum tossed his friend the leading reins.

Samuel caught them in midair. James dug his heels into his horse's sides, clutching John to his chest. Though Samuel would have waited with Callum, Callum slapped the horse's rump and got it moving too.

The horses disappeared around a hillock. Samuel couldn't have been comfortable at that pace with his wounded leg, but the horses were Scottish, not war horses. They were bred to the hills. They wouldn't let the men down and could start to move even faster as they descended into the village. The starless darkness on the western horizon threatened to swallow all light completely, but the moon took that moment to shine out brightly. It would allow them to see where they were going for a little way at least.

Callum stepped off the path and crouched down. The trees were sparse up here and he was counting on his stillness to hide him from the sight of whoever was coming. The patter of feet came closer and as he listened, Callum realized that the noise came from a single runner. He straightened and stepped into the road. "It's me!" He caught Cassie by the arms as she barreled into him.

"God! You scared me!" Cassie gasped for breath. "We need to keep moving. How far ahead are the others?"

"I just sent them on—a matter of minutes," Callum said.

Cassie looked behind her, and they both stilled to listen. "I don't hear anything," Callum said.

"That doesn't mean they're not on their way," Cassie said. "They followed me east for a little way, but then it looked as if I hadn't convinced them sufficiently. I shot one. Once they figure out that nobody is shooting at them anymore, they'll come after us. I'm out of arrows."

"If they come, they come," Callum said. "Can you keep running?"

"Of course." Cassie said.

Callum accepted her assessment. Few qualities in a woman were more attractive than quiet competence, something which Cassie had in abundance. "If we hurry, we can catch James and Samuel before they reach the village," he said.

Callum and Cassie set off, but it seemed the horses had moved more quickly than Callum had thought they might. Cassie and he approached within half a mile of the village and still hadn't caught up with them. Callum slowed. "Could they have taken another path?" he said.

"There is no other path," Cassie said.

Then Samuel stepped from a stand of trees near the river where the terrain flattened out. "Callum!"

Cassie and Callum hurried to greet him. James remained on his horse with John. "His breath is more shallow," said James.

"We've made it to the village," Callum said. "Let's see if we're welcome."

A river ran from a northwestern loch to a second loch further east. The village nestled between them. The horses clip-clopped across the wooden bridge that spanned the river and along an earthen road, hard packed from years of use, which led into the village. The quiet was absolute. Not even a dog barked.

Cassie's head was near Callum's shoulder and she spoke in a whisper. "I know it's after midnight, but surely our presence will bring someone out? Don't they keep a watch?"

"It doesn't seem like it," Callum said.

The village consisted of a dozen houses clustered around a central green. A little church sat on the north side of the village, a little way from the other buildings. The white plastered stone walls reflected the lingering moonlight. The church possessed a slate roof, the only one in the village, and sported a tower and a metal cross above the doorway. The grounds were protected by a low stone wall pierced by an archway with a bell above it.

"What's the name of this place?" Samuel said.

"Duncraggan." Cassie pointed to a one-story building attached to the west side of the church. "I'll go and ask for help, shall I?"

"Not alone, you won't," Callum said.

Cassie made what sounded like a *grrr* at him but didn't otherwise protest his involvement. She and Callum ducked through the archway and walked down the path towards the front door of the church, before cutting across the graveyard to reach the back door. Samuel followed to a point halfway down the path but stopped to wait twenty feet away. Once at the door, Callum knocked.

Nobody answered. Callum turned to look at Cassie, who shrugged, and he was about to knock again when a shout came from the road. "You there!"

A dozen men, maybe all of the men in the village, each armed with an axe or a farming implement, stomped toward them. Several of them also held torches. The man who led them had obviously hurried from his bed because even as he walked, he swung his cloak around his shoulders and fastened it at his throat.

Callum strode to meet him, with Cassie and Samuel in tow, and arrived at the archway in time to set his feet and present a composed face before the leader reached him.

Ten feet away, the man pulled up. "Who are you?" he said in Gaelic, "and what do you want? We aren't accustomed to being woken in the night by strangers."

"We don't wish to make trouble," Callum said. "We come seeking shelter. Several of us are injured and need healing. One is only a boy."

Callum could see the leader studying him, taking in his armor and sword, and then his eyes went to Samuel and James, still on the horse with John. Cassie remained just behind Callum and not in the man's line of sight.

The man was six inches shorter than Callum and ten years older, with bristling gray hair and a close-cropped beard. "Tell me your name," the man said.

"Callum. But my name isn't important." Callum gestured towards James. "This is James Stewart, Guardian of Scotland, and the young lord Graham, from Mugdock."

It wasn't often that Callum had seen a man's jaw actually drop, but this man's did. He recovered quickly, however, bowing abruptly. "My apologies, my lord. My home is your home." He spun around, organizing the men of the village with a wave of his hand. James and John were helped from their horse and they, as well Samuel, were swept towards the leader's house. Callum heard the leader tell one of the others to run ahead and wake 'old Hetty' and bring her to his home, which sounded promising to Callum.

The leader's hut looked like all the others in the village but for its larger size, and like the other buildings, was built in stone without mortar. It had a thatched roof, unlike the church, and was good-sized for a medieval house: close to twenty feet long with its related buildings clustered behind it. The headman's much younger and very pregnant wife met him at the door and gave way as Samuel and James were herded inside, along with the two men carrying John.

Cassie and Callum didn't go inside, instead remaining on the threshold. The leader glanced at them and tipped his head. "Please. Come in."

"We dare not," Callum said. "It's possible we have been followed by men who do not come in peace."

The leader stepped closer, crowding Callum out of the doorway, and shut the door behind him. "What are you saying? You've brought disaster to my people?"

"I hope not," Callum said.

The man's chin jutted out. "How many?"

"We hope no more than a dozen," Callum said.

"We're farmers and herdsmen!" the leader said. "How can we defend against even that many soldiers?"

James pulled open the door behind the man. "I'm sorry to bring trouble to your village. Our horses are tired, but not blown. If you have a man to spare, he could ride to my family's holding at

Callander. I would go myself, but—" James swayed and Callum caught him by the shoulders.

"Are you wounded?" Callum said. "Where?"

James had been holding his left arm across his torso and now turned his hand palm up to show Callum the blood on it. "It's not serious or I would have said something earlier. The exertion of riding has opened the wound again."

Callum looked at the headman. "What is your name?"

"Martin."

"Do you have someone we can send as Lord Stewart suggests?" Callum said.

"Yes." Martin's bluster was gone in favor of brisk certainty. "I will see to it." He walked off quickly towards the village green where several men still gathered.

"I should be the one to go," Cassie said as she helped Callum ease James back inside the hut. The only place to sit him was on a bench against a side wall. He needed the bed, but that was taken up by John.

"No, Cassie," Callum said. "How many of these villagers have real weapons? I need you to fight."

"I'm not a soldier, Callum." Cassie's voice was soft.

"Maybe not," Callum said. "But you think more like one than any other able-bodied man here."

Callum meant it as a complement of a sort, but he could see why Cassie might not see it that way, even if she'd made it clear that she didn't want him to treat her like a medieval woman. She *was* a woman, and a beautiful one at that.

"I don't have any arrows left," Cassie said. "I'm not going to be much use to you."

"The villagers might have a stockpile." Callum tugged on the end of her braid and then dropped his hand at her narrowed eyes.

"I'll ask Martin when he returns," Cassie said. "But for all that the MacDougalls and Bruces employed archers in their companies, most men in Scotland don't know how to use a bow. They use snares to trap small animals, but the lords forbid the hunting of big game. Archery requires years of practice to be able to take a bow into battle."

"That's how it is in England, too," Callum said. "Until they fought the Welsh, they didn't understand how powerful a regiment of archers could be."

"Given that, do you think it would be better if I stayed here and guarded James and John?" Cassie said.

Callum bent his head to hers. "You're actually willing to stay behind?"

"No, but I thought I'd give you the illusion of control," she said.

Callum laughed and shook his head. "I wouldn't mind having you at my back."

Cassie turned to the healer, who had slipped in the back door while they were talking to Martin. "How is Samuel?" she said.

As the first order of business, Hetty had bound Samuel's leg so he could walk if he had to. "He'll do," she said.

Hetty went to James next, tugging up his shirt to get at his wound. Cassie moved to crouch in front of Samuel. "How does it feel?"

"I'm fine," Samuel said.

"Uh huh. You must be James and John's last defense," Cassie said.

"I can fight too," said James from his bench.

Callum glanced over at him. "No." He held out his hand to Cassie. After a brief hesitation, she grasped it so he could pull her to her feet. "Cassie and I will take care of this."

Callum rotated his shoulders to loosen his back and shoulder muscles as he and Cassie left the hut. The darkness would have been complete if not for the torches in the hands of the men that Martin had posted on the green and on the bridge, waiting for the MacDougalls to come, if they were going to come.

"There's no denying I feel naked without my bow," Cassie said. "I don't have any other weapon but my knife."

"I wish Samuel and James still had their swords," Callum said. "I'd give one of theirs to you, even if they protested. As it is, I think our village chief is arming his men. Maybe he can arm you too."

Cassie and Callum followed the sound of men's voices around the back of Martin's house. In many medieval houses, the byre for the animals was attached to the house, but Martin's home was more advanced than that. He had a barn and a shed, and it was to the shed that he had brought his villagers. Callum and

Cassie watched Martin pass out axes and roughly made swords to each man who asked for one.

Cassie approached and fingered the hilt of one of the swords. "Where did you get these?"

"We've been collecting them over the past few years," Martin said. "When you live as we do, surrounded by powerful lords who think nothing of crossing your fields on their way to marauding, you learn to defend yourself."

"Do you have any arrows?" Cassie said.

Martin shook his head regretfully. "None in the village have the skill to make them." Carrying a seven foot long pole arm, he headed to where his villagers waited patiently on the green.

"Maybe Martin doesn't need our help after all." Callum picked up a weapon that resembled nothing less than a goblin sword from *The Lord of the Rings*. It was composed of a thick, flat strip of metal with a leather grip wrapped around one end.

Cassie eyed what Callum had chosen and then picked out a similar weapon for herself, this one with a wicked point. "This is one hell of a sword."

Callum glanced to where Martin waited with his villagers, whose numbers had grown in the last hour. Men who lived in the surrounding countryside had come at Martin's call. Martin lifted a hand to Callum, who nodded, understanding that the men were waiting for him to instruct them. First, however, Callum put a hand on Cassie's shoulder, focusing her attention away from her weapon and towards the green.

"Look at Martin's pole arm," Callum said.

"I've never seen anything like it," Cassie said.

"That's because it's made of steel."

"How is that possible? Where did he get this stuff?" Cassie said.

"My guess—and I think it's a good one—is that we've just found Meg's friend Marty. These weapons are the remains of his airplane."

14

Cassie

They'd stayed up all night again, and Cassie had never been so glad to see the sky lighten. Callum had left Cassie to give a pep talk to the women, while he oversaw the men who would stand as their first and only line of defense against the MacDougalls. While all but a few of the villagers appeared to be shivering in their boots, Cassie had to trust that they would find their courage and do what had to be done when it came to it. The fact that they would be defending their families helped.

"We could have hidden James, Samuel, and John and waited for the MacDougalls to pass by," Cassie said when she finally had a chance to talk to Callum again. "Surely Marty could lie sufficiently to send them on their way?"

"Martin and I talked about it while you were overseeing the setting of snares on the path," Callum said. "If we let the MacDougalls into the village, we lose any advantage we might have gained by confronting them with a strong force. They are fighting men and the villagers aren't. They could wipe the villagers out because they felt like it."

Cassie had lived long enough to have seen the casual brutality that was a way of life for some men. "I'm rethinking those snares, then," she said. "As soon as they see them, the MacDougalls will know we're here."

"I'm not rethinking them," Callum said. "To face fewer MacDougalls when they come—if they come—is worth the the loss of surprise."

Cassie and Callum reached the village end of the bridge. Cassie looked across the river to the hill that the MacDougalls would come down if they were coming. "I'm glad you think so."

"You don't have to be perfect all the time, you know," Callum said. "It's okay to make mistakes."

Cassie found her hands worrying at the fabric of her cloak and forced them to still. "Not in my experience."

"Cassie—" Callum reached out a hand towards her, but she took a step back before he could touch her.

"I should check on the scouts again," Cassie said.

Callum nodded and didn't try to stop her. As she reached the first turn on the trail, a tentative shaft of sunlight broke through the mist and cloud cover that were typical for a morning in Scotland. She glanced back to the bridge. Callum stood where she'd left him looking after her, with a half-dozen men guarding the river.

He noticed her attention and lifted a hand. Cassie nodded, though he might not have been able to see the gesture from that distance. She turned back to the trail and kept walking, forcing herself to think about the coming fight rather than her developing feelings for Callum.

Five minutes later, the ray of sunlight was squelched by the rain that had been threatening from the west all night. The first drops pattered on the trees above Cassie's head. She'd gone two hundred yards when two men who'd been sent to watch the path came running back. The first one practically leapt over her in his fear, while the second caught Cassie's arm as he passed her and spun her around. "They killed Rod!"

"How many come?" Cassie said.

"Two dozen!" The first man shrieked the words.

Cassie hesitated, listening, letting the men get ahead of her. Even through the plopping noises of the rain on the leaves in the path and on her hood, she could hear the progress of the MacDougalls. Cassie wanted to doubt the man's guess at their numbers. If the MacDougalls had brought two dozen men, the villagers would be outnumbered.

Cassie gave up on the idea of getting an actual count. They'd know how many men came against them soon enough. She ran back down the trail after the villagers, almost losing her footing several times as she skidded in the dirt that had turned to mud in the last ten minutes. The wind blew her hood off her head and a wash of rain flew into her face. She didn't mind the coolness of it, since she was hot from running. It also helped to calm that first rush of adrenaline brought on by the villagers' panic. Cassie slowed as she reached the bottom of the hill and jogged the last thirty yards to where Callum waited.

He moved off of the bridge to meet her ten paces in front of the men who stood behind him. "You heard that they're coming?" Cassie said.

Callum nodded. "I heard."

"Do we know how far it is to the nearest ford?" Cassie said.

"The men tell me there isn't one." Callum shrugged. "The MacDougalls could swim the river and come at us from another direction, but if they really have twenty-four men, they'll have too much bravado not to challenge us here."

"We could destroy the bridge," Cassie said.

"I would do it if we had archers and arrows," Callum said. "You alone could decimate their ranks. A few spears aren't enough, and the villagers wouldn't throw them accurately anyway."

Cassie glanced behind her. The MacDougalls hadn't yet appeared. "It would be easy," she said.

"As it is, we may just have to fight them with what we've got," Callum said, "because at this point, I don't have a better plan."

William, Martin's captain, a man in his middle thirties, stepped to Callum's side. "We only have to hold them off until the Stewarts arrive." Martin himself was staying to the rear, though Cassie gave him credit for being there at all. He was neither a soldier nor built for war. Even so, he still carried the giant pole arm.

"Here they come," Callum said. "Get behind me, Cassie."

Cassie obeyed, as did William. "We need to survive this, Callum," Cassie said.

"I have every intention of doing so." Callum spoke softly, but Cassie heard the steel in his voice.

She nodded, more to herself than to him since he couldn't see her and was focused entirely on the men coming towards him. They bunched together in a tight grouping, gathering in the cleared space between the bottom of the hill and the bridge. Most of the MacDougalls carried round shields, two feet in diameter, which they held in front of them. Even with the shields, Cassie could have taken down half of them before they crossed the space if she'd had arrows to shoot. The rain continued to fall steadily, but it had become the more familiar Scottish rain, a drizzle rather than a deluge.

The MacDougalls slowed and then stopped. The way they huddled together made it hard to get an exact count, but they didn't have two dozen—more like fifteen—and three injured: two in the rear were hobbling and a third had a blood-soaked pant leg. Either Rod had done some damage before he died, or the traps had done their work. Cassie would need to remove them when this was over before an innocent person got hurt.

The leader pushed between two shields that had protected him and stepped to the front of his men. He swept a hand through his red hair, brushing the wet ends out of his face. He held a sword, but stood with it down, thirty feet from Callum. The MacDougall leader's jaw was set and he appeared angry more than concerned at the resistance that faced him. These were MacDougall warriors. Peasants didn't fight back.

Callum spoke first. "Turn around and go home. You are not wanted here."

The man's nostrils flared and he glanced behind him at a taller man who stood half a pace to his right. He held his axe in the middle of the haft and was beating time on his thigh with the end of it.

"Give me the boy and we'll be on our way," the leader said.

"What boy?" Callum said.

"John Graham."

Cassie pursed her lips, wondering why John Graham was more highly prized than James Stewart.

Callum laughed. "I don't think so."

"Give way now and nobody gets hurt," the leader said.

"It is not we who are outnumbered," Callum said.

The man lifted his chin. "You lead a motley band of farmers and sheepherders. They are good men who will die today if you resist us."

Callum took three steps backwards. William and Cassie backed up with him until all three of them stood on the bridge. "You have only one way across this river," Callum said. "Do you think you can take this bridge from us?"

The man grinned. "I won't have to."

He waved a hand at the men behind him. They dropped their shields to reveal a girl with her hands bound behind her back. A man held a knife to her throat.

A man behind Cassie, a farmer from an outlying homestead, gave a cry and ran forward. "That's my daughter!"

William spun around and caught him with a hand pressed flat to his chest before he could cross the bridge. "Don't."

"What do you say now?" the leader said.

Callum's hands fisted. "Let her go."

"Give me my prisoner," the leader said. "As I said, I'll let you keep the big man and the Stewart. All I need is John Graham and I'll let the girl go."

"Why do you want him?" Callum said.

"That isn't your concern. Give me the boy or the girl dies."

"If you kill her, you will have no leverage against us," Callum said.

The girl was holding herself very still, but now the man who held her ran the knife blade across her neck, breaking the skin. The girl sobbed.

"In a moment, all you'll have is a dead girl and a grieving family," the leader said.

"John is near death himself," Callum said. "He can't be moved."

"Let me take him and I will determine that for myself, or bring me his body."

"Let her go," Callum said.

Tears streamed down the girl's cheeks and she gasped, breathless, while at the same time trying to hold herself stiff and away from the knife. Cassie had thought her captor would have only pricked the skin, but there was a lot of blood on the girl's neck and dress for a flesh wound.

The leader took a menacing step forward. "You will obey me now!"

Callum's shoulders went rigid. He held himself still for a count of three, just staring at the man—and then he reached underneath his cloak, drew out the gun, and shot the man holding the girl through the forehead. Then he moved the barrel six inches and double tapped the leader in the chest.

Callum and Cassie sat together on overturned buckets in the middle of Marty's barn. The smell of farm animal had Cassie wishing they'd found a different place to confer. Callum held his head in his hands. The gun was hidden away again in its holster. "I had to do it, Cassie," he said.

Cassie knelt in front of him and took one of his hands in hers. She understood that his war had taken its toll on Callum. She'd grown up among veterans, since Indians had a long history of service in the American military. The aching loss, shame, and guilt, punctuated by intervals of pure fear, drained a person. Like some of the other veterans she'd known, Callum was a control freak and sometimes turned inward so far he stopped communicating. Callum also seemed to have this thing about how stuff smelled.

"I know," Cassie said, worried about the bad memories Callum had awoken in himself. "What were your choices, Callum?"

He just shook his head.

After Callum had killed the two men, the girl had screeched and collapsed to the ground. Her cry had released the men behind Cassie and they had surged onto the bridge and then past her. The MacDougalls found themselves down two men, one of whom was their leader. At the sight of twenty villagers coming at them, screaming that banshee wail that the Highlanders seemed to have perfected, all but a few turned tail and fled. The men who hesitated were cut down where they stood, run over by the anger and fear in the men they'd threatened.

Four MacDougalls had escaped outright but the rest were dead, including the three men who couldn't run and who'd been killed before they'd taken ten steps. Martin would be dealing with the aftermath of this battle for weeks to come.

Afterwards, Callum, Cassie, and Martin had conferred hurriedly, a conversation in which Martin repeated "My God!" about a dozen times as he absorbed the idea that Cassie and Callum were time travelers too. Then it had taken some time for him to settle his people. By noon, though many remained on the green, some of the shock had passed. A few still stood guard on the bridge. A posse of ten men had followed the remaining MacDougalls up the trail. Callum had tried to stop the villagers from killing whomever they found, but his exhortations had gone unheeded. Even Martin couldn't control his people in this.

And now they had to deal with what Callum had done. "How bad do you think it is?" Callum said.

"It depends," Martin said in American English. He came forward from the doorway to his barn, a bemused expression on his face. He still looked the part of headman of his village, but now that he knew Cassie and Callum to be kindred spirits, he came across as more comfortable in his surety and less pompous. Cassie studied him. Perhaps it was Martin, of all of them, who had found—rather than lost—himself in the Middle Ages.

"It depends on what?" Callum said.

"On what we want to say you did," Marty said.

"I fired a pistol at two men and killed them," Callum said. "How do we pretend otherwise?"

"The same way we always do," Marty said. "Surely, you haven't gotten this far—" Marty gestured to the whole of Callum's appearance and presence, "—by telling the truth about yourself? It has been all lies and half-truths for me. Until I had enough of a history here, I couldn't speak of my life without deception." He chewed on his lower lip, thinking. "I should have known something was up with you two by your reaction to my weapons."

"They're not exactly standard medieval issue," Cassie said.

"My guess is that you salvaged what you could from your airplane," Callum said.

Marty went very still. "How do you know about that?"

"Because David, the new King of England, is your friend Meg's son," Callum said.

Now Cassie knew how Callum had felt when he'd told her that she wasn't alone in this world. The expression on Marty's face was, quite frankly, awesome to behold: a mixture of stunned surprise, disbelief, and incipient joy.

"Meg—Meg's alive?" Marty said.

"Callum knows her well." Cassie didn't think it would have been possible for Marty's eyes to widen, but they did. Cassie nodded. "Yup. You're standing there thinking it can't be possible, but it is."

Marty paced around in a circle, shaking his head. "I just can't believe it!"

"So tell me this." Callum leaned forward. "You flew off and left her. How could you do that?"

Callum's accusation cut through some of Marty's shock. "I wasn't in my right mind—as I'm sure you can understand—and I was pretty confident she wasn't either. I thought I'd give her some time to cool down." He stopped his pacing and sighed. "By the time I came to my senses, I'd run out of fuel and had to put down." He tipped his head, pointing to the west. "In the loch, if you must know."

"And then what?" Cassie said.

Marty snorted. "And then I discovered Meg was right and we were in the fucking Middle Ages. The people in this village took me in."

"And the plane?" Callum said.

"It's slowly rusting just below the surface of the loch. The carcass is just enough out of sight to be out of mind for the most part." Marty paused. "So Meg made it."

"No thanks to you." Callum wasn't ready to forgive him.

"Tell me more ... that would make Meg the Queen of Wales?"

Cassie thought Marty was so caught up in the story, he hadn't noticed Callum's disapproval. Cassie, who hadn't even met Meg yet, had to admit that she wasn't ready to forgive him either.

"I believe Meg told you before you abandoned her that she had come to the Middle Ages and been with King Llywelyn twenty years ago?" Callum said.

"Yeah, she mentioned it," Marty said, "right before I dumped her off. I knew that she had a kid named David, and that he and his sister had disappeared a few years earlier. You're telling me the truth—they came here too?"

Callum nodded. "As I said, David is the new King of England."

The repeat of that bit of information hardly fazed Marty. He lifted his chin. "What about you two?"

Cassie didn't think trusting Marty was necessarily the best plan, but Callum said, "Cassie was caught in the vortex of the time-space anomaly caused by your airplane and came here when you did. She's been living twenty miles to the south of this village nearly the whole time."

That, of all Callum and Cassie's news, seemed to surprise Marty the most. He jerked away and went back to his pacing, his eyes focused on the floor of the barn. "I'm sorry."

"My coming here wasn't your fault," Cassie said, "and it occurs to me only now that I need to stop blaming Meg for bringing me here. It wasn't her fault either."

"What do you mean?" Marty said. "Of course it was."

"You'd lost your instruments, right?" Cassie said.

Marty nodded. "A storm blew up out of nowhere. Blew us right out of the sky."

"Right," Cassie said. "Your airplane was about to crash into a mountainside right on top of me. If Meg hadn't brought you here—and unintentionally brought me too—all three of us would have been killed."

Marty rubbed his chin. "I suppose you have a point." He eyed Callum. "What about you?"

"It's my own fault I'm here," Callum said. "Because I didn't believe time travel was real, I tried to stop Meg from returning to the Middle Ages."

"What—what was that?" Marty said, freezing in mid-stride. "Stop her?"

"Six months ago, Meg and Llywelyn came to the twenty-first century," Callum said. "I was with the team that tried to detain them and prevent their return to the Middle Ages."

"She *wanted* to come back here?" Marty said. "What—what is she—insane?"

"Her son is the King of England," Cassie said.

Marty actually laughed. "There is that." He stretched his arms above his head and bent back and forth at the waist. "So, how many jumpers are there, exactly? Just Meg? Or David too?"

"What—what do you mean by *jumpers*?" Callum said.

"Jumpers." Marty snapped his fingers impatiently. "Time jumpers—how many are there compared to how many of us?"

"Meg and her two children, David and Anna, can time *jump*, as you say," Cassie said, kind of liking the nickname Marty had concocted. "You, me, Callum, and Bronwen, a friend David brought back with him a few years ago, can't."

"So it's genetic," Marty said.

"It looks like it," Callum said.

Marty nodded. "What about their kids?"

"Whose kids?" Callum said.

Marty gave Callum an exasperated look. "Isn't David's wife pregnant? Didn't Meg have twins? I heard about it all the way up here. Are their kids jumpers too?"

Callum gazed at Marty, his mouth open. "I've never considered it. I don't know. I guess we won't know until somebody tries it, willingly or unwillingly."

"Hmm. It might be interesting to be there when they find out." Marty clapped his hands together. "Well … what a day, huh? I suppose it's time to see to my people."

"What are you going to tell them about the gun?" Cassie said.

"What they'll believe: England is experimenting with hand-held cannons, and that as a confidant of the king, David gave you the prototype."

"That could be dangerous," Cassie said. "Wouldn't it be better to say nothing? Callum has put it away. In this case, rumor might be no worse than fact."

Callum hunched forward on his bucket, his hands gripping his knees. "I agree you have to tell them something, and what you suggest is as good as anything I've thought of. I'm going to have to say the same to James and Samuel, who have probably heard about it already. Thank God they didn't witness the shooting. If they had, I doubt that explanation would suffice.

"It might be best to say that the gun was destroyed in the firing," Cassie said.

Callum nodded. "Early cannons often broke apart after a few uses."

Marty pursed his lips. "Maybe you should come too. They'll take it better if they think you have nothing to hide." He headed for the door. Thirty seconds later, Cassie could hear him talking to his people and responding to questions he couldn't possibly answer with the truth.

Cassie held out a hand to Callum, as he had to her earlier in Marty's hut. "Ready?" she said.

"I suppose."

Cassie squeezed Callum's hand and then hauled him forward, leading the way out of the barn. Callum didn't exactly balk, but he moved slowly. "I feel like I'm headed to the gallows," he said.

"You're not. It's going to be fine," Cassie said, more to comfort him than because she felt confident herself.

The rain had temporarily ceased, though the clouds hovered twenty feet above the ground, coating everything in a fine mist. Men, women, and children had gathered on the green to hear Marty speak. At the sight of Callum, everyone hushed. They stood, nearly fifty people, staring at Callum in total silence for a count of ten, and then the girl who had been abducted gave another screech—this time of joy—and launched herself at him.

"Thank you!" She wrapped her arms around his neck, almost choking him. "Thank you!" Her smiles turned to tears and she pressed her face into Callum's shoulder, sobbing and laughing at the same time. A bandage wound around her neck but she seemed otherwise undamaged from the confrontation. Upon closer inspection, the girl was nearer to sixteen than twelve and knew it, given how tightly she held Callum.

After a moment of hesitation, he put his arms around her and patted her back. "It's okay," he said, forgetting to speak Gaelic, but the girl didn't seem to mind and Cassie had actually heard 'okay' twice in the last few hours from two different villagers. Marty's influence, she guessed. After another twenty seconds, Callum managed to extricate himself from the girl's embrace, and as he put her to one side, the girl's father came forward with his hand out.

"I was angry when you brought the Stewart here, but today will be remembered as a good day," he said.

"Thank you." Callum clasped the man's forearm. The motion seemed to remove the villagers' suspicions completely and they crowded around Callum, offering their thanks. The fight at the bridge would be the talk of the village for many days—maybe years—to come. Cassie was glad that her part in it was over.

Or maybe not. As the crowd was beginning to disperse again, the messenger whom Marty had sent east rode out of the mist. A company of twenty men followed, led by a tall soldier in mail armor.

"I must speak to James Stewart!"

15

Callum

The man who spoke sat at attention on his horse. He had a narrow face underneath his helmet, and was so thin that Callum wondered how he could possibly stay in the saddle, much less wield a sword. Though he'd come prepared for war, not for a village full of merry people, he recovered quickly and directed his men to dismount.

Callum was glad that he'd already put the girl aside, though not at all sorry that Cassie had been looking daggers at him while he held her. He might have known Cassie for only a few days, but that was three months in medieval years. It was about time she started thinking about him as something more than a friend.

Besides, Cassie should know better than to think that Callum was remotely interested in the girl. He was twice her age. Whatever the acceptable practice in the Middle Ages regarding relationships between older men and younger women, no thirty-four-year old man should be satisfied intellectually and emotionally by a sixteen-year-old girl.

"I'm here, Walter." James stood in the doorway of the hut, resting his shoulder against the frame and holding his hand to his newly bandaged side.

"You're hurt!" Walter's sternness dissipated in his concern for his master. "When the boy rode into the castle this morning, we feared the worst."

"It definitely could have been worse," said James. "The ruffians have been vanquished, at least for now. I don't see the point of further pursuit." James looked past Walter to Callum.

Callum shook his head. "The MacDougalls are long gone."

"The boy you sent mentioned that the MacDougalls were to blame." Walter swung around to look at his men. "Secure the perimeter."

The men moved to obey him, and Marty started shooing his people away from the green again. "Show's over," he said, though before he said it, Callum wouldn't have thought that the phrase meant the same rendered in thirteenth-century Gaelic as it did in their old world.

Walter turned back to James. "Are you able to ride, my lord?"

"I will be able to." James looked at Callum again. "The boy is awake."

Callum nodded and canted his head at Cassie, inviting her to come with him into Marty's house. John wasn't actually sitting up in bed, but he had his arms clasped behind his head and was gazing up at the ceiling. He lifted his head to look at them as they entered. His pinched look cleared and his face split into a grin. "Cassie!"

She walked to the bed. "Hello, John. So you aren't completely out of your head after all. James said you were raving."

James choked from behind her. "I did not—!"

"He what—?"

Cassie laughed. "I'm teasing you both." She took John's hand in hers. "How do you feel?"

"My head aches." John's grip tightened on Cassie's hand. "Can you help me to sit up?"

"Of course." Cassie pulled him to a sitting position on the bed with his back against the wall behind him. She handed him a cup of water.

"Why did the MacDougalls abduct you?" Callum said.

"I-I don't know," John said.

"It was you they wanted even more than James," Cassie said.

Callum allowed himself a smile at Cassie's continued use of James Stewart's first name. She should have said 'Lord James' at the very least. James didn't correct her, however, and John acted as if he didn't notice.

"I went to bed in my father's house and woke up in the bed of a cart," he said.

"How were you injured?" Cassie said. "It's just your head, right? They didn't beat you?"

"That I banged my head was my fault," John said. "I tried to escape too soon instead of lulling them into a false sense of security."

"An honest mistake," said James, coming forward. "I did the same thing."

John looked at James as if he didn't believe a lord such as James could possibly have done such a foolish thing.

James ignored the look. "Will you speak to the Bishop of St. Andrews, William Fraser, of all that has befallen you?" He paused. "And us."

"Yes," John said.

It seemed that the honor of the Grahams ran true in this son.

"I will send word to your father of your survival just as soon as we arrive at my castle at Doune," said James.

John nodded. "Thank you."

While James stood beside John's bed, quietly talking to him, Callum tugged Cassie towards the door. "I'm almost afraid to ask you this, but you're coming to Stirling Castle with me, right?"

Cassie wrinkled her nose at him. "In all our running around, I almost forgot what you were doing in Scotland in the first place."

"I was supposed to figure out what was going on among the players for the throne," Callum said.

"Admittedly, you've made headway on that issue," Cassie said.

"And then I was supposed to find out who murdered Princess Margaret," Callum said. "I haven't even started on that yet."

"David doesn't think she died like they said?" Cassie said. "From the flu?"

"Do you?" Callum said. "I think everyone's pretending it was natural so they don't have to think about it. They've convinced themselves that King Alexander fell off that cliff all on his own, too, but I don't believe that either."

"They're going to love you in Stirling," Cassie said, unable to hold back a smile.

Callum laughed. "David envisioned a week of state dinners, not that we'd get ambushed before we'd even started. I haven't even *met* Balliol and Grampa Bruce yet."

"David thought you could have politics in the Middle Ages without murder and mayhem? I thought you said he'd lived here since 1282?"

That prompted another laugh from Callum. "So, what do you say?"

Cassie chewed on a nail, her eyes on James and John. Samuel had fallen asleep on his stool, his back propped against the wall and his chin on his chest. Finally, she nodded. "I'll come. I want to know how this turns out, too."

Callum let out a breath. He'd been worried that he'd have to do some serious persuading. "At the very least, with whatever is between the MacDougalls and the Bruces still unsettled, I don't want you returning to your house alone. It wouldn't be safe."

Cassie met Callum's eyes. "You don't have to worry about me. I can take care of myself."

"I can't help worrying," Callum said. "Daddy Bruce is marching on Dunstaffnage. The countryside won't be safe for anyone."

"I'd almost forgotten that too." Cassie turned to James and switched back to Gaelic. "You know Robbie's father better than we do. Do you think Robbie would have gotten into trouble for helping us?"

"The Bruces and the Comyns hated each other long before this week. I trust Robbie's instincts, and if he helped you to leave his father's camp, we have to assume he knew what he was doing." James glanced at Callum. "We need to have a conversation."

Callum woke Samuel with a hand to his shoulder. With John watching bright-eyed from the bed, Callum sat on the bench next to Samuel while James and Cassie pulled two stools close. James eyed Cassie for a second, and then seemed to come to the decision that whatever needed to be said could be said in front of her. By now, James had to know that he shouldn't expect Cassie to behave like any other woman he'd ever met.

"I am concerned about how to approach the other Guardians and Parliament with what has happened," said James.

"That makes two of us," Callum said.

James looked hard at Callum. "Kirby is a bishop and an advisor to the King of England. Before I make any move against him, I must consult with my advisors. I would hope that I might include you among them when I reach Doune."

"Of course," Callum said.

"Kirby should be locked in a dungeon, sooner rather than later," Cassie said.

"Do we have definitive proof of his duplicity?" Samuel said.

"We have the testimony of Robbie Bruce and of Cassie," Callum said, with a glance at her.

Cassie nodded. "I witnessed the ambush; I saw Kirby's decoy fall. Robbie was the only one to escape before the ambush, and Callum was the only man left alive after the MacDougalls marched the prisoners away."

"Which means that for Kirby to have reached Robert Bruce's forces before Robbie, he had to have already been on his way there when the MacDougalls attacked," said James.

"Yes," Cassie and Callum said in unison.

"Robbie himself reported what Kirby did and said?" said James.

"Again, yes," Cassie said.

James rested his elbows on his knees. "That should be enough for the other Guardians and any reasonable man. Kirby will deny all culpability, of course."

"He's very good at talking," Callum said, "and plotting. We need to have a clear plan for dealing with him when we encounter him again."

"There's still too much we don't know," said James, "and won't until we reach Stirling. Has Comyn retaliated against Bruce for the burning of his castle? Has he sent men after the Bruce army? What have Robert Bruce the elder and John Balliol been doing all this time?" James shifted on his stool, holding his hand to his side. Blood hadn't penetrated the bandage—yet.

"I feel as if time is short, but we can't answer those questions today. You need to rest, my lord," Callum said.

James nodded. "Today we will break bread with the people of this village, who will forever have my thanks, and then we all must rest. We will ride to Doune in the morning." James paused to nod at Callum. "If that is acceptable to you, my lord."

"Of course," Callum said. To ask for Callum's approval was diplomatic of James. The man had class. Besides which, staying the night in the village was fine with Callum. Despite his heroic efforts to keep upright, if he were driving a car, he would have had to pull over and take a nap.

As James was aware (and fortunately for Marty and the villagers), Walter and his men had brought enough food for a two- or three-day journey. They broke it out. In turn, the villagers emptied their homes of tables and stools, a few unsuspecting rabbits were brought out and cooked, and by late afternoon, everyone gathered on the green for a meal. Nobody mentioned Callum's gun again. Callum took that fact for the gift it was and tried to put it out of his mind.

Marty seemed in his element, the center of accolades from James, who toasted him and his village more than once as the meal progressed. Eventually, however, Marty left the main table and came to where Cassie and Callum shared a bench. They were both exhausted from days of nonstop activity and not enough sleep. Cassie sat with her chin in her hands, chewing laboriously on a tough piece of meat.

"What happens next for me?" Marty planted himself in front of Callum and spoke American, though in a low voice that didn't carry.

Callum looked up at him. "What do you mean?"

"I mean—what does the future hold for me? I have a wife and a child on the way, and I need to know what you intend to do with me."

"I don't intend to do anything with you," Callum said.

"Are you worried that we would force you to leave? That King David would demand it somehow?" Cassie said.

Marty's brow furrowed. "I imagine neither he nor his mother have a favorable view of me. With a word in the ear of the Earl of Menteith, King David could make life very difficult for me."

"I've never heard either the king or his mother speak badly of you. They only spoke of you at all to wonder what became of you," Callum said. "You are under no obligation to change your ways or your life. Stay here or go as you please. I guarantee that you'll be welcome in London or Caerphilly if you want to go there, whether for a visit or to stay."

"Besides, it looks to me like James Stewart has taken an interest in your village," Cassie said. "Even if he hated you, King David currently has bigger fish to fry than pursuing revenge over a five-year-old grudge."

Marty turned to look at his people, eating and talking among James's soldiers. "I like it here," he said softly. "When you told me how Meg had gone back to our time, I was excited at first, but I've been thinking about it. Maybe I wouldn't go back even if I had the chance, not unless I knew I could return."

"That's always the question, isn't it?" Callum said.

"We're stuck here, too," Cassie said. "Same as you."

Marty nodded. "I started out just having to make the best of it, and now that I've taken a step back to examine what I have here, I'm thinking it's pretty good." He put his heels together and gave Callum a quick bow before heading back to the table and his seat beside James.

Cassie watched him go while Callum watched her. "I think about my family back at home every day," she said.

"Would you go home if you could?" Callum said.

"I would," Cassie said. "I'm not committed to staying in the Middle Ages forever. I spent most of my first year here hiking around Scotland, looking for a way home. Correctly as it turned out, I'd decided that I'd fallen through a fault in the space-time continuum, though I didn't know that the fault was in a person and not a cave or a ring of standing stones, or I might have lived differently."

"You didn't meet Marty when you visited this village, though?" Callum said.

Cassie shook her head. "I don't remember him. He wasn't the headman then, but he obviously fit in well. They trusted him enough to ask him to lead their village." She moved her hand as if she would put it on Callum's knee and then stopped herself and clasped her hands together. "You've done the same thing—you and David and Meg. It's like you were born to be here."

"But you don't think you were?" Callum said.

"Meg and David believe coming here was their destiny. I don't believe in destiny." Cassie coughed a laugh. "I don't really believe in anything, to tell you the truth. All the same, I can't help but ask why this destiny was mine."

"I'm not so conceited as to think you were put here to save me," Callum said.

"I'm not sorry for this week. I'm glad I could help." And now Cassie did touch Callum, nudging his side with her elbow. "What do you think? Do you rail against fate and wonder *why me?*"

"I have at times, that's for sure," Callum said. "I don't have any answers for you. Mostly, I'm just trying to survive and make a difference for the people here as much as I tried to serve my country at home. It's the only thing I know to do."

Cassie tsked under her breath. "Serve your country." Callum almost didn't catch the words, she said them so quietly. She looked down at the ground and stabbed the toe of her boot into the dirt at her feet but didn't elaborate.

So Callum didn't either. In the army, he did what he was told and told others what to do, believing all the while that he was making the world a better, safer place. He had never said it out loud, but he'd thought of himself as a knight, even if he might have laughed at such a romantic notion if someone had challenged him on it. At the same time, he knew that he could never live up to that code. After a single week in Afghanistan, even the greenest recruit knew how flawed the mission was, and that Britain had gotten itself involved in a war it couldn't win. But still, Callum tried. The best men tried.

Ironically, it was once he got back home that his world fell apart. He found the civilian world messy and complicated. Morality was all shades of grey. Honor was a quaint concept. Backstabbing and gossip, social niceties and norms were just as real and almost as deadly to the soul as IEDs had been in the war.

Callum didn't think Cassie would mock him if he told her any of this, but she didn't understand it either. He wanted to be of service, and whether he did that here or at home didn't matter to him so much anymore.

The next morning, having slept for nearly twelve hours uninterrupted by dreams, Callum stepped out of the door of Marty's hut. He'd shared the floor with Samuel and been happy to do it. Cassie had found a pallet in the healer's hut. Although Callum couldn't see the sky because of the mist that hovered above the ground, it had the look of burning off sooner rather than later and might give them a clear day for the ride to Doune Castle.

Because they were short on horses, Callum arranged for Cassie to ride behind him. It allowed her not only to wrap her arms around his waist, but for them to talk privately.

"It has been years since I've been this far east," she said. "The lowlands are less safe for me."

"And why is that?" Callum said.

Cassie tried to peer around Callum's shoulder to look into his face. He turned his head to look at her.

"Are you one of those people whose brains don't work until they've had a cup of coffee?" Cassie said. "You're not thinking. Have you looked at me recently?"

"I can't actually look at you very well when you're behind me." Callum knew his voice sounded complacent, but he didn't care. "I know well what you look like. What's the problem with your appearance?"

Cassie let out a sharp burst of laughter. "I'm dressed as a man and I wear a bow. They don't like that where we're going."

"That's just too bad," Callum said.

"Easy for you to say," Cassie said. "You're the emissary from the King of England. I'm a nobody."

Callum opened his mouth to argue with her, closed it, and then decided he had nothing to lose in asking about something that had been troubling him for a while. "Why does this bother you so much? Did something happen to you that makes you not want to leave the Highlands?"

Cassie clenched his cloak and put her forehead into his spine. "You've been in the Middle Ages for six months, Callum. How can you not know what might have happened to me?"

"That's it." Callum reined in and pulled to the side of the road. They'd been riding towards the rear of the company, and it was a matter of thirty seconds to let the last few men pass them. Several looked at him with raised eyebrows, but he lifted a hand to indicate that all was well and said, "We'll catch up."

"What are you doing?" Cassie said.

"Off, Cassie."

That 'v' of concern had formed between her brows again, but she slid off the horse and then Callum dismounted too. Cassie gazed at him with a perturbed expression. Even though he knew that she had started to avoid contact with him again after a brief interval where she'd actually initiated it, Callum caught her hand in his and slid his fingers through hers. He tugged her close. "You were hurt?"

"Callum—" Cassie tried to pull away, but he caught her around the waist with his other hand.

"Tell me."

Cassie dipped her head, staring at the brooch on Callum's cloak. "No. Not like that. That's not it."

"Then what is it?"

Deep breath. "I ran into several men who mistook me for someone I wasn't."

Anger boiled inside Callum and he deliberately eased the tightness of his hold on her, though he didn't move away even an inch. "And?"

"And I got away but not before two of them had arrows in them," Cassie said. "I heard later that the men in question were nobles. Young, rich, and powerful nobles."

"Son of a b—" Callum bit off the word and ground his teeth. Rich and powerful young men were the same the world over—and apparently, in alternate universes and times, too. "Are you afraid you'll run into them and they'll remember you?"

Cassie actually laughed. "If you were shot by a girl carrying a bow, wouldn't you remember her?"

"Did any die?" Callum said. "Do you know their names?"

"One of them was a Douglass, I think, and a Cunningham from Dumfries," Cassie said. "And no—I told you the truth when I said that I'd never killed anyone, not that I know of anyway."

"Well that's both a surprise and a relief," Callum said. "It wasn't that I didn't fear for you, a woman alone, but ..."

"I've been afraid a lot," Cassie said, "but less so in recent years. I've found my place."

"And now I'm taking you out of it," Callum said. "I'm sorry you got dragged into this."

"You didn't drag me. Don't take that on yourself. I could go home right now." She was still staring at his brooch. "I'm choosing not to."

Callum swallowed hard. She was very close and he really wanted to kiss her. He'd wanted to for days, but he couldn't imagine worse timing than this. Still, he looked down at her—and found that she was already looking up at him. She put her hands on his chest. He had a second to think *what is she doing?* before she rocked him back on his heels by pushing up on her toes and pressing her lips to his.

Callum held still, afraid that by doing anything other than accepting the kiss she offered he would ruin everything. But then she put her arms around his neck and he was able to pull her tight against him.

"So ... are you coming or not?"

James Stewart's drawl came from behind Callum. Cassie and Callum broke the kiss, but Callum didn't let her go and they stood with their foreheads just touching. "Yes," Callum said.

"Glad to hear it," said James.

Hiding a smile, Cassie bit her lip and peered over Callum's shoulder. At that point, Callum had to give in and look also. James sat on his horse, resting his forearm on his saddle horn and laughing.

"I called a rest a half mile up the road," said James. "I mean for the company to continue as soon as I return."

"We were just talking," Callum said.

"Talking," said James. "I'll remember that one."

Cassie kept her face averted, but her shoulders shook as she fought laughter. And then Callum laughed too.

Cassie had *kissed* him!

16

Cassie

It had been at least a year since Cassie had been inside any castle but Mugdock, and to call both Doune and Mugdock castles was to wildly underestimate Doune and exaggerate Mugdock. Mugdock was a fort, of the same stature and utility as a fort out on the plains when the American west was 'wild' (though not, of course, to the Indians who were there first). Twice as large, built in stone to withstand a long siege, Doune was a different matter entirely.

If Cassie had been riding her own horse, she might not have gone inside at all. But short of sliding off the back and fleeing—from Callum, society, everything—she had no choice but to enter it.

She was still shaking inside from when she'd kissed Callum. Although Cassie had been raised in a world where holding hands and kissing were something you did twenty seconds into a first date—sometimes before you'd even figured out whether or not you really liked the guy—that world was far away. To people here, Cassie might as well have a sign on her forehead that said *Callum's*. Compounding her confusion was the fact that *she* had kissed *him*, not the other way around, and effectively taken their relationship to another level. She didn't know what she was going to do with herself or Callum now.

"That's real power in the medieval world," Callum said as he and Cassie watched James drop to the ground and become instantly besieged by advisers and sycophants.

While Walter had ridden to rescue James at the little village, he'd also sent messengers to Stirling Castle and in the cardinal directions, rousing those loyal to the Stewarts. The men he'd called had responded—more than responded—and the bailey was filled with men and horses.

Callum held Cassie's arm as she dismounted, followed suit, and then tossed the horse's reins to the stable boy who ran to take them. Callum clasped Cassie's hand in his. "Don't run away on me."

"How did you know I was thinking about it?"

"I can see it in your face. You look wary again, more so than the whole time we've been together." He looked down at her. "Considering what we've been through since we met, that's saying something."

"They're going to want me to wear a dress," Cassie said.

"True." Callum canted his head as he looked at her. "Is it the dresses themselves that you don't like, or what they symbolize?"

Cassie ground her teeth. That was way too perceptive for him to have said out loud.

"Besides," he said, "today their expectations are their problem, not yours. If you don't want to wear a dress, we'll find some other clothes for you. You can at least be clean."

"I haven't found medieval people to be as tolerant as you have," Cassie said.

"I know," Callum said. "But my patron is the King of England and that means that I—and the woman with me—can do pretty much whatever we damn well please."

A man hurried up to them and bowed. "My name is Amaury, my lord. I'm the steward of Doune. May I guide you to your quarters?"

"That would be delightful," Callum said.

The steward's eyes skated over Cassie and he looked quickly away, though he managed a bow in her direction. "Madam."

Cassie tried to look as if this treatment was normal and stopped herself from shrinking into Callum's side. Instead, she nodded back as magnanimously as she could manage. What did she care what this man or anyone else thought about her relationship with Callum?

The great hall and the lord's private apartments had pride of place on the north side of the castle. Cassie and Callum were taken to a building on the western side that consisted of several wooden structures built against the curtain wall. Storage areas, an adjacent kitchen, and a bath room took up the lower level. Above were guest apartments, one of which the steward gave to Callum, and then he opened the door to an adjacent room for Cassie. She peered inside. Eight pallets covered the floor. This was where the women slept.

Cassie eyed Callum, who still stood in the doorway of his room, watching her. He was the king's emissary, so of course he got his own room. The steward bowed, indicating that he would return to escort them to the bathing room when it was free, and in the meantime would send up food and new clothing. The instant his back was turned, however, Callum stepped towards Cassie, grabbed her elbow, and tugged her into his room.

"What are you doing?" she said.

"I want to talk to you and I certainly can't hang out in your room while I'm doing it," Callum said.

"This is very Indian of you." Cassie closed the door behind her.

"How do you mean?"

"You know what the rule is—unmarried girls should *never* be alone with a man in his room—and you're breaking it anyway when nobody is looking," Cassie said. "I approve."

Callum sat on the bed, sinking into it with a sigh. "It's better to ask forgiveness than permission."

Cassie leaned against the door. "My senior year in high school, my family traveled the pow wow circuit—dancing—so I missed a lot of school. I had straight A's, but the school counselor only cared that I wasn't in class like I was supposed to be."

"She sounds like a bitch," Callum said.

Cassie laughed. "My mother actually called her a *racist bitch*."

"What did you do?"

"Kept dancing," Cassie said. "We didn't make a fuss; we didn't protest or ask to see the principal; we just quietly continued as we'd been."

"That's exactly what you've done here, in the Middle Ages, isn't it?" Callum said. "You've gone your own way and if someone objects to how you dress or talk, you avoid them and keep doing what you're doing."

A gleam appeared in Callum's eye making Cassie almost sorry she'd started this conversation. He was trying to figure her out. And she was letting him. "You should have seen the counselor's face when I won an arts scholarship to college for my traditional dancing and she had to present me with the award."

Callum laughed with Cassie but then sobered. "We all impose our own cultural expectations on other people. When I first came to the Middle Ages, I didn't expect an opportunity to bathe at all. I believed the stories that medieval people lived in squalor."

Cassie scoffed. "They used to say that about Indians too."

"Exactly. On my first day, Meg told me that while it was always difficult for peasants to bathe in winter, the habit of not bathing came about among the nobility during the Spanish Inquisition when nobody wanted to be confused for a secret Jew."

"I hope you didn't ever mention that to Samuel," Cassie said.

"Of course not." Callum flopped full length on his back on the bed with one arm above his head. Cassie walked to the bedside and looked down at him. He took her hand, gazed at her for half a second, and then pulled her down on top of him.

Cassie *whuffed* a laugh as she collapsed onto his chest. Then she wiggled away so she could lie on the bed beside him, though he wrapped both arms around her to keep her close. Cassie capitulated and put her head on his chest. It wasn't like she didn't want to.

"That's better," he said.

"You're insane," Cassie said. "This is improper, even for me."

"I thought you didn't care what people thought?" Callum said.

"I didn't say I didn't care," Cassie said. "I just don't care enough to do what they want."

"That is a conundrum." Callum gave Cassie a quick squeeze. "Still, I can't say I'm currently sorry about any of this."

Cassie closed her eyes, deciding she could live with being this close to him for now. The worry of the last few days seeped out of her body and into the bed covers. Given how soft the mattress was, it had to be made of down. In other words, it was expensive. At least it hadn't rained recently, so they weren't getting it wet.

"I may never move again," Cassie said. "I slept okay last night, but I still feel like I could sleep for a week."

"Fine by me."

A few minutes passed, but to Cassie's surprise, sleep didn't overtake her. "Callum?" Cassie said.

"Yes?" Callum's voice, on the other hand, was thick with impending sleep.

"Do you know what you've never told me?"

Silence.

"Your last name."

"Callum is my last name," he said. "Somewhere along the way, the family dropped the 'Mac'."

Cassie pushed up so she could see his face. His eyes stayed closed.

"That's what I've always gone by," he said. "I never thought about mentioning it."

"So what's your first name, then?"

"Alexander," Callum said.

"You don't look like an Alexander," Cassie said.

"That's why I go by Callum." His arm had relaxed onto the covers, but he lifted one hand and gently rubbed her arm.

Cassie looked around the room, taking in the thick blue drapes around the four-poster bed and the woven tapestry of a stag hunt on the wall. Her mind was whirring away about everything that had happened since she met Callum and didn't want to stop. Somewhere along the way, probably about the time she'd kissed Callum and he'd kissed her back, she'd gotten a second wind. "What happens next?" she said.

"Bath." Callum's eyes were still closed. "Food. Bed." He really was tired if he was speaking in one word sentences.

"That's not what I meant," Cassie said.

"Oh—you mean *what's next for us?* Well, since you kissed me and now have compromised my virtue by coming in here and lying on my bed, I guess you'll have to rescue my reputation by marrying me."

"*Callum,*" Cassie said.

Callum opened one eye. "What? You're not going to do the right thing by me?" He surveyed Cassie for a second and then sat up. He had that *look* about him that told Cassie he didn't feel as flip about marriage as he was trying to sound. Like he actually might be serious.

"Talk to me." He weaved his fingers through hers.

"I meant, *what's going to happen next for Scotland?*" Cassie said. "Our trip to Stirling Castle. The succession and all that."

Callum took in a deep breath, bent back his head to look at the canopy above their heads as if asking God for patience, and then lay back down, pulling her with him. He closed his eyes again. "Given the muster of men and horses at Doune, I'd say we're looking at war. Or something like it."

"Can't anything be done?" Cassie said. "Can nothing stop it?"

"You're the one who said that we were talking about the MacDougalls verses the Bruces," Callum said. "Daddy Bruce is already on his way to Dunstaffnage. We can't do anything about his choices."

"But we can stop this from getting worse." This time when Cassie sat up, she sat cross legged on the bed, resting her elbows on her knees and her chin in her hand. "You're the king's emissary. You speak for him."

"So I've been told," Callum said, "but Kirby is the one he charged with negotiating among the Scottish barons, not me."

"Kirby's gone off with Daddy Bruce," Cassie said. "You're the only one left." She stabbed a finger towards the bailey. "Stewart is marshaling men even as we speak. Who's he planning to march on?"

Callum groaned and levered himself to a sitting position. He hung his head. "I was looking forward to my nap." And then he visibly shook himself and rose to his feet. "Come on. A time traveler's duty is never done."

They found James Stewart in the great hall, conferring with his captains. They huddled around a rough map of Scotland, which was held to the table by stones on the corners. James hadn't had a chance to bathe either.

As Cassie and Callum approached, Callum put his mouth to her ear. "Did you shoot any of these men four years ago?"

Aargh! He'd made her laugh again. "No," Cassie said.

Several of the men raised their eyebrows at Cassie's approach, since she was still dressed as she had been, in shirt, breeches, sweater, and cloak. Their expressions ranged from shock to amusement. Cassie ignored them all. It wasn't as if she wasn't used to it. Most likely (and most annoyingly), it was only the fact that Cassie was clasping Callum's hand that made them treat her politely.

"I'm glad you came, Cassie," said James. "I suspect you know the terrain north of Mugdock better than any of us."

Cassie could have kissed him for being so welcoming, and she felt bad for maligning him in her head. "I don't know about that, my lord, but I will help if I can."

James turned to Callum and bowed. "Doune is honored by your presence, my lord. I am sorry that we haven't welcomed you to Scotland properly before this."

"Thank you," Callum said.

James then introduced some of the men around the table. They included Andrew Moray, who evidently *hadn't* been included in the MacDougall raid, Patrick Dunbar, James's brother-in-law, and a half-dozen other noblemen whose names Cassie instantly forgot.

"What are your intentions?" Callum said.

"We have word that Bruce is hard beset. The MacDougalls didn't run as he'd hoped, and they set an ambush for him on the road to Dunstaffnage," Andrew Moray said. "It is thanks to you that we have so many men already mustered to relieve him."

"How so?" Callum said.

"You sent one of your men, Liam, to Stirling, and he has roused the countryside on our behalf," Andrew said.

Tension Cassie hadn't known she'd been feeling left her shoulders. She was very glad they hadn't sent Liam to his death.

Callum rubbed his chin. "Why doesn't Bruce retreat?"

The rest of the men stared at him in disbelief. "Retreat?" said James, as if he had never heard the word before and didn't understand its meaning.

"You would allow the MacDougalls' act of war to go unchallenged?" Andrew said. "You of all people cannot condone what they've done."

"I don't," Callum said. "And yet, you plot as if your country has no leaders. What of the Guardians? Shouldn't it be they who bring the MacDougalls to justice?" It was essentially what he'd said to Daddy Bruce a few days ago.

"The Black Comyn is one of those Guardians," Andrew said. "Bruce burned him out. How likely is it that he will abandon his allies and work with Lord Stewart?"

"You won't know until you ask," Callum said, "and surely taking a moment to convene the Guardians—not to mention Parliament—is better than all-out war. The MacDougalls aren't going anywhere."

James gritted his teeth. "You don't know what you're saying, my lord—"

"Up to a point, it is understandable that Bruce took matters into his own hands," Callum said, "but he loses the moral high ground if he pursues a vendetta against the supporters of Balliol. Better to back down now than for the father to lose the kingship because the son acted too hastily."

Cassie wasn't sure that these medieval men would know what a moral high ground was, but it involved military imagery, and Callum's tongue-lashing had several men chewing on their lower lips.

"I would add that King David will surely see it that way," Callum said.

James ran his tongue around his teeth while Callum kept his expression calm. James glanced at his men, several of whom looked down at their feet. Andrew Moray continued to glare defiantly, but after he and James exchanged a long look, Andrew canted his head as if to say *okay*.

James took in a deep breath and let it out. "I see the wisdom in your suggestion, my lord. Bishop Fraser, who holds Stirling, may well share your view. As you know, the other Guardians and Parliament were summoned before any of these events took place. They are already gathering at Stirling."

James turned to Patrick Dunbar. "Will you ride to Bruce and convince him to back down from this fight? He can't win with the men he has. Tell him that the Stewarts support him, but he must come to Stirling and seek justice under the law."

"What if the MacDougalls follow?" Andrew said.

"Then they will get the war they're looking for," said James.

Cassie eased out a sigh. She had pushed Callum to assert his authority as a representative of King David. Even though he had no actual power here, the weight of England was behind him. In practice, that was no small thing, even if many of these barons despised the notion that the King of England was involved in their internal disputes at all. Callum, for his part, had risen to the occasion.

James's face was tight with tension. "What of King David? Will he interfere?"

"Not if he doesn't have to," Callum said. "I think you're doing the right thing—"

The door to the hall slammed open and one of James's men strode into the room, followed by a second man in a travel-stained cloak and mud-spattered boots. The second man strode past the first and went down on one knee before James. "My lord, I have news."

"Rise," said James.

The man stood. "I have just come from Stirling Castle. King David of England received word of the ambush of his men and is even now preparing to leave London with an army. He's coming to us, my lord."

James turned his gaze on Callum.

"No one should have assumed he would take the death of his men lightly," Callum said.

It was a desirable trait in a leader, even if it meant one more headache for James. An angry King of England was not what he wanted at this time, especially one with his own claim to the Scottish throne.

"Damn pigeons," said James.

"It was a feat for your man to ride here from London in five days," Cassie said, trying to find the silver lining for James.

"What the King of England chooses to do or not do is out of our control," Andrew said. "It's four hundred miles from London to Edinburgh. It will take him weeks to get here with an army."

"Then we have time to straighten out this mess before he even reaches York." James spun on his heel and glared at the noblemen who gathered around the table, all of whom gazed back at him with firm jaws and new resolve. "We ride for Stirling Castle within the hour."

17

Callum

"You haven't told anyone but James about Bishop Kirby," Cassie said.

"I know," Callum said, "but I think we're better off not talking openly about what Kirby has done just yet. Given that he's far away with Bruce, he's not our concern right now."

"He might be if he's telling everyone he encounters that John Balliol conspired with the MacDougalls," Cassie said.

"We have a little time, I think, before that rumor becomes widespread," Callum said. "If I can send a message to King David, maybe he'll have a few words of wisdom for me as to how to proceed from here."

Callum hoped that Rhodri, David's man in Stirling, would make himself known once they arrived at the castle and spare Callum the trouble of seeking him out. It would have been Rhodri who sent the pigeon informing David of the ambush—and of Callum's death. David needed to know of Kirby's perfidy as soon as possible and that Callum himself was alive and still working for him.

Located five miles south of Doune, Stirling Castle sprawled across the top of a crag in splendid medieval fashion and sat above the farthest downstream crossing of the River Forth before it flowed into the Firth. If Cassie's eyes were big when they'd ridden into Doune, they were saucer-like at the sight of Stirling. The company came to the castle from the north as the early evening sun shone from the west, lighting up the rock on the west side of the river. Given Cassie's silence on the topic of *them* as a couple, even more than at Doune, Callum felt a little sick at the thought that she would turn around the second they hit the gatehouse and fly back the way they'd come.

"I am very far from home," Cassie said, showing Callum that he'd read her thoughts correctly. "I have often wondered how different our world would have been if my people had built castles."

"From what I understand, they had different priorities," Callum said.

"Conquest not being at the top of the list, you mean?" she said. "Yes, you're right. But still, if the Incas could do it, why not the Umatilla?"

"Maybe they're doing it right now in this world," Callum said.

"I hadn't thought of that," Cassie said. "I hiked to the west coast once, you know, so I could have a look at the sea. I wondered at the time what it would take for me to reach America."

"A big boat," Callum said, making Cassie laugh. That got them inside the outer curtain wall, but as they came to a halt amidst a hundred other men, Cassie went very quiet.

"What is it?"

"One of them is here."

"One of the men who attacked you?" Callum said, going still himself. "Where?"

"Over there. By the blacksmith works." Cassie ducked behind Callum, though with that five-foot bow on her back, if the man looked her way, he would see her.

"Just dismount," Callum said. "If we stay calm, there's a good chance he won't notice us. Even if he does, you're with me. Everything's going to be fine." With Cassie's hand in his, Callum headed across the courtyard to the keep. He looked straight ahead and made sure he didn't make eye contact with anyone but James, who had made it to the top step already and stood there with another man, waiting for them.

"My lord Shrewsbury." As Callum reached him, James Stewart held out a hand to him. "May I introduce Bishop Fraser."

"Welcome to Stirling Castle," Fraser said.

Callum bent his head slightly in Fraser's direction. "Thank you."

James gestured that Cassie and Callum should precede him into the main hall.

"Callum," Cassie said, in something of the same voice she'd used when he'd mentioned marriage, "Why did James just call you 'Shrewsbury'?"

Callum and Cassie had resolved to use their English only when they were alone, so she'd spoken in Gaelic. Thus James, who was walking a pace behind them, overheard her question. "My lord, in all this time you haven't told her who you are?"

Cassie came to a halt, forcing Callum to stop too. "It's not important, Cassie."

"Not important?" said James with disbelieving laughter, looking from Callum to Cassie. "My dear Cassie, Lord Callum is the Earl of Shrewsbury."

Cassie kept her face perfectly still as she turned on Callum and said without expression or inflection, "Really."

"The blame lies with me as well," said James, a low chuckle still evident in his voice. "I didn't include his title when I introduced him to my counselors at Doune. I failed in my duty."

"As I said, it isn't important." Callum took Cassie's arm to escort her, but he glanced at her as they walked towards their rooms, wary now. It was so hard to read her sometimes.

Fortunately, Cassie didn't give him the silent treatment, even if he might have deserved it. "I was wondering about all the *my lording* everyone always did around you. Why didn't you say something?"

"I didn't want you to think I was trying to impress you," Callum said. "You knew I was a knight and King David's representative. That seemed enough to be going on with."

As before, Callum got his own room, whereas Cassie had to lodge with other women further down the corridor. James stopped when they reached Callum's door. "My lord Callum, back in the bailey, I noticed that the Cunningham boy, Gerard, caught your attention. Has he offended you in some way?"

James was interested in everything. Callum wasn't sure what to tell him, but Cassie spoke up. "I shot him once."

A grin split James's face. "Did you, now?"

"I'd rather avoid him if I could," she said.

"He's a spoiled pup," said James, but then sobered. "If he hurt you, Cassie—"

"He didn't," she said. "It was a long time ago and ended with both of us being equally scared of each other."

"I'll keep an eye on him," said James.

"Is Gerard's father here?" Callum said. "Should I speak to him?"

James pursed his lips. "I would hope there'd be no need. Let me feel him out first."

James bowed and departed. Cassie eyed Callum, her face set.

"You're mad at me," Callum said.

"No," she said. "I'm not at all mad at *you*." Callum spent a silent ten seconds trying to figure out what she meant by that, but then she enlightened him. "I don't like needing someone to protect me."

Callum hovered in the doorway, trying to think of what to say. Women had little power here, no matter how smart or capable they might be. Many medieval men saw women as good for sex and heirs, and if by chance a woman inherited land, she could enforce her will only through the actions of men. Callum could see why it might make Cassie mad.

"I want to go home," Cassie said, and then she gave him a rueful smile. "To my cabin, that is."

"I'll make sure you get back there if that's what you want in the end," Callum said. "I promise."

But in promising to do what she might not be able to do for herself, Callum suspected he'd only made her anger worse.

Callum was given the opportunity to bathe and got in a good hour-long power nap while Cassie was prodded into a complete makeover elsewhere in the castle. When he was finally reunited with her again, Cassie didn't express resentment about the dress James had found for her or the elaborate way the maidservant had arranged her hair. Callum wasn't so naïve that he thought she'd somehow accepted the reality of life in the castle, but he hoped that she could tolerate it long enough to get through the next week. He didn't want her to be the object of gossip and speculation, nor a target. And—holy hell—she was beautiful.

"You're smiling," she said, as he walked her down the steps that led to the great hall. "Why?"

"Because the most gorgeous woman in all of Scotland is on my arm," Callum said.

Cassie's lips pinched, but not in anger. She was holding back a laugh. "You see what you want to see."

"No doubt—" Callum cut off his words when they both stopped short in the entrance to the great hall. Callum felt his own lips twitching. Cassie could deny what he saw all she wanted, but she looked unlike any other woman in the castle, as different from them as a wild rose amidst a field of tulips. Both could be beautiful, but only one turned the head of every man in the room. With Cassie's particular coloring and bone structure, her beauty was unique. Nobody in all of Europe had her genes.

Callum should have known there was going to be trouble, however. She was gracious to everyone who spoke to her or came to greet her, but her laughter was hollow. Callum was required to spend most of the meal speaking to William Fraser, who sat between him and James, while James related in great detail all that had happened over the last week, including—finally—Kirby's treachery.

As the meal drew to a close, William excused himself and James turned to speak to the man on his other side. Soon he was deep in conversation. At last, Callum could focus on Cassie. She stared down at the wine in her cup without drinking it. As Callum thought back over the last hours, he realized she'd drunk very little and eaten only a few bites of her food.

"What is it, Cassie?"

She looked up at him. Callum was afraid she'd be near to tears, but her eyes were clear. "You know what it is."

"The meal?" Callum said. "The dress?"

"The expectations," Cassie said.

Callum tsked through his teeth, irritated for the first time that she couldn't play along, even for one night. "What kind of world did you live in back in the twenty-first century that you were able to be yourself all the time?"

Cassie laughed without humor. "Is that what you think? That's not it at all. Quite the opposite. I couldn't be myself there—not ever. Growing up as I did in my grandfather's house, I lived with expectations about language and dress, about family and career, expectations that were impossible to meet most of the time. And don't get me started on the infighting and gossip within the Tribe. But still, outside in the world—" she gestured to the hall at large, but she didn't mean the people here, but those back at home, "—I never faced discrimination because I was part Indian, but nobody understood those expectations either, or where I came from or why I made the choices I did. Everybody just wants you to conform, no matter where you live ..." She looked down at her plate.

Callum leaned in. "Don't you think I understand that, Cassie? We all live inside our own heads most of the time. I came back from Afghanistan to a world that has no place for someone who's most comfortable with a rifle in his hands, and yet can't handle it if his hands don't smell exactly right." Callum touched Cassie's shoulder and then dropped his hand because he knew she didn't want him to touch her. "I had nightmares about the war every night until this week. I haven't had a single one since I met you."

"It could be because we've hardly slept," Cassie said.

Callum had to smile. "I grant you that."

To Callum's left, James had risen to his feet and Callum caught a gesture out of the corner of his eye that meant he wanted Callum's attention. "Earl Callum."

Reluctantly, Callum turned away from Cassie to look up at James.

"If it pleases you, Bishop Fraser feels we must meet in council now," said James. "Both John Balliol and the Black Comyn have arrived."

This was going to be a fun meeting. "Of course," Callum said. "Just a moment—" He turned back to Cassie.

"I know. You have to go," she said, "though I imagine sitting in a meeting with men at each other's throats has to be your least favorite thing on the planet to do."

"I'd rather be on the wrong end of an ambush." Callum leaned in and kissed Cassie's temple. "I know I'd rather be with you."

Though Cassie gave Callum a quick smile, it didn't reach her eyes. As Callum stepped off the dais with James, he turned to look at Cassie one more time. She had already left the table, however, and was just disappearing through a door on the other side of the hall.

18

Cassie

Cassie was ready to leave, with or without saying goodbye to Callum, even if it meant behaving like Maria in that horrible scene from the *Sound of Music* after which her mother had always made her go to bed because the movie was so freaking long. Except that no duchess was telling Cassie lies to make her leave. She was doing that all by herself. It would be dishonorable to go, and hurtful, but Callum couldn't see how wrong this all was.

Cassie saw what was in his eyes when he looked at her. They'd known each other for a week, and she knew what she saw in him because she felt the same as he did. How could they not, after what they'd been through? But he didn't really know her if he didn't see that she couldn't *do* this; she couldn't be a medieval wife; she couldn't be the Earl of Shrewsbury's wife, for heaven's sake!

Back at the village, Callum had told Cassie how he felt about this life, and she had talked about her feelings. But the truth was, despite his issues, Callum handled being in the Middle Ages better than she did. He actually thought she could just *adapt*.

Cassie's ire carried her out of the hall and up to her room. It started to wane, however, when she realized that her clothes hadn't returned from the laundry (and might never do so) and that she still hadn't restocked her quiver. She could at least do that and pretend that she had something real to occupy her time instead of simply looking pretty on Callum's arm. Callum would be gone for hours meeting with the other men, determining the course of Scotland's future.

And that probably would have sounded as sour spoken out loud as it did in her head. Poor Callum, though. The deep circles under his eyes were going to become permanent if he couldn't rest in a real bed soon.

Cassie swung her fine new cloak around her shoulders and unsnapped her quiver from her backpack. She held the quiver in one hand and her bow in the other. Somehow, she couldn't leave the bow behind, even for the time it would take to find the armory and fill her quiver. If she didn't get her old cloak back, she'd have to cut slits in this one so she could wear her pack on her back as before.

Cassie found her way to the inner bailey of the castle, but when she reached it, she came to a halt at the sheer number of men in front of her. Not only the Black Comyn and John Balliol, but the Scottish parliament—a council of bishops, earls, and minor lairds from all over Scotland—had come to Stirling. At the same time, she was glad of their presence because it would be easy to get lost in the crowd.

It was full dark by now, and Cassie threaded her way to the outer bailey by the light of fifty torches. The armory lay by the outer gatehouse. The second bailey was even more crowded than the first, what with so many retainers and hangers-on who needed a place to sleep tonight.

Then a drawling voice said, "Well, well ... what do we have here?"

Cassie felt herself spun around, her wrists clamped so tightly she had to drop her bow and quiver. The Cunningham boy, Gerard, buttressed by two of his friends, grinned at her as he pressed her to the stone wall of the armory.

Cassie looked past him, searching for anyone she knew. Nobody paid them the least attention. Cassie tried to keep herself composed, even as she struggled to free her wrists. "What do you want?"

"You know what I want." Gerard hauled her around the corner to a narrow space between the armory and the blacksmith's works. The alley smelled of wet hay and manure. And fear.

Cassie drove her knee towards Gerard's groin, but one of his friends was quicker and jammed his leg between her and Gerard, putting the full weight of his body into her side. "Now, now," Gerard said. "We can't have that."

Real panic rose in Cassie now, along with a blinding rage that this could be happening to her. She wouldn't have thought it possible for her to be so alone in such a crowd. But if anyone had seen the men grab her, they might have thought nothing of it. Everywhere men went, whores followed. Cassie kept up her struggles, but even though Gerard was the same height as she, he was stronger and had two friends to assist him.

"Help—!"

Gerard cut off Cassie's cry with a hand clapped over her mouth. "Let's get her under cover—"

And then suddenly Gerard was grabbed from behind and thrown—literally thrown—ten feet towards the blacksmith's works. The man to Cassie's right took a gloved fist in the face, and because the second friend was backing away, not looking at her, Cassie was able to stab at his knee with her foot. Callum stepped in to finish him off with an uppercut to the jaw.

"My God, Cassie!" Callum pulled her to him and wrapped his arms around her so tightly she almost couldn't breathe, even as her breath came in gasps.

"Is there a problem, my lord?" One of James's soldiers came hurrying up.

Callum loosened his grip on Cassie enough to turn to the man. "Do you know who I am?"

"The Earl of Shrewsbury, sir."

"These men were assaulting my betrothed. I want them locked up until Lord James decides what to do with them."

"Y-y-yes, my lord!" If the man had been a modern solider, he would have saluted. As it was, he waved an arm at four members of the garrison who'd followed him. Callum urged Cassie back around the corner and into the bailey. He held her head between his hands and kissed both eyes, her cheeks, and then her lips. "What could have happened—"

Cassie started to shake with delayed shock. Callum held her in a full embrace, rubbing at her back and arms to warm her. Cassie's heartbeat began to slow. "I'm okay, Callum."

"I'm not," he said. "And you might not have been."

Which was only too true.

"Let's get you out of here." Still with his arm around her, Callum turned to head back across the bailey.

"Just a second, Callum." Cassie shrugged out of his arm so she could pick up her fallen bow and quiver.

Callum stared at the weapon. "Christ, Cassie! What were you thinking?"

Cassie clutched the cloth of his tunic at his breastbone. She found that she couldn't speak, couldn't get mad at him like he was mad at her.

Callum glared at Cassie. She could feel the force of his gaze even before she lifted her head to look at him. "You were running away. Away from me."

"I actually wasn't, Callum. But you have to know that what ... almost happened has shown me again how much I hate this world and what I have to be to fit in it. That I needed you to save me ..."

"I didn't save you from those men because you're a woman," Callum said. "If three men had jumped me, I would've needed saving too!"

"Yeah, but—"

Callum cut her off. "Just because you need a little help once in a while doesn't make you a lesser person. Believe me, that wasn't what was going through my head when I saw those men surrounding you. David Beckham never won a game all by himself. You're good at some things and I'm good at some things. Why can't we be good at them together?" He wiggled the tip of Cassie's bow, which she held with the quiver in her other hand. It was probably how Gerard and his friends had noticed her in the first place.

"How'd you end up in the bailey?" Cassie said. "Weren't you supposed to be in a meeting?"

"The council adjourned for the night," Callum said. "I might have met you before you left your room, but as I left the hall, David's pigeon man at Stirling, Rhodri, came to find me. After I sent him off with a message for David, I again intended to return to my room, but before I could, I saw Gerard leaving the inner bailey. I followed him. Cassie, why—?" Callum broke off and looked away from her, as if he couldn't bear to look at her.

"I won't lie. I was thinking about leaving," Cassie said. "I hadn't yet decided to. I wanted to restock my quiver."

Callum's brows drew together, but his gaze wasn't directed at her. He looked over her shoulder, towards the entrance to the armory.

"What is it?" Cassie said.

"You need arrows. I agree that we should do something about that. Come with me." He moved towards the steps that led up to the building behind them.

"You've lost me," Cassie said, taking two steps for every one of his. "What are we doing?"

"I could have sworn I just saw Red Comyn and ... well ... Kirby enter the armory."

"Really?" Cassie said. "If it is Kirby, what are you going to say to him? Are you going to confront him?"

Callum shook his head. "I can't. I promised James that I wouldn't until he could speak to the other Guardians. I certainly wouldn't do it on my own—not until we've ferreted out more of his plan. As James pointed out, Kirby is a bishop and England's representative to Scotland, and if I expose him, I call David's power and authority—and wisdom—into question."

"James is too cautious," Cassie said. "Kirby is responsible for the death of dozens of men, whatever his overall plan might be."

"James knows the nobility of Scotland better than I do, and because of that—and because I think James is a good man—I'm willing to give him the benefit of the doubt, though what he'll say when Kirby shows up in the council chamber, I don't know."

"You have to get to James first," Cassie said.

Callum nodded. "For now, I will be polite to Kirby and lie through my teeth if I have to. We don't need him punished today. I know where to find him when the time comes. I'd rather lull him into a sense of complacency."

"You like it when people underestimate you, don't you?" Cassie said.

Callum just looked down at her and took her hand without replying. They went up the steps and through the doorway, but the barracks were dark. With no light switch to flip, the torchlight coming through the open door was their only light. Callum turned on his heel, looked outside, and then back into the main room where the armor and weapons were kept. "Huh." A stairway went up to his left, but no sound came from the floor above.

"Where did they go?" Cassie said.

"Maybe I was hallucinating," Callum said. "I'm tired enough. We can at least get those arrows while we're here."

An unlit candle rested in a holder on a barrel by the door. Cassie lit it with the fire steel left beside it and brought it with her, weaving among the storage crates after Callum. In a far corner near an open door into another room, he bent over a barrel containing a stockpile of arrows. Cassie was glad they had something to distract them from what had happened to her. It was a relief to talk about casual things, even if what was going on between them was fast becoming the elephant in the room.

"This is a pretty meager collection," Callum said. "The MacDougalls and Bruces had archers among them. Why aren't there more arrows here?"

"Archery takes years of practice and good arrows aren't something just anyone can make," Cassie said. "We saw that at Duncraggan. Nobles use swords, and if the men they recruit don't know how to shoot—"

"You end up with a single barrel as Stirling Castle's entire stash of arrows," Callum said.

Cassie gazed with him at the arrows he'd found—a hundred at most. Two bows leaned against the wall. She glanced around. In contrast, an entire wall was given over to spears and poleaxes. Swords, axes, helmets, and armor of various sizes and kinds were stacked in trunks or lined the walls. "Let's hope Stirling Castle doesn't have to defend itself any time soon. It would be in trouble," she said.

"They haven't had a king here for a long time. William Fraser's a bishop and probably doesn't think about having to defend Stirling or about war at all, other than how to avoid a fight." Callum reached into the barrel, pulled out a handful of arrows, and presented them to Cassie.

"Let's talk in here."

Cassie swung around at the voice in the same instant that Callum blew out her candle, tugged on her arm, and whispered, "This way."

They ducked behind the door to the adjacent room. "Is it—?"

"Red and Kirby, yes," Callum said. The two men stood three feet from the front door, thirty feet from Cassie and Callum.

"What is our position?" Kirby said.

"Better than it was, but not good enough," Red said. "Lord Callum has not revealed himself sufficiently for me to judge what he plans, though I feel certain that the positions of both Bruce and Balliol have been weakened."

"For all that he's a jumped-up earl, Lord Callum is not a fool," Kirby said. "When did he arrive at Stirling?"

"Today. He's already met with the other lords in the council chamber," Red said. "I would have thought you would have been there too."

"I needed to determine the lay of the land, first. I owe Robbie Bruce that much," Kirby said.

"Is that regret I hear in your voice?" Red said. "What we do, we do for the good of Scotland."

"I have come to admire the boy and his father," Kirby said. "I regret the deaths of Robert Bruce and Alexander MacDougall, even if they were necessary."

Cassie gasped and then immediately clamped a hand over her mouth, but it was too late. They'd heard her.

Kirby swung around to peer towards the back of the room. "Who's there?"

Cassie stepped into the room, already pulling an arrow from her quiver. Callum was there too, however, shaking his head *no* and pressing down on her arm so she'd lower her bow. Cassie gritted her teeth but assented as Callum strode towards Red and Kirby, who held up his lantern so he could see further into the room.

"My lord Callum!" both men spoke in unison, followed by a low bow.

"Save it," Callum said. "I overheard you speaking of Bruce and MacDougall. They're dead?"

"They were both wounded in battle, my lord," Kirby said. "I have been given to understand that neither can survive."

"And it had nothing to do with you," Cassie said, under her breath, in American English.

"What was that?" Kirby peered past Callum.

Cassie came forward into the flickering light, which was enough to illumine everyone's faces. Callum rubbed his chin. He had said that he wasn't ready to accuse Kirby of treason, and Cassie could see the merit in saving what they knew until both Callum and Kirby could stand before King David and tell him the whole of it. But she didn't have to like it.

"Why have you come, Kirby?" Callum said. "I thought you'd thrown in your lot with the Bruces."

"I come to Stirling on behalf of Robbie Bruce," Kirby said. "He fears retaliation for his father's actions against the Comyns. He asks for peace and forgiveness for all parties, including the MacDougalls, though they do not deserve it."

"What of John Graham?" Cassie said.

"Who?" Kirby said.

"Patrick Graham's son," Callum said. "He was taken captive along with James Stewart and my friend, Samuel."

Kirby and Red exchanged a glance and both shook their heads. "I don't know anything about him," Kirby said. "He was not in our party on the road to Stirling."

"I know that," Callum said. "What would MacDougall have wanted with him?"

"Why would I know anything about how Alexander MacDougall thinks?" Kirby said. "I have never met the man."

Kirby kept his eyes wide and they didn't skate away. He was doing everything in his power to put on a mantle of innocence. Didn't he realize that Callum and Cassie had overheard the earlier part of his conversation with Red? Didn't he realize that they knew his story about the ambush was full of holes big enough to drive a truck—or perhaps a carriage—through?

Cassie had dozens of questions she would have asked him, but Callum stepped past Kirby and Red and looked out the door of the armory. As they'd been speaking, a great tumult of noise had arisen in the bailey.

"What is it, Callum?" Cassie said.

Callum turned back to Kirby. "Now that you are here, it's time you did your job. Bring your message from Robbie to the Guardians."

Kirby gazed stonily at Callum. "I have done nothing to betray King David's trust."

Whatever, Cassie felt like saying, but again, didn't.

"If you achieve what we set out to do," Callum said, "I will put in a good word for you with the king. He might just name you Archbishop of Canterbury when Peckham dies. It's what you want, isn't it?"

Kirby maintained his poker face, but from Red's expression, Callum had gotten it exactly right. Callum didn't wait for Kirby's answer. He tipped his head towards the door, asking without words for Cassie to leave the armory with him. Cassie slid past Red and Kirby and followed Callum outside.

"Something's happened," Callum said.

Samuel stood underneath the inner gatehouse, looking this way and that. At Callum's raised hand, he raised his own and then steered his way across the bailey. "You said to come find you if I had news," Samuel said. "Well, I do."

"Is it the council or—"

"Erik of Norway has come. He has sailed his fleet up the River Forth and his army is marching on Stirling Castle as we speak."

19

Callum

"That's just what we need." Callum headed under the inner gatehouse to the keep, holding Cassie's hand, with Samuel hustling to keep up.

"Maybe it is, at that," Cassie said.

"What do you mean, Cassie?" Callum said.

She tugged him to a stop at the top of the steps to the keep. "None of the Scots will take kindly to Erik of Norway's attempt to grab the throne by force. Along with their hatred of England and fear of King David, it is one of the few causes that could unite them."

"She's right, my lord," Samuel said. "They just need that fact pointed out to them."

Callum turned around and saw Kirby and Red crossing the bailey, thirty paces behind them. He lifted a hand and made a 'come here' motion at Kirby. The man was cowed enough to quicken his pace. "Yes, my lord?"

"I am counting on you to be the voice of reason," Callum said. "Erik of Norway has come, and all these bickering Scots need to pull themselves together and throw him back into the sea. I want you to be the one to say it."

Kirby gazed at Callum for a count of five and then nodded. "I would argue that it would be better coming from you, but I appreciate your confidence in me."

Callum tipped his head in the direction of the council chamber adjacent to the great hall. The acrimony in the room was such that shouts could be heard through the closed door. Kirby marched towards the noise, Red in his wake.

"Why are you trusting him?" Cassie said.

"I'm not," Callum said. "I don't trust him at all."

"But—"

"Look," Callum said. "I can't control Kirby, but I can keep him busy. Whatever his grand plan, Erik of Norway is in the way. It is in Kirby's best interests to do as I ask."

"I gather Bishop Fraser and James didn't reveal everything yet?" Cassie said.

"No, not yet," Callum said.

"So, the other barons might actually listen to Kirby," Cassie said. "You and James were right to delay exposing him."

Callum eyed Cassie, unsure whether her tone was approving of him or disappointed that she'd been wrong. "Besides, getting these noblemen to agree to anything is going to take days," Callum said. "I hate meetings and the three of us have more important things to do."

"Excuse me, my lord?" Samuel had been staying close, waiting for instructions.

"Saddle up the horses," Callum said. "We're leaving immediately."

"We're going to flee Stirling before the fight?" Samuel was shocked.

"Of course not," Callum said. "We're going to find the Grahams and the MacDougalls and whoever else doesn't want to see Erik of Norway as king of Scotland and get them to march together to Stirling."

Cassie openly laughed. "That's brilliant. Knowing the MacDougalls, they're already halfway here."

"Exactly." Callum pointed a finger at her. "I'll be right back. Stay here."

"Yes, sir," Cassie said, though she smiled as she said it.

Even with midnight approaching, James Stewart had seen the merit in what Callum was suggesting and had gathered a mixed company of men to ride with them. Before they left, Callum related to James what he and Cassie had witnessed in the armory and the apparent alliance between Kirby and Red. James promised to keep an eye on both men. With Erik of Norway about to surround Stirling, they weren't going anywhere.

Callum rode with Cassie, who'd rescued her breeches from the laundry. Samuel came too, along with a dozen noblemen representing half of the competing interests in Scotland, and Andrew Moray who joined them at his own request. Callum was pleased that he'd chosen to come. Even if the timeline in this world was playing out a bit differently, the man had a lot of history behind him. A companion of William Wallace, he had played a pivotal role in the Scottish wars for independence against King Edward after 1300.

It took nearly an hour to get everyone together, by which time Callum was worried that they were too late to get out of Stirling before Erik surrounded it. At last, the horses pounded down the road as fast as they could go, winding around the crag upon which Stirling Castle was built. Callum's heart was in his throat the whole time.

When they reached the valley floor, they met riders coming the other way, seeking the safety of Stirling. "They're almost upon us!" the lead scout said. "You must turn back!"

"Not tonight," Callum said.

"But my lord—!"

"Tell James Stewart that we got through," Callum said.

"Yes, my lord." Then the riders were past them, racing up the road to the castle.

Callum's company continued on. The valley Stirling Castle overlooked stretched west and south from the crag while the River Forth wound southeast in a sinuous curve. Looking to his left, Callum could see a swath of light along the river. He imagined that he could hear the Norwegians' marching feet. Erik's army didn't have horses, however, or at least not many, and by the time Callum's company had ridden a mile and a half from Stirling, they'd left the army and the river in the distance. They'd escaped in time.

Callum glanced at Andrew, who nodded. The horses slowed as they turned onto the high road that would take them west to Glasgow—the same road upon which the MacDougalls had ambushed Callum's company nearly six days ago.

Cassie's head was down. "I really thought I was going to get to sleep tonight."

Callum groaned. "Don't remind me how tired I am."

"Is there any chance of sleep occurring again in this lifetime?" Cassie said.

"Actually, there is," Callum said. "We needed to get out of Stirling before the Norwegians trapped us inside, but the plan is to ride to Kilsyth, which is less than ten miles from Stirling, and sleep there."

"Thank God for that," Cassie said.

"James felt—and I agreed—that it was better not to attempt to travel through the Highlands in the dark. This time, we want the MacDougalls to see us coming."

"I'm glad we got out, but I'm worried for those inside Stirling," Cassie said.

"I am too, but Erik won't begin the assault tonight," Callum said. "He'll talk first, and James said he would stall him for as long as he can with platitudes and promises he doesn't intend to keep."

"Erik wants the throne but will take it without bloodshed if he can," Andrew said, riding on the other side of Callum. "Half the nobility of Scotland is in Stirling Castle tonight. In marching on

Stirling, Erik proclaims both his right and his power, but at the same time, he risks all in a single move. Therein lies both Erik's hope and his fear."

"What do you mean?" Cassie said.

"Erik can't rule Scotland without the consent of the barons," Andrew said. "He needs us cowed, but not dead and not desperate."

"I think it's already too late for anything but desperate," Cassie said.

Two hours later, at some point past midnight which Callum didn't care to calculate, they reached Kilsyth and entered the rudimentary castle that guarded the road. It consisted of a single tower surrounded by a curtain wall. Tonight, everyone would sleep on the floor of the hall, high and low alike. Callum put Cassie's pallet between his and the wall, and Samuel lay crosswise at their heads. Though Samuel started snoring immediately, Cassie and Callum lay looking at each other, their fingers barely touching under a blanket while they waited for the room to settle down.

"I've been thinking, Callum."

Whenever Cassie started thinking, Callum started worrying. But he just nodded.

"I've been thinking that I love you."

It was like she'd punched Callum in the gut. He couldn't breathe—couldn't get enough air to make any kind of response. At the same time, if his men weren't asleep around him, he would have found the wherewithal to sit up and cheer.

Then she spoke again. "But I'm also thinking that love isn't going to be enough for us. You only like me because I'm the first single time traveler you've met. You don't know anything about me, really, and I can't imagine I'm going to be good for you in the long run. Just because you love someone doesn't mean you should marry them."

Callum went from joy to desolation in the space of four sentences. A million things passed through his head, but all he said was, "You're wrong, Cassie. I need you to give me—and us—a chance."

She slowly untangled her hands from his. "I don't think so. I've never been one to lie to myself, and I just don't see where our two very different worlds can ever intersect."

"They're not so different and they intersect in the middle," Callum said.

"But they don't. We worked well together almost this whole time, up until we got to Stirling Castle. But Stirling Castle is the world you live in. I don't see how we can be partners there." Cassie bit her lip and shook her head. "I'm not as good a person as you are, Callum. When this is over, I need to go home and you need to go back to London, or to wherever David sends you next, and make this world a better place."

"Cassie—don't be this way. I love you too."

She shook her head again. "You'll find someone else. Someone who will be the person you need her to be. I can't—I just can't—" Cassie rolled over to face the wall without finishing the thought.

Maybe in their old world, Callum wouldn't have pressed her—he'd only known her for a week, after all—but this was the rest of their lives they were talking about. This could be the only chance at love either of them were going to get. Cassie was still giving Callum the cold shoulder, but he scooted closer and put his arm around her. What he had to say had to be said up close.

"I don't know where you got the idea that I wanted a medieval wife," Callum said. "I don't. I don't expect you to be one, even if you could. I don't expect you to change a single thing about yourself."

"You want me to leave the mountains for you," Cassie said.

Callum closed his eyes. She'd hit upon the one thing he was asking her to change. "I can't stay in the Highlands, Cassie."

"And I can't leave."

Cassie refused to talk to Callum about it again. He stayed close to her as she fell asleep, and even managed a few hours of sleep himself, though his heart was heavy.

Because their mission was urgent, they rose early, breakfasted quickly, and left Kilsyth two hours after dawn. Although Cassie rode near Callum as they headed up the river valley to Mugdock, she remained quiet. Callum and Andrew had a quick debate about which path to take and in the end determined that a visit to Patrick Graham on the way to wherever the MacDougalls were fighting the Bruces was in order.

While the morning had dawned clear, once the company left the main road for the smaller track heading north, a swift mist came down from the mountains and settled on their path. If others in the company hadn't known the way—Cassie among them—Callum would have gotten lost immediately.

"Whatever has happened, sir?" Samuel pulled in close to Callum's left side, his eyes on Cassie, who rode ten yards ahead near the front of the company. "When did you two have time to quarrel?"

Callum glanced at Samuel, surprised that he would bring up such a delicate subject—and lied through his teeth. "We didn't quarrel. We're fine." Callum eyed Cassie's straight back. She was giving nothing away. Callum feared that her words of last night would become entrenched in her mind and no amount of pleading on his part would change them.

Callum had experience with keeping people he cared about at arm's length. Who knew better than he about the perils of opening up? It wasn't even the possibility of getting hurt that made him unapproachable. It was the knowledge that what was going on inside his head was so horrific, if those he loved knew what he was really like, they would turn away from him. It was better—and easier—to push them away first. But for the first time since the war, he didn't feel that way. He wanted to share himself with Cassie.

Samuel snorted. "You may be, but she's not."

"Let it go, Samuel. She'll come around." Callum paused. "I hope."

Mist or no mist, they found their way to Mugdock unmolested and circled to the north of the loch, through the site where Daddy Bruce and his men had camped a few days before. The Bruce forces had left behind burned circles from their campfires and trampled grass—and a castle in far worse shape than when they'd found it.

Much of the palisade had burned, though repairs had already begun. Not a single intact roof peeked over the curtain wall. If the castle looked this bad from the outside, the interior damage must be considerable. Even though the only banner that the company carried was a white flag, nobody came out to greet them. Callum couldn't blame Lord Patrick for his anger.

Cassie and Callum dismounted just outside of arrow range, and Callum waved at the rest of the company to stay astride. "Wait."

"My lord," Andrew Moray said, "this is foolish. He may be hostile."

"He may," Callum said, "but I trust him not to shoot first and ask questions later." Callum reached for the pole upon which the white flag hung, lifeless in the fog with no breeze to fill it.

Cassie put a hand on Callum's arm to get his attention but then quickly dropped it. "Stay back with the rest of your men. I would speak to Lord Patrick alone."

"That's not a good idea," Callum said.

"I'm a big girl, Callum. I can do this."

Callum had to catch her by the arm to stop her from heading off immediately—and then had to stop himself from shaking some sense into her. "Just because you're capable of doing something all by yourself doesn't mean you have to, Cassie. You don't have anything to prove. Not to me! Why to you?"

Cassie glared at Callum for a second and made to wrench away, but then she took in a deep breath and let it out. "You're right. We did this together before. We can do it again."

Thank God for that. Carrying the white flag, Callum walked with Cassie towards the gatehouse, through the churned-up earth, debris, and refuse of war that hadn't yet been cleared. The fog had made the day cold, but Callum wore no helmet or hood so his face would show to Lord Patrick and he would know who was coming to speak to him.

One of the guards peered down at them from the top of the palisade. He jerked his head at Cassie. "The lord doesn't want to talk to you. The last time you were here, you took a prisoner with you, our only leverage against Robert Bruce."

"Oh, be quiet, Rory." Donella popped up beside him. "Don't speak unless you have something useful to say." She looked down at Callum and Cassie. "He's coming. He's angry, but he's coming."

"Thank you," Callum said.

As the gate opened, Cassie stirred beside Callum. Lord Patrick came through it all by himself. He looked past Cassie and Callum to the men who waited on horseback a hundred feet away, nearly invisible in the heavy fog. "Is this all you have brought to finish us off?"

Callum stuck the flagpole in the ground in front of him.

"We're not here to fight," Cassie said.

Lord Patrick kept his eyes fixed on Callum, resolutely not looking at Cassie. "I only came to speak with you because I understand that I have you to thank for my son's rescue. I would not want you to think me ungrateful."

Cassie wasn't giving up. "You're welcome. Now we need your help."

Lord Patrick lifted his chin to point behind them at the motley crew of Balliol and Bruce supporters, as well as a few undecideds. "I see Andrew Moray rides with you. And—good Lord!—is that Henry Percy? You clearly don't need me."

"You don't know what we're asking of you yet," Cassie said.

He glared hard at her. "You betrayed me."

"I didn't," she said. "Or at least, not in any way that mattered. It was Callum and I who convinced Robert Bruce to break off his attack on you."

"Bruce and I were conferring on a truce when he discovered your absence from his camp," Lord Patrick said. "His anger was a sight to behold."

"You don't need to concern yourself with Bruce," Callum said. "He will not trouble you further."

"So you say."

"So I do say," Callum said and held Lord Patrick's gaze for a count of ten.

Lord Patrick broke off the staring contest to turn to Cassie. "So ask."

"Erik of Norway has come to claim the throne of Scotland," Cassie said. "He besieges Stirling Castle even now. We ask that you gather all who support you and come with us to Stirling."

Lord Patrick's surprise made him forget that he was supposed to be angry at Cassie. His mouth opened and closed, and then he rubbed at his chin as he looked at her.

"My lord—" One of the men on the battlement called down to him, but Lord Patrick raised a hand to stop him speaking.

He glared at Callum and swept out his arm to indicate the destruction around them. "Do you not see what Bruce has done to us? How can I leave Mugdock when we have been so ill-used?"

"What if I asked you to do it?"

Cassie and Callum wheeled around to see Robbie Bruce swing down from his saddle. A host of men, twice the number of those Callum had brought, came to a halt on the far edge of the clearing beside Callum's men.

Lord Patrick's face reddened. "How dare you—"

Robbie bowed before him. "My father is dead, my lord, as is Alexander MacDougall, both felled in a fight that should never have been fought."

Lord Patrick pressed his lips together. "I'm sorry for your loss."

If the face hadn't been the same, Callum wouldn't have recognized Robbie by his manner.

"Thank you," Robbie said. "I know now that Alexander MacDougall abducted your son to force you to do his bidding. I have just heard that John is alive and free."

"Yes." Lord Patrick wasn't giving anything away, but this was the truth Callum had been waiting for. Lord Patrick had been fearful when they'd spoken to him a week ago. Now Callum knew the cause of his fear had been the worst thing that could happen to a parent: the loss of his child.

"Erik of Norway must not be allowed to take Stirling Castle. Regardless of your feelings towards my family, we need you—Scotland needs you—to speak to the men of your party—the MacGregors, the Comyns, and the MacDougalls—and convince them that they must fight, even if it means fighting beside us."

"John Balliol is among those besieged at Stirling," Cassie said.

"And my grandfather, too?" Robbie said.

Cassie nodded.

Robbie turned back to Lord Patrick, an expectant expression on his face.

Lord Patrick gave Robbie a long look and then nodded. "I will come."

A valley separated Callum's company from Stirling Castle. Smoke rippled from the homesteads and little villages that Erik of Norway's army had burned, avenging the death of his daughter and hoping to subdue Scotland before it could marshal its forces against him. The army circled the crag upon which the castle perched. Roofs within the castle walls were on fire too. Despite the speed at which they had ridden once they'd left Mugdock, they had come almost too late.

Callum waved a hand to his captains. "Spread the men along the cliff. I want Erik to see the force that comes against him!"

Callum's captains shouted orders to their men, following his commands. Cassie sat on her horse to his right. "They have to know they can't maintain the siege under these conditions," she said. "James will charge out of the castle with as many men as he can muster and they'll be caught between us."

Robbie's horse danced up to Callum, Robbie's eyes alight with what he believed already to be a victory. "See them cower behind their shields! In a moment they will turn and run."

Callum looked into his face and then at the men behind him. Unlike Robbie's, their faces were set, grim with the knowledge that they would lose men in the battle that was to come. Experience told them it was inevitable. Erik of Norway would make a stand, even if he had to fight on two fronts simultaneously. He hadn't come all the way from Norway to run away with his tail between his legs at the first sign of resistance. His men would never countenance it and he wouldn't be able to call himself King of Norway, much less King of Scotland, if he did that.

"No," Callum said, under his breath.

Only Cassie and Robbie heard him. "No?" Cassie said.

"Erik of Norway has a genuine grievance," Callum said. "He lost his daughter who should have been queen and now other men fight over her throne. Why shouldn't his sins be forgiven as much as Robert Bruce's?"

"Bruce is dead," Cassie said, dryly.

"True," Callum said, "but the question still stands." He turned to Robbie. "I don't know if you will ever become king, but I do know that Scotland would be ill-served by any man gaining the throne over the bodies of his rivals. When you expressed as much to me, you showed wisdom beyond your years."

"My lord?" Robbie said. "I don't understand."

"I don't either, Callum," Cassie said.

Callum turned in the saddle and waved at Lord Patrick, who sat on his horse a few feet away. "I want twenty noblemen to ride into the valley with me. And I want my white flag again."

"Yes, my lord!"

Robbie seemed to have been struck speechless that Callum wasn't going to order his forces to attack, but Cassie sidled her horse closer. "What are you going to say to Erik?"

"I'm going to force him to see that he cannot win," Callum said, "any more than Bruce or Balliol can win without the consent of the governed. I'm suggesting that we begin as we mean to go on."

"Who do you propose should be the King of Scotland, then?" Cassie said. "King David?"

Callum shook his head. "That's not my decision to make. It's not any single man's decision to make. It occurs to me only now that David sent me to Scotland because he believed I could find a solution to the problem of Scotland's succession out of my experience, one that only we few have. He understood what might be possible, and if it was, I was the only man in Scotland who could see it through."

"What might be possible?" Cassie said.

"Democracy."

20

Cassie

Callum's small party rode into the valley under a white flag, leaving the bulk of the army on the heights to be as intimidating as possible. Cassie feared Erik of Norway would be intransigent, but once Callum explained to him the size of the enemy forces arrayed against him, and the fact that King David was marching north to deal with the succession personally, he turned pragmatic. Erik ordered his men to stand down and to wait for him at a camp to the south of Stirling, while he joined Callum's company to ride up to the castle.

There would be another council and maybe this one would actually reach an agreement. As the company cantered up the long road to the top of the crag, Cassie eyed Callum, riding ahead of her and surrounded by a dozen noblemen. She didn't know what the other men thought of him, but she saw in him what King David must have seen. Callum had taken charge of the proceedings. It was as if he'd been born for this. While Cassie knew that a relationship between them would never work, that didn't mean she couldn't be proud of him.

The company rode under the gatehouse and such was the press of men and horses in the bailey that it took her a moment to notice the uproar occurring at the far end. She dismounted beside Callum and together they elbowed their way through the crowd to find that it wasn't Erik or James, Balliol, Red, or Grampa Bruce who'd brought the entire matter to a head, but Liam, Kirby's nephew.

Liam held his uncle at sword point. A blood-stained bandage covered Liam's head, and his arm was glued to his chest by a second bandage, but he stood tall in the center of a ring of men that surrounded him and his uncle. It could have been a middle school fight, except for the real sword Liam held and the bishop's staff his uncle clutched as a meager defense.

Liam's accusation rang through the clear air. "I name you traitor!"

"This is just what I need right now." Callum shot Cassie a weary look.

Kirby sputtered, "Liam—" Then at the sight of Callum shouldering his way through the crowd, Kirby went from dismissive to pleading in the space of a breath. "My lord, please—" He held out his hand to Callum.

"You will not speak!" Liam said. "I have lain in my bed since I arrived, half out of my head to be sure, but I can no longer remain silent in the face of your treachery. I cannot allow you to weave your webs of deceit upon innocent men!"

Liam's wrist wavered as he pointed his sword at Kirby, and his face was nearly as white as his linen shirt. He looked like he might collapse at any moment. Still, he kept his shoulders back and had the wherewithal to flick the point of his sword towards James, who stood under the gatehouse to the upper bailey, watching the proceedings with a preternatural stillness. "You must listen, my lord, to the tale I have to tell!"

Kirby tried again. "You don't know what you're saying—"

"You left me for dead!"

The shout echoed around the bailey. Callum slid around the last few men who blocked his way. He crept up to Liam from behind, trying not to draw his attention from Kirby or James, but Liam sensed him and swung around.

Callum brought his hands up. "You don't need to do this, Liam."

"Don't I?" Liam jerked his head towards Red Comyn, who stood beside his father ten feet away. "Did you know that the Comyns pretend to support Balliol, but really seek the throne for themselves and are servants to a greater master?"

Cassie believed Liam instantly, but Callum kept his face impassive, as if Liam was telling him something he already knew.

"Put away the sword, Liam," Callum said. "Nothing good can come of this."

"My uncle's death! That can come of this!" Liam leapt at Kirby, slashing his sword. Kirby brought up his staff and jumped back just in time to deflect the sword's tip. Callum moved closer, but as Liam recovered, he spun back to him. "Stay away from me!"

By this time, both Samuel and Robbie Bruce had come to stand on either side of Cassie. Robbie watched intently for a moment and then strode forward, elbowing his way through the crowd until he was inside the circle too. "Let him speak, my lords! I have lost my father over this matter. Let him speak!"

Kirby really wasn't good at keeping quiet, even if it was in his own best interests. "My lord Callum, I don't know what he's talking about—"

Callum made a slashing motion with his hand in Kirby's direction. "Quiet!"

Meanwhile, the Comyns had taken a step backward, out of the first ring of onlookers gathered to watch the fight. Cassie nudged Samuel, tipping her head towards them, and said under her breath, "Don't let them get away."

Samuel disappeared from Cassie's side and twenty seconds later reappeared behind the Comyns, with Andrew Moray beside him.

"Tell me, Liam," Robbie said. "Tell me what you know."

But it was James who answered, finally moving to where the combatants stood. "Those who know more than you, Liam, have been aware of Bishop Kirby's treachery for some time. I wish you'd come to me first, Son."

Liam's mouth opened and closed like a fish. "M-m-my lord—"

James halted in front of Kirby. While Kirby dipped his head in obeisance, James gazed stonily back at the bishop. "I've been making my own inquiries since I learned of your treachery,

Bishop. It is my understanding that you've recently spent some time in France."

"That's what I've been trying to tell you." Liam had reached the end of his rope. "He met William de Valence in Avignon! Night after night they schemed together!" This last accusation seemed to exhaust Liam completely and he stumbled. Callum reached him, going down on one knee just in time to keep him from collapsing on the stones of the bailey.

Kirby stood as if his feet were frozen to the ground, a fixed smile on his face. Cassie wanted to see something else from him—hatred, anger, loathing—but he kept his expression mild, as if nothing untoward was happening. "I did, my lord."

"William de Valence is the sworn enemy of England and plotted against King David's life," said James, "and yet you admit to meeting with him?"

"As a bishop of England, my role is to foster peace, no matter how acrimonious the grievance ..."

"You were not there to make peace!" said James. "You were there to conspire with Valence to put the Black Comyn on the throne of Scotland."

Cassie gasped along with the rest of the crowd. How could they have been so stupid as not to see it before? She could understand Callum's ignorance, since he'd only been in the Middle Ages for six months, but the marriage of Joan, William de Valence's daughter, to Red Comyn had been the talk of the clans in the spring. Red had married Joan despite Valence's disgrace and exile, and the wedding had apparently cost Valence a small fortune in dowry. One rumor suggested he'd spent more than he could afford.

"You dare to call yourself a man of the Church?" Robbie advanced on Kirby. "You saw to the murder of all but a handful of the king's company; you manipulated MacDougall and my father to their deaths. All for what? Money? Power? A place at the new king's side? A post in Rome?"

"I have no idea what you're talking about," Kirby said.

"I don't either, but I'm looking forward to finding out."

Cassie swung around at the commanding voice. Arriving next to where Callum and she had left their horses was a man in his forties, helmetless, with a full head of red hair going grey at the temples. He had arrived unannounced amidst the turmoil, but here was a man who could never go anywhere unnoticed.

"My Lord Clare!" Callum released Liam to two guards and strode out of the circle of men.

Gilbert de Clare—Earl of Gloucester, the fifth Guardian of Scotland, and King David's right-hand man—dismounted. His traveling cloak was stained and his boots were caked with mud, but he rode at the head of a company of men and looked more like a king than most of the claimants to the Scottish throne. The crowd gave way, allowing Callum and Clare to greet each other a pace from Cassie.

"Thank God you're here," Callum said in a low voice as the two men clasped forearms. "Only you would believe the intrigue and deception I've had to wade through since I got here."

Clare's eyes crinkled in the corners, the only indication of his emotions, and then he looked past Callum to his fellow Guardians: James and the two Scottish bishops who had come to stand beside him. "Sorry I'm late. Perhaps someone would care to explain the problem?"

21

Callum

Kirby and the two Comyns had been arrested and locked away in one of Stirling's towers. Liam was back in bed under careful watch, though more for Kirby's safety than because James felt the need to hold him. The time had come to speak truth to power, as one of Callum's Cambridge professors had liked to say.

Callum leaned heavily on the table before him and looked at the twenty men who faced him. "I will lay out your choices. You can do this now, or you can do it later when it's King David who suggests it."

"Why should we listen to you?" said the still belligerent Erik of Norway.

Callum stabbed a finger towards the western wall of the chamber in which they were meeting. "You think your chances of defeating the entire might of Scotland out there in the valley are that good, do you?"

Erik glared at him, but Callum didn't back down.

"I speak for King David, who countenances this plan." If it wasn't what David wanted, Callum would ask his forgiveness later.

"King David—" Erik scoffed. "Upstart boy."

That brought James to his feet. "His claim to the throne is more legitimate than yours, and he had the sense not to bring an army against us to force our hand. He, at least, believes in Scotland."

Balliol and Grampa Bruce also rose to their feet. When they realized that they both wanted to speak at the same time, neither gave way by sitting down again. In the end, Balliol went first. "The crown is mine by right of birth."

"I beg to differ," Grampa Bruce said. "Mine is the superior claim."

Balliol sneered. "An election would be a waste of time. We already know who would win."

"I would," Grampa Bruce said.

Balliol turned on Grampa Bruce. "You always were the most arrogant—"

"Put that confidence to the test," Callum said, cutting through their argument. "Put your weight behind an election. Both of you."

"Lord Callum is right," said James.

Callum cheered inwardly that James had made up his mind to support Callum's plan. It had been by no means a sure thing.

"Every claimant to the throne needs to swear—right here, right now—that he will abide by the decision of Parliament and support the man they choose to rule." Callum canted his head. "You never know. It could be you."

In the old world, it was really only Balliol and Grampa Bruce whose claims had serious merit, and it had been Balliol who'd ultimately triumphed—at least until King Edward had set about systematically undermining his rule. Balliol had died in exile and Robbie Bruce had risen to power, ultimately throwing the English out of Scotland entirely for a time. Now, with Callum's plan, even Erik of Norway and Patrick Dunbar, an agnate son from the House of Dunkeld, had a chance of winning the throne. Callum saw the men before him glance to their rivals, calculation in their eyes.

"I agree," Erik said. Callum had guessed he might be the first. His was the lesser claim. A vote was his only chance, even if vanishingly small.

As the other men began to nod, Callum heaved a sigh. He remained standing at his place as they filed out, leaving him the last man in the room. Before leaving, he leaned his shoulder into the frame of the door, allowing the wood to take his weight. He was more tired than he'd ever been in his life. The physical exhaustion was one thing, but to have Scotland's future resting on his shoulders had him stumbling under the burden.

He looked up at the sound of an indrawn breath. Cassie was standing a few feet away. The corridor between the meeting room and the great hall where Parliament was gathering was empty except for them. Cassie reached up a hand to brush his cheek with her fingers. "You look so tired."

"I feel like I've aged ten years this week," Callum said. "Only a little longer, though, and this might be over."

"I hear you pushed it through," she said. "The men were talking of it as they left the room."

"It seems I did," Callum said. "We'll see in a minute what Parliament has to say to the idea."

"There's an additional factor that we haven't taken into account, you know," Cassie said. "It's already starting."

Callum glanced up. "What is that?"

"Politicking," Cassie said.

"The foundation of democracy," Callum said with a half laugh. "I expect the Scots will learn the art between the main course and dessert tonight."

"Surely it's the only reason Erik of Norway agreed to the vote, don't you think?" Cassie said. "Nobody is going to vote for him, but if he offers to throw his support behind another candidate ...?"

"I suspect every man in that room was thinking about how to get an edge," Callum said.

"There'll be no stopping them now," Cassie said.

Callum took a step towards the open door at the end of the corridor. "I need to go, Cassie."

"I know," she said. "My only consolation is that Samuel isn't allowed to attend either."

"If the medieval world can change in this way, it can change in other ways too," Callum said.

"Women didn't get the vote in the United States until 1920," Cassie said. "That's a lot of change."

"You don't know David," Callum said. "Give him a chance."

And then Callum really did have to go. He entered the great hall, finding that he had to force his legs to stride forward instead of faltering in the doorway. The host of men who made up Scotland's Parliament were packed to the rafters and still men kept coming.

If this was what politics was like all the time in the Middle Ages, Callum hoped David wouldn't put him on a job like this again. The only thing that was keeping him upright was the urgency of the task before him and the need to see it through.

James Stewart stood to Callum's left and gazed out at the men in the hall. He lifted his chin so that his voice would project to the far corners of the room. "So that we all have the same understanding, I will relate what has occurred over the last week, so that you may make your own judgments as to the course of action we now must take."

"Please," Clare said under his breath.

Callum glanced down at him. Clare had found a seat to Callum's right and tapped his fingers impatiently on the table, his eyes glinting. Callum found Clare's lack of personal interest in the succession a relief from the intense emotions of everyone else.

"We now know this to be true: John Kirby, Bishop of Ely and England's ambassador to Scotland, conspired with William de Valence to place John Comyn on the throne of Scotland," said James, beginning his tale at the end of the story. "He incited

Alexander MacDougall, a Balliol supporter, to ambush the king's company along the road to Stirling; he encouraged Robert Bruce to exact his revenge, first on the Comyns, and then on MacDougall. Kirby saw to the murder of fifty men in the hopes that in our anger, we would act unjustly, sacrificing tradition and law in favor of his choice for the crown. He intended that the Black Comyn would come forward as the voice of reason."

James held up a piece of paper. "We found this document in Kirby's possession. It is a testimonial by John Balliol, signed and witnessed, urging Alexander MacDougall to eliminate King David as a way to ensure Balliol's own ascension to the throne. We now know this document to be a forgery."

If David had been here, he would have recognized Kirby's tactic. It was Kirby who'd fabricated the documents claiming that David's mother was the illegitimate daughter of King Henry and Caitir, a daughter of Alexander II. Someone would need to pry out of Kirby the name of his expert forger, but for now, that knowledge could wait.

Then it was Bishop Fraser's turn to speak. "We have unmasked a devious plot and implicated a Guardian of Scotland in the process. The time has come to anoint a new king. It is long past time."

Fraser looked to Callum, who nodded. James and Fraser sat, leaving Callum the only man standing. He waited for the men in the room to fall silent, and when after two minutes they didn't quiet, he lifted a hand to gain their attention. Finally, they settled down and Callum waited another fifteen seconds until he could have heard a pin drop.

"Your Guardians asked King David to come to Stirling to help Scotland choose their new king," Callum said. "Perhaps it was even the Black Comyn himself who suggested King David act in this role." Callum glanced towards Bishop Fraser, whose face paled. Callum had guessed right.

Callum continued. "Not knowing of Kirby's treachery and wishing not to confuse the matter by putting forth his own claim to the Scottish throne, King David sent Bishop Kirby in his place. If King David were here, he would apologize for this mistake and take up the task in Kirby's stead. King David, however, is not here and that role has fallen to me. I am Alexander Callum, the Earl of Shrewsbury, and I say that the question of succession should be put to a Parliamentary vote."

Dead silence.

Clare's mouth twitched and Callum almost kicked him for his insolence. Then the room went from silent to raucous in a matter of seconds. It started as a murmur and then swept through the hall as each man spoke to his neighbor. The Guardians and the dozen claimants to the throne remained silent, some standing, some sitting, but all impassive. They had known what Callum was going to say, of course, since he'd already said it to them earlier.

Andrew Moray lifted a hand and Bishop Fraser gestured that he should rise and take the floor. The uproar in the great hall had continued for ten minutes, but it was time to talk about it as an official body.

"Among my people, King David's plan isn't without precedent," Andrew said. "We choose our clan leaders through the ancient tradition of tanistry."

Many of the men nodded, though not Erik, who said right on cue, "And what is tanistry?"

"Upon the death of the clan chief, succession doesn't fall to the eldest son, but to the most capable man of the clan, even if he isn't the son of the man who died," Andrew said. "Moreover, the man is chosen by election." Although much of the nobility in Scotland were Lowlanders, everyone in the room but Erik of Norway had some Highland blood and should have recognized the practice.

"If you accept what I'm suggesting," Callum said, "the only claimant whose name will be withheld from the ballot is King David's."

"Of all the claimants, he's the only one who *should* be on it," Clare said, though under his breath and only to Callum.

Callum glanced at Clare, trying not to smile at his sour tone.

"That's the deal," Callum said. "Take it, and you and your people get to truly decide the ruler of Scotland. Leave it, and you will have King David to deal with."

"You're threatening us?" said a man from the back of the room.

"Only if he has to," James Stewart said.

Callum had wanted to propose that an election be held every five years, and Cassie had demanded that Callum include women, but James had talked him out of both. Even Cassie had eventually admitted that such an agreement would be too much for the noblemen of Scotland to swallow. Callum couldn't force it down their throats and he would prefer not having to do it at the point of King David's sword. Personally, Callum thought Scotland was like a wild horse and didn't envy any of these men trying to tame it. He didn't blame David for not wanting the crown.

Bishop William Fraser dropped a fist onto the table. "We will adjourn for dinner and meet again later tonight."

The hall filled with noise again, but those at the high table continued to sit. Clare tapped his fingers rhythmically on the table. "If Parliament elects the new king of Scotland, no body of men has employed such power since ancient Greece."

Callum shouldn't have been surprised that Clare would know such a thing. "Will this work, do you think?" Callum said.

"You have boxed them into a corner with the threat of war against England as their only alternative," Andrew said. "Parliament will accept the power—gleefully, I imagine—though some of the claimants to the throne may in the end, when they lose, come to think that war would have been the lesser of two evils. The new king may also regret the extent to which he is answerable to the men who elected him."

James ran a hand through his hair. "How did you come by this plan, Lord Callum? Don't tell me that King David wrote to you of it. There's been no time for messages."

"This has been King David's dream for Britain since he was fourteen years old," Callum said.

"I would like to meet him," said James. "When I was fourteen, I'd just discovered lasses."

Callum smiled. "King David knows that he sits on the throne of England because the people chose him to rule. It gives him power that you can't yet understand."

"So be it." James put his hands on the arms of his chair and pushed to his feet. "Come, Andrew. We have noblemen to appease. Best get to work."

22

Cassie

Callum and Cassie stood on the battlements of Stirling Castle, alone for the first time since their conversation at Kilsyth.

"Just tell me what's wrong, Cassie," Callum said. "I can take anything but your silence."

"I'm going to leave."

"Cassie—"

She turned to Callum. "I can't do this, Callum."

"At least wait a few more days until I can take you home," Callum said.

"You have a job to do. I'm going to let you do it while I go home. Alone. I can't stay for even one more day."

"Then let me send Samuel with you," Callum said. "It's not safe for you on the road by yourself."

Cassie rolled her eyes. "I was alone for five years, Callum."

"Please, Cassie—"

"You deserve better than me."

"I don't think better exists," he said. "And isn't that my decision?"

"I'm only going to hurt you."

"Not worse than you're hurting me by leaving."

Cassie looked away. "You'll heal."

But Cassie wasn't sure she would.

Callum no longer tried to stop her from going. Within the hour, she was on her way out of Stirling on foot. Because Grampa Bruce had demanded to speak to Callum yet again, Callum hadn't even been able to see her off and sent Samuel in his stead.

"Are you sure you want to do this, Cassie?" Samuel said. He'd walked twenty paces with her out from the gatehouse.

Cassie had talked with Samuel only a few times and wasn't sure that now was the time for confidences, but she answered him anyway. "Yes. I'm sure."

"The love Callum is offering you is special. Do you really want to toss it aside?" Samuel said.

Cassie stopped in the act of adjusting the straps on her backpack. "Is that what you think I'm doing?"

"Isn't it?"

"This isn't about love," Cassie said. "It's about living. Besides which, you're a fine one to talk. Callum tells me that you've been secretly courting a woman for years. Why haven't you married her?"

"She's a Christian. I'm Jewish."

"The times, they are a'changing," Cassie sang. "You should be embracing the change, not running from it. King David and

Callum both would support your request for her hand. You know they would. That should be enough for anybody."

"You don't understand."

"*I* don't understand?" Cassie said. "You're a coward, that's what you are."

"And that makes you—what?" Samuel said.

Cassie shot him an aggrieved look but didn't reply. His issues were not hers, nor her business. The only thing left to say was *goodbye*.

She slept rough the first night, as she had in those months of wandering Scotland during the first year she'd lived in the Middle Ages. The next day, she woke early and set off again. She was just approaching the place where Callum's company had been ambushed when the cantering hoof beats of a single horse sounded behind her.

Cassie spun around, bow in hand and arrow nocked. Her heart pounded in her ears, but even as the adrenaline rushed through her, she acknowledged that she wasn't afraid of whoever was coming; she wasn't afraid because she thought it might be Callum.

That won't do at all!

Cassie leapt up the slope that buttressed the road and crouched in the brambles to hide herself from the rider, all the while telling herself that of course he couldn't be Callum. Cassie had told him how she felt and he would respect her decision. Even so, as the man rode out of the mist, Cassie's breath caught in her throat. He wore mail, sword, and a helmet like Callum's. But then he was past her and he wasn't Callum, and Cassie was alone again.

She arrived home, unscathed but not unchanged. She spent the next week mending her relationship with Donella, renewing her supply of herbs and foodstuffs, and tending to her garden. May turned to June. Lord Patrick returned to Mugdock with the news that Scotland's Parliament had chosen John Balliol as their new king. Cassie thought it appropriate that the man was given a fair chance, given what had happened in the old world.

Five days later, Cassie was in the midst of picking the first vegetables from her garden, with dirty knees and sweat-soaked hair tied back from her face with a leather thong, when a rider appeared in the clearing in front of her house.

Cassie had been so absorbed that she hadn't heard him coming. She glanced up, her heart pounding with the idea that it was Callum, and then she recognized Samuel. Cassie hastened to him, brushing at the dirt on her hands and trying to batten down her flash of fear, since he wouldn't have come if all was well. "What's wrong—?"

"He's sick," Samuel said. Neither of them had to clarify who *he* was.

All the blood drained from Cassie's face. "With what? Who's tending him? What have they tried?" She ran to wash her face and hands in the bucket of water she'd left by the door to her house. Cassie plunged her hands into the cool water and scrubbed at them, internally cataloguing what herbs and salves she had on hand that she might need to bring.

"Nothing anyone does for him seems to help," Samuel said. "He needs you."

"Did he ask for me?" Cassie straightened, mopping at her face with a cloth. At the silence behind her, she lowered her hands and spun around.

Samuel stood with his hands behind his back, studying Cassie. A small smile played around his lips.

"That was a dirty trick," Cassie said. "You mean he's lovesick. For me."

"I had to be sure of how you felt," Samuel said. "Now I am. Why did you really leave him, Cassie?"

"I told you why. I told him why."

Samuel gazed around at Cassie's little steading. She kept it neat and clean, probably more so in recent days than she had in the past. It had been important to keep busy. "You're really so happy here?" he said. "You like these Scottish mountains that much, do you?"

"I do." Cassie swept loose strands of hair from her face. "You wouldn't understand."

"I understand that you're afraid," he said. "I understand that you aren't as happy here as you want me to think."

Cassie laughed, though the sound came out strained.

Samuel went on. "Callum has become my friend, and I hate that you left him. He mourns the loss of you as you do him, and you're both too stubborn to fix this."

"Who says I'm unhappy?" Cassie said.

"As soon as you learned that he was ill, you could think of nothing but going to him."

Cassie swallowed down a scathing retort. Samuel was right, of course. "Does Callum know you're here?"

"He'd have my head if he knew. As I said—stubborn."

Cassie folded her arms across her chest. "Whether or not we miss each other doesn't change the fact that I'm not the right girl for him."

"He thinks you are."

"But *why?*" All of a sudden, Cassie's throat was thick with unshed tears. "I don't want him to love me. I don't want to need anyone as much as I need him. Everybody I have ever loved is *gone.*"

As soon as Cassie said the words, she wanted to take them back. But God help her, they were so much the truth it left her breathless. She couldn't believe she had shared so much of herself with Samuel when until now she hadn't admitted how she felt, even to herself.

Samuel, however, was neither moved nor sympathetic. "Everybody needs someone, Cassie." He turned and waved a hand. Cassie's mouth dropped open as a woman rode out of the woods and came to a halt beside Samuel. He reached his hands up to her waist and helped her to the ground. "You see, Cassie. I accepted your challenge. This is my betrothed, Elspet. It seems to me that if I've had to change my ways, you have to change yours too."

* * * * *

"You're wearing a dress."

Cassie smiled at the amusement in Callum's voice and turned around. "Ah ... but I'm wearing pants underneath. Don't get too excited."

Callum entered the room and closed the door behind him. He leaned back against it and looked at Cassie, while she drank in the sight of him. His quarters at Stirling Castle were well appointed and private, indicating his high status. "It's about time you showed up," Callum said. "Another day or two and I would have come looking for you."

Cassie clenched her hands into fists. Now that she was here, her confidence had evaporated. "You would have?" It felt like she hadn't taken a full breath since she'd seen him last.

Callum pushed off the door and came closer, stopping two paces away, his hands loose at his sides. If he didn't know what to do with them, Cassie had some good ideas. Before she lost her courage completely, she stepped closer and put her arms around his neck. His hands went to her waist.

"Is this a change or am I reading too much into this?" Callum said.

"You can read whatever you like into this," Cassie said.

Callum bent to touch his forehead to hers but didn't speak.

Cassie didn't have a lot of practice with this sort of thing, but she recognized that for the moment, she was going to have to do the talking for both of them. "What's next on your list of things to do and countries to save? Are we off to London to give Bishop Kirby his comeuppance?"

"Actually, no," Callum said. "King David still isn't satisfied with the official story of what happened to Princess Margaret. Since I'm already here, he is sending me to Orkney to see if I can uncover what happened to her. It's his guess, as it is mine, that we may find Valence's hand in that as well. At the very least, I can get the full story from those who witnessed her death." Callum bit his lower lip. "Did you say *we*? Last I heard, you wanted to stay here."

"I do," Cassie said. "Part of me still does."

Callum pulled Cassie a little closer. "I can't stay here, Cassie. The election is over and I have so much to do."

"I know," Cassie said. "That's why I told Lord Patrick that I would be leaving my house and most likely, unless I entirely misunderstood your wishes, not coming back."

Callum swallowed hard. "You mean it?"

Cassie nodded.

"What changed your mind, if I may ask?"

"You did," Cassie said. "You never wavered, even as I kept trying to make you out to be someone that you're not, with ideas that you don't have, just because I've known so many men who aren't as amazing as you are."

Callum actually blushed. "As for this dress issue, I really don't care what you wear."

Cassie laughed and looked down at her feet. "I can wear a dress sometimes if it keeps people from asking too many questions. I don't have to be a medieval woman, even if I look like one occasionally. I just need you not to expect it."

"I never did." Callum seemed to be having difficulty getting any words out, and when he did speak, his voice was thick with emotion. "I love you."

Cassie was having trouble breathing herself, but if she was going to do this, she was going to do it right. No half measures or second thoughts. "*For as long as the rain falls on these green hills, I will stand with thee.* Isn't that how the vow goes?" she said.

Callum drew in an audible breath. "Every day—every day—I thought about what I would say to you when I saw you again. I meant what I said. In another day, I was going to beg you to come with me."

"I don't want you to beg," Cassie said. "You shouldn't have to beg, though if you wanted to say nice things about me, I wouldn't stop you."

Callum tipped back his head and laughed. And then he looked down at her and Cassie finally got to kiss him again.

"Oh! I forgot to tell you." Callum pulled away a few millimeters. "I received a message from King David yesterday. Have you heard?"

"No," Cassie said, suddenly wary. "Heard what?"

Callum gave Cassie a huge grin. "It's a boy."

The End

A Note from the Author

I'd like to thank each and every reader who has stuck with the *After Cilmeri* series now for six novels. *Exiles in Time* has allowed us to wander off into Scotland, where the culture and history are different from medieval Wales, though no less exciting and complex. Since I was writing a novel and not a dissertation, most of the research I did in creating the book didn't make it into the actual story. For those of you who are interested in the historical context of 1289, I'd like to direct you to my web page and the following topics in particular:

Languages of Medieval Scotland:
http://www.sarahwoodbury.com/scots-scottish-and-gaelic-whats-the-difference/

Medieval Scottish Clans:
http://www.sarahwoodbury.com/medieval-scottish-clans/

The Succession of 1290:
http://www.sarahwoodbury.com/the-succession-of-1290-scotland/

The Welsh Longbow:
http://www.sarahwoodbury.com/the-welsh-longbow/

Early Parliament: http://www.sarahwoodbury.com/early-parliament-and-representative-process/

Medieval Bathing Practices: http://www.sarahwoodbury.com/did-medieval-people-bathe/

Medieval Administration: http://www.sarahwoodbury.com/would-a-medieval-prince-have-had-an-office/

Messenger Pigeons in the Middle Ages: http://www.sarahwoodbury.com/messenger-pigeons-in-the-middle-ages/

Could Time Travel Happen?: http://www.sarahwoodbury.com/could-time-travel-happen/

Acknowledgments

First and foremost, I'd like to thank my lovely readers for encouraging me to continue the *After Cilmeri* Series. I have always been passionate about these books, and it's wonderful to be able to share my stories with readers who love them too.

Thank you to my family who has been nothing but encouraging of my writing, despite the fact that I spend half my life in medieval Wales. Thank you to my beta readers: Darlene, Gemini, Anna, Jolie, Melissa, Cassandra, Brynne, Carew, Dan, and Venkata. I couldn't do this without you.

About the Author

With two historian parents, Sarah couldn't help but develop an interest in the past. She went on to get more than enough education herself (in anthropology) and began writing fiction when the stories in her head overflowed and demanded she let them out. While her ancestry is Welsh, she only visited Wales for the first time while in college. She has been in love with the country, language, and people ever since. She even convinced her husband to give all four of their children Welsh names.

She makes her home in Oregon.

www.sarahwoodbury.com

Made in the USA
Middletown, DE
22 September 2018